THE HARPY

JULIE HUTCHINGS

inked entertainment

For Wayne
I love you

CHARITY

*H*er eyes glowed with barely human heat. Smudges of black makeup didn't conceal her sleepless nights. Her hands were at the ready to close on another throat, but it wouldn't sate her.

The agony of her own hunger left her terrified.

Charity was a monster in every way that mattered. Her days were spent pining for the cruelty she could dole out when night came, when she became something more than punk rock trash without a future; what she became had only a present. The monster—its sharpness, its energy, its single-mindedness—permeated the smallest and saddest parts of her. The fear of it couldn't touch that. Those human feelings that plagued her days were an illness she could only treat with destruction when she turned into the *thing*. When nothing could stop her.

"Charity?" The voice brought her back to daylight. She picked her head up and focused on her boss sitting across from her. Another coffee shop owner, and she had worked at many a coffee shop. This guy was always blinking too much. Dishonest as fuck. Always putting a hand on her where it didn't belong, like he was quietly claiming different parts of her, trying to make her smile and take it like the other girls did for extra hours.

Four more hours until sunset.

"Charity, I'm talking to you."

"Well, I wish you would stop."

"Excuse me?"

She stared at him across the café table, one that she surely was supposed to have cleaned. She sighed, rolling her eyes. "The more you talk to me, the more I have to try to listen. And I really cannot even begin to care."

He licked his liver lips. His eye twitched. He took off his glasses and cleaned them on his shirt, making them dirtier. He gritted his teeth and leaned in, demeanor changing in the blink of an eye.

"Your attitude pisses me off. You come here with your tits hanging out, ass barely covered, wagging it in front of me— You act like you're better than the other girls. *They* know their place. You never have. If you didn't bring in more customers dressing like the whore you are, I'd have thrown you out of here long ago."

Something broke inside Charity at that.

. . .

*S*he put her thin, pale arms on the table, fixing her eyes on his, wishing she could smile wide enough to make the corners of her mouth bleed. She wished to be that other *thing*, that there was no charade to uphold anymore.

"You asshole. My ears die a little more every time I hear your pussy voice telling me some menial bullshit to do. And then you top it off with an ass pat or something, like you own me."

He sat corpse still, eyes fluttering at her brazenness. She zeroed in.

Spit whistled out through her clenched teeth, lips peeled back with feral cruelty. "Watch where you walk at night. You'll scream for mercy, but I won't listen. I'll demolish every bit of you, eat you until bloody bits fill my gut and I'm puking sick with your flesh in me."

His lips were quivering, sweat pasting wispy hair to his forehead. Charity laughed loudly, head thrown back, platinum frizz shaking. Customers stared at her with even more alarm than usual.

Charity stood with a ghastly movement, a jagged gracelessness that clawed the room with a presence of its own. "Needless to say, I won't be serving fucking coffee and cleaning tables anymore." She slammed her chair into the table and walked out, pausing only long enough to wink at him wickedly.

HOW CHARITY MET SALLY

*H*er name isn't actually Sally. We met at my psychiatrist's office—though I use the word "my" loosely. Turns out enough bar fights won me a great choice between community service and therapy, bordering on asylum time. The bar fights counted as a service to the community in my eyes, so I took Door Number 2. My soul itched just knowing what horrors lie on the other side of that gold-plaqued door, waiting to be exposed.

My memories were far scarier than any bar fight. Scarier than the monster I became at night.

I never did master the art of avoiding eye contact. The need to dominate everything around me mixed with the morbid curiosity of how people continue their lives, obviously miserable lives. It made me stare at the most inopportune times.

This time, I was looking at a woman with the least appropriate smile, sitting stiffly in a stiffer chair. The waiting room smelled like despair and dollar store hand sanitizer. She was a nondescript thing in a denim dress, mousy hair that begged to be forgotten, and that infuriating goddamn smile, like she was waiting for someone to smile back at her.

It was not me.

She caught me watching her hand-wringing book-ishness, and said the craziest frigging thing to me: "You look like me."

My disgust was showing. "What?"

"You look like me."

"Not on the inside."

Inappropriate Bookish Girl smiled wider. "Especially on the inside."

I probably caught a doctor's office fly or two in my gaping mouth. "Well, guts do all look alike. I should know." I pierced her with that face that made people look away fast.

She didn't look away. *She laughed.* "That's not what I meant. You've been hurt, like me." Her bottom lip sloped to the side when she said some things, like she'd had a stroke, but she probably hadn't.

"Everyone has, there, dollface."

"No," she said through that smile, like she was letting me in on some ancient wisdom I was formerly not privy to. "Abused." I half expected her to say, "come sit near me, dear child." Fuck me, my appointment was four minutes overdue. And when was *she* going in? What the hell.

"Listen, I'm waiting not so patiently to have my head examined and my soul stripped before I know what fucking hit me, so not really looking to share my pain with you or claim Abused Broads Solidarity right now. Save it for the shrink."

I tried to focus on the pile of late nineties *Sports Illustrated*s, but I could still see her out of the corner of my eye, looking at the wringing hands in her denimmed lap. Her tight, sad smile and fast blinking made me nervous.

"Jesus frigging shit, I didn't mean to hurt your feelings." I tapped my foot and stared at the door with the gold name plaque, willing it to just open already.

My new not-friend sighed hard, a gesture I was more comfortable with than the smiling, so I watched her. She was blinking like crazy. The goddamn smile was inappropriate to the point where I was starting to like it.

"No, I'm sorry. Fuck!" she said, and man, was that unexpected. She was wearing moccasins, for Chrissakes. "I'm just nervous is all, and it makes me blab." The smile disappeared.

"I'm sorta nervous, too," I admitted. "Makes me an even more unbound jerk." I nodded at the looming door. "Going into the unexplored territory that you've explored too many times. Trying to remember things you'd rather forget. Meeting new people, fearing them, trying new things, burning inside, knowing how much you want to kill the motherfucker who made you need any of this store-bought affection from a complete fucking stranger with a piece of paper saying he's better than you, being afraid to be alone in the same room with this guy you're paying to be in the same room with, knowing you never want to see him but you make yourself go because if you don't try *just this once* your life will never be a thing you want, it will be a thing you wouldn't even put in a pawn shop. It will be as worthless as the bastard who ruined it for you."

Silence. The *Sports Illustrated* pile. The smiley girl, not smiling. The fake clean hand sanitizer stench.

"First time here?" she asked.

"No."

The door opened with a deathly squeak and a bee-hived angry woman came out with a clipboard that held our immediate futures and hellhole pasts. The me they thought I was condensed to a piece of particle board. That puts into perspective how easy it is—was—to leave the world behind and start a new life, just disappear.

"Jen Matthews."

My new acquaintance stood up. She turned to look at me with a sadness that I only recognized in the mirror.

"The first time doesn't always hurt the worst," she said. I watched her go until the door closed behind her.

I SWALLOWED A HELL SPLINTER

*T*here was nothing in the office that made me want to open up and spill my bright and shinies all over the floor. Psychiatrist's Cave became more depressing every time I entered it.

"So, Charity, how are we feeling?"

"Well, Psychiatrist, if *we* were feeling good I wouldn't be here. But I most certainly am feeling *myself*."

His little beard and moustache twitched with cynicism. "I can appreciate that. Charity, I'd like to remind you again that you can, of course, call me Dr. Mortimer."

"Okay, Psychiatrist. I'd like to remind *you* that you can feel free to call me 'Patient' or 'Lunatic #854' or what have you. I would also like to remind you that if you don't say 'Charity' in every sentence, I will still remember my name and assume that you probably do also."

He laughed, making the buttons on his tweed vest

shimmy and threaten to pop off. "You always make me laugh, Charity." He brushed imaginary lint off his pants. Should I really trust someone with such an obvious tick to map the contours of my nightmare brain?

"I'd very much like to hear more about your memories of the abuse, Charity." Still calling me by name. Made me think nothing I said mattered to him. And of course, it didn't.

"I don't love talking about 'the abuse,'" I said, using air quotes. "But I wouldn't mind telling you that I quit my job."

No surprise registered on his face. "Did you? How are you going to survive, Charity?"

"I always survive. That's not a question."

"Fair enough. Why did you quit this job?"

"Wait, I forgot my name for a minute because you didn't say it. I quit because I fucking hate doing what a fat-ass letch like Roger tells me to do. He treats all the girls like it's some fifties diner and we're all named 'Flo.' He's all fucking sweaty, too, and I just know he's waiting for me to tell him it's okay to stare or grope me or whatever."

"But you've been conscious of that treatment from him for almost six months. Why the sudden change?"

"I know you're hoping I'll tell you that I realized I'm more than just tits and ass, but that's not it. It isn't sudden. But now I want to claw his eyes out and eat them, sucking on them like bloody little lollipops, hoping I could remember through the taste to kick him as he screams in agony in the dirt. So, that's a change."

Psychiatrist's face totally blanked.

"No, that wasn't for shock value. That's what I envisioned when I told him to shove the job. To answer your next question, no it does not worry me, and yes, of course it should."

He smiled, like this shit was something he heard all the time, and I got pissed. The fire in my veins, electricity in my eyes, claws itching to protrude from my fingertips kind of pissed. My lips peeled back over my teeth in a snarl that I didn't hold back. My eyes glowed hot, and everything about me from the inside out just screamed at being contained in this space. The skin on my back strained, trying to hold the monster in, and my feet tried to Hulk out in my boots.

Where's your smartass smile now, Dr. Mortimer?

"Do you—" He wiped his forehead with a douchebag handkerchief. "Do you feel this sort of anger often, Charity?"

"That time I did forget my name, but just for a minute." My turn to smile.

"Would you say you enjoyed that fury you just expressed?"

"The last time I'd been that happy was when my mother told me she was done with heroin the first time. Blissful. I remember looking in the mirror, not recognizing the smile on my face because I'd never seen it before. This feels like that, like I could never be happier than when that rage takes the sunlight away."

He cringed, but I give him credit, he continued to ask questions.

"Charity, do you *want* to be happy if it means this is

what happens to you?" Sweat dripped down the side of his head.

I leaned forward and his eyes moved from my fishnets to my breasts. "This happiness is the only thing that matters. And what's happening to me isn't real anyway, right? My nightly excursions are hallucinations—that some medication might help with," I added, wagging my finger at him. "Because this is a disorder, and not reality. Isn't that what you told me, Psychiatrist?"

"I believe that *you* beleive you become a monster at night that ravages men and eats their entrails. I believe that to you it is very real."

It was fun to watch him try not to be afraid, trying not to be wrong. It was fun when I killed the men in their beds, in bars, in their cars. It was fun to see when a terrible man no longer believed that he was the most terrible thing there was.

This guy was a good guy, who wanted to help me but couldn't. And it's why I hated being just a person during the day, the same old Charity who controlled fucking nothing. The heat flowed out of me slowly, relaxing my limbs as it went. My eyes didn't burn. My heart did.

"You won't believe what you've just seen in front of you? I was *almost there,* almost changed! You don't think I could become something more than just a girl?"

"Charity—"

"Psychiatrist."

That actually put him more at ease. "Charity, a person can make all kinds of things happen if they believe it to be true. Success, failure, growth, physical changes." He motioned to my body, and I leaned back to let him take it all in. "It is what we want most that we make come alive." He breathed deep. The worry lined his face; he was afraid to see me like that again, if he said the wrong thing. "It is our innermost demons that we give voice to—when we think we can destroy them."

I stared at the shelves of books. "Did you make that up yourself? About the demons?"

Chuckling, he said, "Yes, I suppose I did."

"It was beautiful."

"That struck a chord with you?"

I stood up, finishing the session myself. "I liked it. Except I'm the demon. And I think I'll probably live forever."

~

"Hey there." Denim Dress Sally was waiting for me outside when I left the office, leaning against a Kia Something Dull.

"Hi. You waited here for me?"

"Yeah, I guess I did."

"Do you guess you did or did you?"

The obviously nervous smile again. My fists clenched. "I did. I just wanted to apologize—"

"No you didn't. You already said sorry and you didn't even need to then. What is it?"

She shook once, eyes darting, and I was the fucking jerk again. She was too much like Little Girl Me, and not like Free Me to treat like this. "Shit, I am sorry. Again." We looked at each other, her with her stupid smile, me looking like I just left a vampire club. And we laughed.

Laughing was…new.

"My name's Jen and I have no idea why I waited for you." She held out her hand.

"Charity. Nice to meet you." I smiled, like a happy, regular smile. "You see a different guy than me. How did your appointment go?"

She got shy again. "Fine, I guess. How about yours?"

"Like swallowing fucking splinters from Hell then throwing them back up again."

She snickered, shaking her head. She didn't know what to think of me. Shit, *I* didn't know what to think of me these days, and this new making friends thing was not part of my usual repertoire.

"You want to get some coffee?" Jen asked. "I know it's weird, but I kinda *want* to talk to you. If it's *seriously* weird, I can just go—" She stood up to bolt, but I grabbed her arm before she could.

"No, wait." *What the fuck was I doing?* Wait until she found out I turned into a cannibalistic monster for fun. "That'd be cool. Dunkin Donuts? Meet you there?"

Her real smile was as bright as the sun we stood under and twice as warm. "That would be so nice. Thanks."

"Thank you for waiting for me. For bothering."

She reached out and touched my bare arm. "You're worth bothering with. I can tell." She gave me that smile again, the real one, and got in her car.

Getting into my own car, a rust-bucket convertible living on borrowed time, I thought about how goodness just rolled off Jen, and that it was directed at *me*.

We'd both suffered. It didn't matter that we'd just met, the vulnerable kindness made me like her. She'd become this shining angel of a person and no matter how annoying, I was intrigued. I had become a murderer, an evil beast, and willingly. It scared me to think of what I could do to her soul, just by knowing her.

But being scared never stopped me.

WHEN COFFEE ISN'T JUST COFFEE

*W*e sat down with two Styrofoam coffee cups that somehow managed to take away all the awkward.

"Charity's a pretty name."

"Thanks. I picked it out myself."

Smiley laughed, but it was true. The only way to get away from the junkie bastard who clawed my innocence open with dirty fingernails was to change my name, move out of Boston to the suburbs and leave that girl behind. Hazel Harrington was a child who didn't stand a chance; Charity Blake took chances and made opportunities. That rarely panned out, but hey. *He* hadn't been the only one of my mother's suppliers/boyfriends/pimps to take advantage of me, but he had been the only one to do it with a song in his heart. I was fifteen.

And now anyone I gave my time to was purely charity. Hence, the name.

"So, uh…" Jesus, I was bad with names or caring about them.

"Jen."

"Sorry. What's your story? What are you seeing your own version of Psychiatrist for?"

She wrapped her hands around the cup like it was some kind of life preserver. I admired her for wanting to preserve her life. "Straight to the heart, huh?" The smile.

"Yeah, why not? You waited for me for a reason, and I'm pretty certain it wasn't because I was so friendly."

Her shoulders relaxed and she smiled more genuinely again. "You're right. I just…you're more honest than most." Her eyes darted to my corset, rested for a second on my bright scarlet lips. "You don't hide."

"Bullshit. We're both messes."

"Takes one to know one."

We laughed again, and sipped blazing hot coffees. "God! That is hot."

"I only like it hot," she said. "Iced coffee is just watered down good coffee."

"Right. Tell me about you. I kinda can't believe that I care, to be honest, but please." I motioned for her to start, sitting back in the booth, and waited.

"I was raped," she said like she'd just swallowed thorns, but with the fucking smile.

"Simple enough."

"I was twenty. I got grabbed on the way home from a college party, Bridgewater State." Long sip. "A guy jumped out of a car, the passenger side. Knocked me down, threw a blindfold on me, and tossed me in the backseat." She was reliving it behind her eyes. I wanted to pull her out.

"There were two guys?"

"Four. Two of them held me in the back and hogtied me, drove with me for forty minutes the police said, but it felt like forty days."

"Did they all…"

"No. Just the one guy, the driver, Richard Preston. He was the older brother of one of the passengers who went to school with me. Not that the kid picked me out, I just happened to be in the wrong place at the wrong time."

"I'll say."

Nervous tinkling laughter from her had a guy at the counter turn and look our way, staring at her, not at me. I wasn't used to that. Now that she wasn't just Denim Sally with the Inappropriate Smile, I thought she was pretty in a simple way; sandy blonde hair, no makeup, approachable if not skittish. Not like me. Not at all.

Jen stopped talking to watch the guy walking to our table, unabashed, like he was in a fucking bar, like we wanted him there.

"You have the loveliest laugh I've ever heard," he said. This guy was beyond hot, no matter who you were, or what type you had. Pitch black hair with an unintentional messiness. Five o'clock shadow that went perfectly with the suit. And the eyes, Jesus Christ. Brilliant blue, inquisitive, smart, with zero egotism. He stood next to our table, this unbelievable movie star gentleman, with timid Jen, who was six shades of purple, and me, nightmare white hair that took over the room, in fishnet and sequins and black lace. He totally ignored me.

"Hey, buddy, we were talking, and drinking this mediocre coffee, so if you could just—"

"Miss, I was talking to your friend. If she wants me to go, I will." I'd never been told to fuck off so politely.

Jen had recovered from her blush shock and sized the guy up. "It's okay, Charity," she said, eyes still glued to him. "I'm Jen."

"Evan Hale." He held out his hand to her, and she gave it a limp shake.

Unexpectedly, he turned to me, not the type to ignore a lady, or even me. *Good luck in my company, Evan Hale.*

"Charity, she said?" He held his hand to me, and I shook it powerfully, sitting up straighter and staring him down. He was beautiful. It was intimidating and I hated that.

"Yeah, Charity. So what exactly are you doing over here?"

He smiled wide and uninhibited. I couldn't help but smile back. "You've got fire in you, don't you?" he said with a little laugh. "I won't mince words." He turned back to Jen. "I think that beautiful laugh is probably the tip of an iceberg of beauty in a woman like you."

Jen's mouth gaped, her eyes fluttering. I did her a favor and kicked her under the table.

"Ow! Thank you!" she said with lovesick blankness. I rolled my eyes.

"Let me take over here," I butted in. I focused on

Evan. I was mentally incapable of watching any more of Jen's shy awkwardness. One of us should walk away with this guy, and I'd probably already ruined my chances to see him naked. But man, just once would have been nice. "Give him your phone number, Jen, in case you're unfamiliar with protocol."

Evan glanced at me, amused, like we shared some secret joke. It bothered me that I wanted to share a secret joke with him. Jen rattled off her phone number and he punched it into his phone.

"I'd love to meet you for drinks sometime," he said with a low huskiness. He spoke so civilly, and yet with such intimacy. He wasn't shy about being a deep guy. Sexy.

Jen wet her lips, giving the impression she'd crawled through a desert to find someone like him. He watched her back, like he'd been waiting.

I was not used to being the uncomfortable one. I'd just met these two clowns, for hell's sake. This day had taken a surreal direction.

"Ooookay, so, nice to meet you, Ethan," I said with a huff, waving him away.

"Evan."

"Yup. But we're going to finish our coffee now and get to know each other. You'll have your chance."

He smiled coolly. "Of course. My pleasure, ladies. And Jen," he took her hand in his, and her intake of breath was loud. Embarrassing. "We'll speak soon." He nodded to me and swaggered out, smiling politely at everyone he passed.

"What the hell was that?" I said.

"I don't know. Meeting all sorts of interesting characters today." She waggled her eyebrows and smiled the cute smile. I didn't have one of those.

"He was incredible. Too old for me. Had to be like forty, but incredible," I said.

"How old are you?"

"Twenty-three."

"You seem younger. And older. Never mind."

"I hear that a lot." I'd never heard it.

Jen put her head down on the table, making me laugh. It unnerved me. I liked her. I'd stopped really liking anybody.

"You're going to go out with him, right?" I asked.

She whipped her head up, making hair fly in her face, and said something that made me so angry: "No."

"What? Why the hell not? He's amazing. Even I think so, and nobody impresses me."

"Then you should go out with him," she snapped, and looked down into her coffee shamefully.

"Hmmm. What's that? You're annoyed. What for?"

"He isn't my type," she said.

I laughed loud, getting more stares than I'd already gotten. I winked at a college kid who was staring at my huge, white hair.

"What's so funny?" Jen spat.

"That guy's everybody's type."

She scrunched up her face as if wondering if she should say the thing she was thinking. A huge proponent of saying everything I thought out loud, I egged her on.

"Tell me what's on your mind. This is already one of

the strangest afternoons ever. How much more complex can it get?"

She let out a loud sigh. "I don't really date well."

"Ha! That's all? You don't have to marry him, just go out with him, put him to use, and let him call you again if he isn't a fucking nightmare. Or a nightmare fucking."

"It's one of the reasons I go to the psychiatrist. I date guys for a while, but I can't ever make it work, even if there's nothing wrong. I'm not afraid—I want to find someone, but I can't." She bit her lip, tears welling. "I can't."

"Sure you can. Rape screws you up. Makes you want things you really don't. Makes you think you can't have things that you deserve. It makes you dark when you're not looking." I slugged back coffee. "You're not like that. You're not *bad*. You can have a good guy like that. And yeah, you are too afraid, you'll probably always be afraid. Evan seems to be a good guy. Go out with him."

Calling him a good guy burnt my tongue like eating fire ants. Calling any man 'good' was against my nature, but I also knew when they weren't awful. I could see the roughage in people like I never could….*before*.

Becoming a murderous scourge of the earth had its perks.

Jen's eyes welled. "Oh, fuck, don't cry. Crying scares me." I reached over the table and touched her hand, and the tears spilled over. "We have to get out of here."

I stood with lots of clanking of pins and buckles

and bracelets and pulled her to her feet, pissed to be humiliated by *her* show of emotion. Head hung, she shrank. For the first time ever, self-consciousness like the ordinary folk knew crept in. Idiotic. Dressed like a *Rocky Horror* extra, the way I always was; a spectacle.

"My apartment isn't far from here," she said, eyes wide with rejection fear. "Can you come over for a while?"

She clearly needed me. It was weird, but I had nothing to do for a few hours. Until it got dark and I got dark with it. I choked down the bile that filled my mouth.

"Let's go."

WOUND LICKING

"It's a little messy, sorry," Jen said, laying her purse on the floor. She didn't mumble when she was upset, I realized. Like she was still trying to make sure everyone thought she was okay.

"I live at Spring Hill. So your place is like in a different dimension of class."

I sank onto a chair like I always do, like I owned the chair and it had been waiting for me to find it. The apartment was cookie cutter, like mine, but the paint looked a lot better, and the carpet was tan, not lime green from 1974. Hey, lime green got me a hundred bucks a month off rent when I got around to paying it.

Jen collapsed onto a blue loveseat, exhaustion painted all over her. I remembered that exhaustion, back when I had feelings. I remembered when my feelings didn't make me a monster, and when I didn't like it.

I liked what my feelings had been turning me into.

"You're smiling," she said.

"Oh. Sorry?"

"No, no, it was just sort of a weird smile," she said, laughing, making me laugh. "What were you thinking about?"

"I was thinking about how tired you look, and that I probably did it to you asking hard questions after you just went to your psychiatrist. And then Don fucking Draper showed up."

"I'm okay. I get like this. Tired, you know, just tired of being afraid and stuff." She crossed her legs, kicking her shoes off. Some of her timidity disappeared in her own space. "So, now that I called you weird, you want to know why I can't hold a relationship down?"

"You think you can out-weird me, do you?" I glanced down at my red corset and fishnet stockings, my wardrobe staples.

"Yeah, I do. I always date guys that look like my rapist. Always. Blond guys with curly hair, blue eyes that go right through me. Muscular, athletic."

"Yeah, going for muscular blond dudes is weird." I winked at her. "You're right, that's totally fucked, actually." I was still winning the weird-off, though.

"Then I always crack. Dr. Reed thinks I'm trying to make them love me, and that when they treat me right and don't hurt me, I don't know how to react."

"Yup, sounds like something a shrink would say. If you don't mind me saying, Basket Case, maybe it would do you some good to have a drink with this guy, Evan, then? He doesn't fit the usual fucked up bill."

She grinned. "Well, Lunatic, I think I'd like to hear

your story before I take your advice. Not your fashion advice though."

"My fashion advice? How many Denims had to die to make that Canadian tuxedo you're wearing?"

I saw what Evan Hale meant about her laugh. If clouds being parted made a sound...

"This is so fucking weird, that we're talking like this. Weirder that I like you." I threw my leg over the arm of the chair, kicking off one combat boot, then the other. They fell onto a pile of books, knocking them over. I didn't pick them up.

"You don't like a lot of people?" she asked, her voice with this cute scratchy undertone. She had endearing traits. Jerk.

I smiled that one way that creeped people the fuck out. I did that one best. "A lot of people don't like me."

"Well, I do. You hungry?"

"Always."

She went barefoot to the kitchen that was about a foot away, yelling to me like she was in the west wing. "So, tell me about your major malfunction, Charity."

I chipped red polish off my fingernails. "It's all in the past now."

"It always is, but not for us."

With a sigh, I let it out. "I was court ordered to go to the shrink after a bar fight down at T-Bones. The guy pressed charges—"

"The *guy?*" She stood in the kitchen doorway, eyes and mouth looking like *The Scream*. "You got in a bar fight with a guy?"

"Well, girls don't want to fight me," I shrugged.

She shook her head, eyes wide. She clearly wished she'd been there. "What did he do to deserve a beating?"

"He told me I looked ready for a fucking. In his defense, I did." Her face fell a little, and I didn't understand it. I kept talking until it went away. "I mean, I get cat-called or whatever; you don't look like this and expect to see a lot of doors held open. That's fine, but when this fucking smelly biker dude assumed he was the one who was going to give me a proper fucking, well, I wasn't having any of that. So I punched him in his fat, bearded mug, kicked him in the balls before he knew what hit him, and then punched him again. And again." I gave my finest ugly grin. It made me happy to think of it, made my stomach clench and my heart pound. I was getting closer to the time to be the Other Thing. "He didn't like that. Turns out I did end up getting fucked. He called the cops on me. Pussy."

She shook her head and went back in the kitchen. I hadn't had anyone cook for me in a long time. It smelled good, whatever she was reheating.

"And that's the story of how I came to be Psychiatrist's new favorite friend."

Jen's lip quirked but she wasn't smiling. "That's not your story, though. What made you want to punch a dude to begin with?"

"Channeling Dr. Mortimer! Really, you want the whole story, why I'm this thing?" I hadn't meant to call myself a thing, but if the shoe fits....

I poked around at the stacks of books, a basket of knitting, with a bunch of knitted stuff all around. She clanked around in the kitchen for a minute, and I thought maybe she would forget she asked, but she came out with a piping hot bowl of spaghetti, and trained her eyes on me.

My story was the kind of thing only psychiatrists deserved to hear. But she wanted to hear it anyway.

"This is awesome, thank you. Nobody ever cooks for me. I barely even cook for me."

"Obviously, you're so skinny."

"Yeah, I'm on this killer diet of beer and human flesh with the occasional box of Teddy Grahams."

She sat again, searching my face, biting her lip, waiting. I twisted spaghetti in my mouth and it was so good. Just so good. It tastes different when someone else cooks for you. I couldn't recall the last time someone made a home-cooked meal for me. I guess you gotta have a home for that stuff.

"You don't really have to tell me what happened to you."

I swallowed, not looking at her, just eating like I hadn't ever eaten anything so good. "You know what? It's okay. You told me your shit, and it's like Voldemort or something, you talk about it and it loses its power."

"I think that's the other way around."

"Well, Voldemort didn't get abused by every Tom, Dick and Harry his mother brought home, so I'm making the rules here."

She stopped moving or eating. "What happened?" she asked in a whisper.

Fork noisily scraping the bowl, I started leaking the slow poison. "My dad left us when I was a kid, like everybody's dad did. That wasn't a big deal. I always expected it because why would he deal with my mother's shit if he didn't have to? She was nasty to him, always yelling and being awful. Then the drugs started." Slurp of spaghetti. Jen was unmoving but that was all I could see without looking at her directly, and that I couldn't do.

"She worked at Walgreens, and when they switched her to nights, she'd show up at the school bus stop to meet me, high as a kite."

"How old were you?"

"Ten." More spaghetti. It was forming a lump in my throat, but I kept eating. Comfort food, increasingly offering less and less comfort. "Mom started hitting the bottle hard. Then the nasty street drugs came. The men came with them." I hated what my voice was doing, getting lower and deeper. I shoveled in the spaghetti.

"Do you want a drink? Soda or juice…"

"Beer? You got any beer?"

She shook her head, and we made eye contact. I cringed.

"That's cool, it's too late to start day drinking. Almost time for night drinking."

I stood up, unable to *not* move anymore, and brought the empty bowl to her kitchen. She didn't follow me. I washed it quickly, breathing in through my nose, out through my mouth. *I could do this, I did worse than this all the time.*

My hands were clammy; a sign of fucking weakness. I hated nothing more.

Jen said from her spot in the living room, "Hey, I

think I have some leftover vodka from my birthday party."

"I sure would like to meet her, Lady Vodka."

Jen came out to the kitchen, reached up into a high cabinet and pulled down a half bottle of vodka. I wanted to hug it. If any occasion deserved drinking, it was this one.

"I don't have any shot glasses."

"Do you have any regular glasses? Who am I fooling here?"

She poured half a cup, but I waved her on to a full glass.

"You're not having any? Really?" I asked. She hadn't discovered drinking on a weekday afternoon, maybe.

"I don't really drink."

I pulled a glass out of the cabinet. "You do today."

She winced taking the glass, poured a quarter of a cup and raised it to me. "To new friends."

"And old demons."

I threw mine back, drinking about half, but that was twice as much as Jen was able to. I took the glass out of her hand and just shook my head. "My bad." I drank the rest of both of our glasses, and led the way to the other room, fate echoing in my ears with every step. I was glad to be wobbling a little.

"You don't really have to tell me more if you don't want to."

"Stop saying that. I don't do anything I don't want to," I said through gritted teeth. I didn't sit down, but I would not pace. I wouldn't be weak. Looking out the window but seeing nothing, I told her the things nobody wanted to know, least of all me. Nobody got to hear this stuff, nobody got to live it with me, or hear it from my mouth. But I spoke.

"We didn't have any money, of course. Single, junkie Walgreens mom. She blew any money we did have, I could tell by the lack of food in the house. Like, I was too oblivious at that age to really get the idea of "poor," but there was never fucking anything to eat, you know? And the place just kinda smelled like booze all the time, had the ambiance of a shitty bar. Anyway, the first time one of her boyfriends hit me was when he bought a sub and ate half, then put the other half in the fridge. I was so hungry after school, I had to have it. A fucking steak and cheese. Who turns down a steak and cheese sub just sitting there?

"So, I'm sitting at the kitchen table, loving this sub, and I got knocked on the back of the head so hard that I fell out of the chair, sub goes with me, I hit my head on the table leg, and I'm instantly mad that I can't finish eating. Then I realize this huge guy whose name I didn't even know had punched me in the head. I'd just turned eleven. "

Jen was a good listener, which was great because when I had shit to say, somebody had better be paying attention. I finally sat down; the chair enveloped me in comfort in a way id hadn't the first time I sat in it. Maybe I just needed it more.

She looked like she was watching the scariest horror movie ever. She kinda looked like she belonged in a horror movie, actually, that was the bland kind of pretty she was. Girl-next-door type that the superhot girls never saw coming.

"Anyways, he beat me unconscious, not that day, but a different day. I don't remember what I did. Don't remember much of anything, really, but I never saw him again after that. My mom's consolation prize to me. I'd be getting plenty of those."

Voices out in the hallway. It surprised us both, reminded us we weren't all alone in the world.

"What time is it, Jen?"

She glanced at her watch. I didn't even own a watch. "4:30. Wow, that happened fast."

I didn't have long.

"Okay, well I have a dinner date at six, so I'd better get rambling."

She didn't believe me, and I bet she thought I was too scared to tell the rest of my story. That wasn't it.

"Dinner date, huh?"

"Yeah. But I can stay for a little while." I looked around again, sudden panic rising in my throat. What the fuck was I doing there, telling this goddamn stranger what Psychiatrist had barely squeezed out of me after our many visits together? I stopped myself from biting my bloody fingernail. *Weak.*

She was giving me that face, like she wanted to hug me from across the room. So I went on, fast.

"Anyway, without the sordid details, as I got older and mouthier, and the men came and went, I got hit plenty. So did Mom, but we never spoke of it. That or anything. I don't know if she even noticed, she was so strung out. I learned to fight fast, so there's that. Turns out, though, the ones who want to fuck kids liked it when I fought."

"Oh my God," she said, hand up to her mouth like she just saw a car accident, eyes wide like it was someone she knew. I suppose it was both.

I shook my head, happy to be both comforting and the comforted. "No, I'm good now. Tip top. My mother's choice in men, or her necessity for men, was piss poor, but that wasn't my choice. I learned a lot fast. *That* was my choice." I gritted my teeth as I pictured his face, *that* one, the one that broke me. "Nobody makes my choices for me now."

I stood up fast, the booze and memory combo making me stumble, brain buzzing. I was so ready to let the claws come out that my fingers itched and my heart burned and my chest screamed and my stomach quaked.

Jen threw her arms around me in a way nobody ever had. The way that says she didn't want anything back. It hurt all over.

"I'm so sorry," she whispered into my ear.

I backed away, gazed in her pretty blue eyes, and smiled. "Don't be. Doors that are kicked in are still open doors, baby."

HARPY

I smiled to myself, leaving Jen's apartment. I couldn't believe I'd told her those things, and after we'd just met. Like, *just met.* Telling that story was something I only did when shitfaced and wanted to scare someone off or when I met our good Psychiatrist. It wasn't the kind of story to tell and then ever want to face the person with this new knowledge ever again. But something about the softness of her, like her stupid fucking smiling for no reason, and all the books piled up everywhere, like she'd close herself up in one if she could, it made me think how easy it would be to just be *regular*. Regular person, regular problems, regular pain, and leftover spaghetti and books and a couch that I went shopping for and smiled when I found. That would never be me.

I was angry every time I pictured *his* face; even more since talking to Jen. Soon, that memory would change me into a monster that could do something about my suffering.

My keys left another scratch on a broken chair as they landed. I observed my own place like I'd done to Jen's. She had new things; I had former trash. Used things, without the fucking romance of being hunted-down antiques. Necessary crap that survived and got uglier with every move and bump, more battered with every minute they endured. There was so little of me here, I realized. I didn't have a lot of things. Didn't need things. And what I did own was hidden from wandering eyes—not that many came by. It wasn't really a home, I guess, but I wouldn't know *home* if it fell on me Wicked-Witch-style. This particular hidey hole was just *mine* to run to.

A place to wait.

Anxiety had me grinding my teeth, I couldn't rest my eyes on one spot, just waiting for dark to descend. I got more fucking nervous every night. For the past fifteen days, the change had happened. The monster makes the woman.

I went straight to my bedroom, which was a bad idea because I realized how hideously beat I was. Emotional strain and all that.

I didn't even tell Jen the worst of it.

"Sweet Jesus, you look good," I said to my futon. It was tucked into this alcove that served no purpose but to hide sleeping people from the world, and I loved it. Collapsing onto it, I pulled off my boots and curled under the blankets.

I was well aware of how ridiculous my unicorn bedspread was. I wasn't trying to be fucking ironic. My eyes flitted to the shelf of unicorn and fairy statues, to the unicorn stuffed animals, to the fairy pictures and wall hangings. I actually laughed, not for the first time, about them. It had a youthful ambience, like a demented fifth grader lived there, but I guess one did. Forever trapped in that hellhole I'd "grown up" in. In my room now with those ridiculously glittery, soft, pure, dreamlike things, I didn't feel trapped in that kid's heart. I hadn't owned anything as cute as this stuff when I lost that girl.

I rolled over, willing myself not to fall asleep, pulling the cotton candy pink and rainbowed blanket up, but my mind drifted as I lost focus on the wall shelf, to the gift shop on the waterfront where I'd bought it, *John Alden* something. Everything in Plymouth was named after that guy. I'd gone in for a cold drink, Hades-hot from walking aimlessly downtown, and it was staring at me from a shelf with a bunch of other crap. A snowglobe with a unicorn inside, standing on green grass. It was chipped on one side, the only one on the shelf, an imperfect thing that had once been perfect. A useless, shattered, nothing that no one believed in. I brought it home, cradling the bag to my chest.

My alarm went off, little bird chirps because fuck all if I would allow myself to be woken up by the incessant buzzing noise of a regular alarm clock. It was set for 5:30 every afternoon. Just in case. But I never missed dusk. Not anymore.

I threw off the blankets, kicking my legs free, stretching, the hum of adrenaline already in my head.

"Come on baby, let's see what you can do," I said out loud, shaking my arms and legs. I waited.

His image danced in my head, the one who broke me, like a demon clown, taunting me. It happened every night. I bared my teeth and pleaded with the clock to let me sprout wings.

I sweated. I drank a glass of water, chased it with a beer. I needed to loosen up and enjoy myself. And oh, I most certainly would be enjoying myself.

He'd always said that when he showed up in my room, when my mother was out cold; how much he was enjoying himself.

I screamed a guttural, thirsty scream at his face in my head.

The clock on the stove flashed to six. It would be an early night.

My body went ice cold and clammy like a corpse pulled out of a river. It was starting. Every night the first thing to hit me was the odor. Rotten carcasses, carrion. Roadkill. Like dried blood and viscera in the blazing sun.

My stomach growled.

A spasm shook through my feet, and they grew, and grew, all the while the soft skin thickening, hardening, becoming scaly and rough, ripping apart the tender flesh on the outside. My red toenails split down the middle and curled back, and black talons burst through, waiting for someone else's blood to be caked underneath them. I watched, detached, the inevitable pain something I gave into every time.

My knees snapped backwards, the ungodly pain snapping me back, and I stifled the screams through a spasm of tears instead; three other apartments were on this floor alone, a footstep away. Body buckling, I hit the floor as my legs broke—*snap, snap, snap*—and reshaped into those of a larger than life bird. Dingy white feathers ruptured from my legs in waves like dominoes, soft and filthy. They went up to my waist, meeting the bottom of my red corset, winding around the backs of my arms.

This was the best part. My heart pounded, a smile spreading across my face at the agony in my feet and legs.

It was faster each time. This time the wings sprouted in seconds, monstrous and strong. Not from my back like some fallen angel, but from the backs of my arms like a beast. I barely winced as they ripped through the muscles, banana-split the skin from my wrists to my shoulders. Any amount of pain was worth what they did for me; they could carry me anywhere, no matter how tattered they were. I thought they were perfect. They brought the monster to life. *I* was the intimidating one.

I gawked at myself in the hall mirror that I'd put up especially to watch the transformation. My blonde hair had gone bleach white when I started turning into the creature fifteen days ago. At night when I became the bird-thing, it filled out into wild tight waves that stood around me like I'd been electrocuted. My lips were black, but my eyes were mine. I wished they would go away, too.

I was a cracked and blistered thing behind them.

Getting outside was a bitch, but I was getting quicker and quicker at it. I put my arms at my sides, wings folding like any bird's, and stuck my face out the door, hair getting caught in the deadbolt. "Motherfucker," I muttered as I ripped it out. Nobody in the hallway. I couldn't know if anyone was looking out the peepholes of one of the other three apartments, but it was a chance I looked forward to taking every night.

I squashed a tiny flutter of happiness that Robbie, the next door over, might see me. There'd be no explaining myself to anyone, but to Robbie I don't think I'd have to.

I made quick time up the stairs from my basement apartment and out the front door, hearing muted voices from the second floor. The second I hit the landing outside, I stretched my arms. Every muscle in my back and chest flexed with power, and a surge of adrenaline burst through me as I jumped off the steps, flexing my wings once, twice, three times, then soared. To say it gave me freedom is an understatement; it gave me dominion.

I laughed until my lungs hurt, relishing the ugliness of the hyena-vulture sound. To use my arms that way, to actually *fly*… No matter what I'd suffered to become the beast, the purpose and strength it gave me was worth a thousand childhoods.

My teeth ached. It wasn't the wind, it was the need to rip something to shreds. Gnashing them hard, I let out a screech and descended, unaware of where I was and caring even less. Time, space wasn't the same when I was the bird-thing. It didn't just move faster, it went slower too, and I covered area in odd bursts that didn't make sense. Like teleporting but with more effort maybe? It was wildly disorienting but took me so completely from being human…it was a drug.

Soaring just above the trees, I zeroed in on a group of guys, a couple of them stumbling. They were probably my age. None of them had that red heat emanating from them that I'd become familiar with. When I started transforming I could follow the red heat and it showed me who was best for killing. Not that I needed any suggestions. Red ripples in the air, the same waves of evil that my mother's bastard boyfriends emitted when they grabbed me, pushed me, hurt me and made me a loveless thing. As *he* tore my guts in two, taking what he shouldn't have from me. When I was that winged beast, I could always see the evil in front of me. These guys weren't good enough. Bad enough.

I kept going, until the air changed, became warmer, the trees less dense. I still didn't know where I was, but I'd gone far in time and space, the sky changing colors in no particular order. Then I saw it.

The cloud of molten haze, and inside of it, a man. No shirt, skin bared like some god of debauchery. He laid on a beach in the darkness, a woman next to him, and down I swooped.

I landed on the sand with a great flap of my wings, causing it to tornado around me in the briny air. They were alone on the beach, these two, and I wanted him bad. She was asleep on the sand, or more likely passed out drunk, but he was wide awake. He hovered over her, and there was no doubt what he was ready to do.

It had been done to me so many times.

I lifted my arms just enough to propel me across the beach, my shoulders tensing, every muscle alive, and I landed beside him. He screamed, eyes like satellite dishes, but she didn't stir. He scrambled backwards into a wall of rocks. I loomed over him in a second, standing easily eight feet tall in that form. My claws dug into the sand, and my tongue hung, panting. My face, my torso, were still human but the heart that beat inside was all animal after dark. I threw my head back and screeched from my gut, the corset tightening with my breath.

"Please!" he blubbered at me, like they always did. Fucking coward.

I cocked my head. "Please?" My voice was nature and broken glass and evil incarnate. "Would you have heard her say it?"

He shook his head, not understanding through his fear, certainly not understanding that a thing like me could talk, or exist, but he glanced at the girl on the sand, stirring, and understood enough.

"She knew what she was getting into when she came here with me," he said.

That was all I needed.

I fell on him with demon screams, digging the claws on my feet into his thighs, holding him down, while I ripped at his torso as fast and hard as I could with taloned hands. Blood rained all around us. The smell drove me wild with need.

I tore into his neck with my own teeth, as human as they were when I woke up that morning, and I lashed my head back and forth, tearing ragged holes in his skin. Fucking delicious, the best steak I could find. He was far from dead, the way I liked my prey, but his red haze was turning a dull pink. Pink like my skin was before it was covered in bruises. I bit harder.

"Giving up already?" I snarled, and plucked out an eyeball with one talon, popping it in my mouth. His screams flared up the red aura again, adrenaline surging, blood flowing, ready for me. I laughed.

Behind me, the girl came to. She screamed bloody fucking murder, of course, and it didn't get any better when I turned to look at her with my human face, covered in blood—her boyfriend's, or whatever he was. He twitched under my foot.

"What the—what the hell *are* you?!" she screamed.

What the hell is wrong with you, I thought. *I'm not the scariest thing you've seen tonight, just uglier on the outside.*

"I'm a Harpy." The word erupted as though it had always been there, as if I'd always known. I loved the sound of it slipping off my gore-slick lips and said it again. "A Harpy. Now, calm down," I said, smiling to show her the flesh bits stuck to my teeth. "He won't be bothering you again." The words sounded as bitter as they tasted, and I drenched my throat in his blood to wash it away.

～

*A*fter I'd drained him and conveniently thrown the bloody bones out to sea, I flew off, head high against the rushing wind, zero guilt for leaving the shocked girl there. I'd done her the most massive favor, one nobody else could ever do for her, and nobody was about to believe that a massive, dirty bird lady flew down and ate the hell out of her man-friend. She wasn't telling anybody, that's for sure. I made it abundantly clear to her that it would not be a good idea to do so. After that, not my problem.

"Shut the fuck up and be glad the blood isn't yours." Comforting? No. True, yes. She could use a dose of reality. After all, what the hell had she been thinking going alone to a beach with some dude? *Please, like he wouldn't have done the same thing in one of its forms on the subway, at 7-11, on the White House lawn...* And he certainly would have thrown her to me for my next meal if it meant saving his ass.

Nothing could have saved him once I set my sights on him. His blood was as good as spilled the minute he stepped on the sand.

I spread my arms and took off at a run, the wind billowing under my wings. Seagulls raced away from me as I rose high above the sand and rocks, and the crying girl who had nothing to cry over. Both tired and energized after the kill, I knew from experience that one a night was enough. The high I got from it wouldn't carry my exhaustion away. I passed out cold the first time, in the woods, and woke up half naked, covered in blood, no idea where I was. I waited there, exposed, terrified, until the change took me again that night.

Not the first time I'd been exposed and terrified, waiting for the night.

My claws hit the wet grass and I reluctantly folded my arms down. Funny, it never occurred to me to care if I was seen returning home. Any inhibitions I did have—and there weren't many—disappeared after being the Harpy. I threw my arms out one last time, sucking up the cool air, and the utter sense of being me and *not* being me all at once. A creature to be feared and admired. Invincible.

I let the change happen with tears in my eyes. Mortality crashed back into me with the gentle hush of feathers, and I was Charity again, half naked and shivering. I went back to the human world a defiled queen.

Back in my bathroom, ordinary bathroom for ordinary people, cookie cutter and personality free. My relection stared back at me in the mirror, face covered in dried blood, wild hair matted with it, and a coating of it on my teeth. My eyes were crazed, lips still black, a thing in-between. I loved myself this way more than I could ever love myself as a person.

I stripped off my corset, caked with bits of flesh and yet more blood, and dropped it in the sink to soak. Time for a hot shower to wash away that part of me, the part that consumed rather than be consumed.

I wouldn't be stripped anymore.

THE THING NO ONE BELIEVES IN

*T*he morning after was only ever hard because I remembered what I had to face: life. That particular morning, I had no job to go to, again, giving me both nothing to do and no fucking money to do it with.

My wiry body creaked hatefully as I rolled out of bed. I'd become really grateful that bed was just a futon right on the floor. My body ached in weird places, like I'd wrestled a donkey or something. When I was a kid, in that house, I woke up the mornings *after* just like this —I didn't cry these days. Waking up after being goddamn raped as a child simply didn't give me the satisfaction that the Harpy hangover did. Go figure. Every morning I wished the wings were still there so I could fan them out, enormous and powerful, drenched in sin. Reminding me that I my head pounded and my body throbbed for good reason. I took another shower, with the massage setting—coffee shop jobs paid enough for a good showerhead if nothing else.

My arms weren't strong enough to power wings, but my heart wasn't strong enough not to do it. The ache in every muscle was worth it. I smiled into the hot stream of water, and only wondered for a second why I suddenly turned into a Harpy every night. It was great to have a name for it—for *me*. I stopped questioning what I was after that first morning when I woke up covered in bruises from flying into shit. From the first time, it gave me a sigh of relief, a natural shedding of the dead skin, transforming into something...*else*. I didn't need more answers than that. Gift horse and all that shit.

Waiting for the last of my good coffee to brew, since I wouldn't be stealing it from work any longer, I started making myself into Daytime Charity Barbie. I loved the white hair that the Harpy had given me. It was shaggy, Debbie Harry-hot. I ran my hands through it with some gel that made it even more a mess. As the day wore on, it would get longer, wilder. By the time I turned into the Harpy at night, it was a huge mass of afro around my head, tight white crimps with a life of their own.

My black lips went away during the day. I missed them. I blended blood red and black lipstick to remember. False eyelashes, black liner, red eyeshadow. Glitter. Ready for a humdrum day in Plymouth, Massachusetts. America's Hometown was never ready for me.

Just because I hid from the asshole who scarred me didn't mean I had to hide from everyone else.

I turned on the TV, falling into my salvage sofa, the coffee I needed with junkie urgency in hand. Always, I was afraid that there would be a report of who I'd killed, but over two weeks with nothing. That, I did wonder about. Nothing, again. I still didn't know where I'd gone the night before, or most nights—the killing and eating always filled me with pure adrenaline, soured my stomach in the most satisfying way. But no one seemed to notice what I was doing.

"What the hell?" I barked at my buzzing phone. It was Jen. I shocked myself by smiling and continued to shock myself by answering it.

"Good morning!" she sang.

"Dial it down. I'll decide if it's a good morning or not."

She laughed that infectious, sunny laugh that made me jealous. My laughing was offensive, even to me.

"I hope I didn't call too early." She paused. "I just… I'm happy after talking to you. Like, not so…"

"Alone?"

"Yeah, alone. And I'd really like to hang out again, but with way less drama."

"I am a huge proponent of less drama. Meet you at Dunkins again later?" I was weirding myself out, instigating more play dates with the girl. But I liked her. I *trusted* her, with little reason to. Trust wasn't something I gave out as easily as my phone number.

"Cool, Chare." She gave me a little nickname. Cute. Next I would be 'Care Chare.'

"Meet you there at like, three. I can get off my ass by then."

"Three it is. Thanks."

"Jen, you don't have to thank me for hanging out with you. Nutcase."

"I guess that was weird. Lunatic." We laughed, and I hung up smiling, but sadness nudged up from underneath it. Strange. Compassion was something I could put in a junk drawer.

I tossed my coffee mug in the sink with a crash and squeezed my eyes shut, like it would take my day away. Like Jen wasn't a helpless girl that I was dragging into my disgusting life. Like I wasn't directionless, broken, worthless. Closing my eyes made me believe it even less. All I could see behind them was the blood I spilled and the flesh I fed from. It shouldn't have made me preen like a peacock.

I jumped when I heard the familiar knock from the other side of the kitchen wall. I put my hand on the tile, and smiled for a second, before finally knocking back. My neighbor, Robbie's way of saying good morning. One of the reasons I woke up at all, if I was being honest. I imagined him on the other side of the wall, and hoped he was smiling. Paper thin walls let me hear him put something in his own sink. We should be having coffee together. Like regular people would do if they liked each other. We liked each other, but I wasn't regular.

Being ordinary was something I didn't do well, and yet, my days were filled with it. That day, I had a date with the job search again. Even that was becoming ordinary, something that truly defined me as a person. And I wanted to be something more than that person; no not more—*different* than that person.

I heard The Ramones start up, more distant into Robbie's apartment, pulling him even further away.

I wanted to be the Harpy and never come back.

~

I didn't go looking for a job. I went back to bed. It was a terrible idea from the get-go, but fuck it, it's not like I had anywhere to be, really. The dream happened, as it did sometimes, and there was no waking from it. Being out and about all night made me too tired to wake up from my memories.

The nightmares about the bastard were always too bright. I could see everything from the dust on all the furniture, to my mother's pill bottles lying open, to his goddamn snarl as he unbuckled his pants. In the dreams there was no hiding. And in life there had been no hiding.

He was big. Tall, muscular, and hairy as a fucking bear. He had a mustache and beard, wild and unkempt dark hair. His chest was covered in it over his old sailor tattoos. He was too young to have been a sailor, I don't know what possessed him to get those. I remembered staring at the big ship one on his chest for too long, focusing on anything but what he was doing.

I only dreamed about that first time he raped me, not about the other times, and not about the things he made me do to his daughter when he brought her over. Even my subconscious ran from those memories, I think. That was the thing that broke me, sucked my spirit out, made me wish for death when I had barely begun my life. I only dreamed ever of the first night, and it always ended the same way; me waking up screaming when he got off of me, pushing on the already-budding bruises he left on my chest and arms and laughing about it. I dreamed of his sneer and how he walked to the door naked like he'd just conquered the fucking world and not a scared little girl. At the door, he said, "This is only the beginning."

Sweat-soaked, I rolled off the futon, unicorn blankets coming with me. I sat against the wall, chewing my lip painfully, concentrating on breathing deep. I opened my eyes and focused on the tattered fairy picture, cut out from a magazine, stuck to the wall next to my bed. Filtered sunshine gently kissed her half-closed eyes, her pristine wings letting her hover just over a dandelion that could swallow her whole. In the picture, it never did.

"Jesus Christ, it's after one?" I grumbled, pulling on a t-shirt and sweatpants. I made my way to the kitchen for more coffee. It was like starting my day all over again. No thanks, once was enough. Sitting on the couch again was déjà vu, and I was not into it. It hurt to start over without having been the Harpy in between; I'd been cheated. Nobody cheated me and got away with it. Guzzling my coffee, I all but ran to my bedroom to get dressed. White fishnets, same old boots, red skirt, black corset, a simple one. My makeup was smudged, but it was me. The wrong amount of imperfect.

Robbie was bringing in a load of laundry as I left the apartment. My breath caught as I wondered if I should quickly back into the apartment and avoid him. Talking to him wasn't horrible, even pleasant at times. Impossibly, we got each other. When he talked to me it appeared as though he actually was paying attention. He'd lived next to me for over a year and we'd hung out a few times. I'd seen his band play a bunch, and we had a standing weekly date to watch *American Horror Story,* getting old seasons on demand when the new ones ran out. We looked good together. He was a little grungy, always in old jeans and work boots, with this floppy hair that girls dreamed about. Pretty skin, Mediterranean or something, and smooth. He did have all the makings of a groupie magnet.

"Hey, what's up?" I muttered.

"Laundry, woman. Where you headed?"

"I need to do something that's not sitting in there," I said, nodding at my door. "Quit my job yesterday."

He put down the basket and leaned against his door, running fingers through his tousled hair. Delicious. Never pick up your neighbor, I say. Makes them harder to run away from, and I really didn't want to have to kill him. He was too attractive.

"Are there any jobs left for you to quit?" Oh my god, that smile was a panty-wetter.

"Yes, I just don't know where they are or if I want any of them."

He shook his head, smile getting wider. "Time to stop working at crap jobs, maybe?"

"Yeah, I'll get right on that CEO position they've been bugging me about at Apple."

"No, I mean why don't you go to school or something? Do something you actually like?"

"I don't like things."

"Yeah, me either." His laugh was honest and loud. He pushed off the door and walked to me with enough swagger to leave me panting. Maybe we could just screw and get it over with. I stood still, pissed that I was holding my breath, and watched him get closer to me. He smelled like cedar and his lips looked girl-soft.

"Charity, you're better than shitty coffee jobs," he said in a low voice that made me squirm. "Let yourself be good at things."

I wanted him to touch my hair that was filled with hairspray, or kiss my lips that were covered in two shades of lipstick.

"Thanks. Maybe I will. You know, try something new or whatever."

His lips curled into a crooked smile that had my heart pounding to get out of this corset. "New is always good, even when it's not."

The air was electric between us, full of life. It made me itch to be liked. By him. It always did and I snuffed it out every time.

"All right, I got to get my laundry finished," he said, backing away. I wished he'd turn around so I could watch his glorious ass. "You have a good one. We on for *AHS* tomorrow?"

"You know it."

I walked to the duck pond across the street and sat on the grass. You used to be able to feed the ducks there, but then they shat all over the place and specific

town-employed duck feeders handled the job to mini-
mize duck shittetry. I took a bag of popcorn out of my
purse and tossed a handful into the water. It usually
settled me down, but not that day. I was nervewracked
by what Robbie had said. He pretty much told me I
wasn't applying myself. I most likely did need higher
expectations of myself, find something that I was
passionate about.

Something that I could do in the daytime, as a
human being.

Maybe I should do more than make great coffee. Be
a nurse? No, too many people, all of them needy.
Computer tech? No, too many pornos start out with
girls like me fixing computers. I tried to think of things
I loved—it didn't take long.

I remembered singing as a kid, the fleeting happiness, and how happiness grew when I did it, like giving
me a kickstart to live through the next day. I knew my
life would only give me what I put into it, like all those
inspirational posters said. Going to Robbie's band's
shows always made me want to get on stage and sing
with them, but I could never. I wasn't afraid to do
things, but I sure as hell didn't want to like anything
too much.

I threw more popcorn on the grass, and the ducks
came closer. I stared at their wings; there was nothing
that could make me want to stay on the ground like
them. Down here was place made for suffering. I had
the heart of a Harpy, and the body I carried around all
day was an afterthought. I didn't need any job or
hobby to action-pack my days. None of that mattered

when nighttime hit and I turned into something beautiful.

I was already a thing no one believed in. I sure as hell didn't need to amplify my lesser half.

Goals and aspirations would do nothing but eventually destroy and disappoint me, and confirm that I was not a person destined for good things. I probably wasn't a *bad* person, but the good in me was shackled to so much misery that it spent more time hiding than it did showing itself.

The Harpy made that all go away.

The bag of popcorn had been empty for a while, and the ducks had gone away. I was alone, wishing I had something more for them.

"Be happy with what you get. You weren't expecting it," I said to them, and threw the popcorn bag into the water.

Almost 2:30. Time to go and see someone who knew what it was like to be half a person.

*J*en was sitting politely as a churchlady when I got to Dunkin Donuts, at the same table we'd been at before. Her face lit up when she saw me, but couldn't mask that embarrassment about my clothes. She was in some mumu thing.

"Hey," I said with my own genuine smile, still scary. Jen got up and hugged me like I was a life preserver in an endless ocean.

"Hi," she said into my shoulder. I hugged her back. She needed it. But not as much as I needed coffee.

"Going to get a cup," I said. "You got one?"

She nodded and I got my cup of black hot coffee, no sugar. The girl already had it waiting. She didn't remember because she liked me, she remembered because she couldn't forget me.

"You dress like this every day then?" Jen asked as I sat down. I had to hand it to her, I didn't think she had the sack to come right out and say something like that.

"Only when my nun's habit is in the wash," I said, running a finger over the edge of my corset. I caught a middle-aged guy ogling me from a booth and winked. "This is me. You dress like *that* every day?"

"Like what?"

"Like a soccer mom who lost her sex appeal in the divorce."

She laughed loud, a nice, friendly sound that made more people look at her than me. "You're right," she said. "I could go on that show where they give you all the money and beg you to let them dress you."

"They'd Jell-O wrestle each other over which of us needed the makeover more."

Laughing and shaking her head, she took a long sip of her coffee, closing her eyes like it was the most peace she'd ever had. I knew from experience that it probably was.

"So, what do you do all day, Jen? Apparently, I'm on the market for new ways to occupy my time. Paying ways."

"Well, I do have a way that pays minimally. I work at Gunther Tootie's. I'm a baker."

Fleeting moment of anger that I had nothing like that. I wasn't a baker, or a coroner, or a farmer. I made coffee like hookers have sex, but not well enough to overshadow my abrasive interactions with the public. I wanted to think I was a singer, but for that, I'd have to sing. I had little to sing about.

"I like to *eat* baked goods. I got that going for me. Actually, I want a donut." I stood up and walked right into Evan Hale.

"Shit, sorry," I said.

"Are there donuts on the other side of that fire?"

"What?"

His eyes drilled right to the heart. "Like 'where's the fire?' but you were… That was bad."

"It really was. Yeah, I want a donut. Do you want a donut? I can get, like, a bunch of donuts." Money spent on donuts was never a waste, regardless of how little money one had.

He wrinkled his eyes, giving the impression that this was a serious decision. "I always want a donut. Sit down."

Nobody needs to tell me to sit down more than once. He went to the counter, and started pointing out donuts with the enthusiasm of a small child, while still maintaining this elegance that real men didn't have. Did he never eat damn donuts or was he just made happy that easily? I watched the muscles in his shoulders and back under his white dress shirt move. Nice.

I winked at Jen across the table. "Nice, huh?" I said, nodding at Evan as he paid the donut girl, who had a helluva smile for him. I hadn't gotten one.

"What? Oh, yeah." She was mesmerized by him. I looked away, a little ashamed of checking out the guy who'd so clearly gunned for her the day before.

"Pushover," he said to me, but with eyes on Jen. He smelled so good, it would be hard not to hit on him, but Jen's googly eyes made it evident that this would be a cruel thing to do. He popped open the box and pushed it to the middle of the table, pulling out a chocolate frosted mess of a thing as he did. I was immediately impressed that he would do this while wearing a white shirt.

"Cheers," he said, smashing my own Bavarian Kreme into his chocolate glazed. He smiled like we did this every day.

"Jen, you're a chocolate donut girl, I can tell," he said as he bit his own. I loved how he sat down with us like he was meant to be there, this incredibly put together man with Moulin Rouge me, and soccer-mom–before-her-time Jen. "Glad I bumped into you two days in a row," he continued. "Never saw you here together before, though. Starbucks girls, are you?" He pointed at me with his half-eaten donut. "You, I've seen here. But you work at that other coffee shop, don't you?"

"Not anymore. Stalker."

He laughed, and wiped cream off his lip with a thumb. I wanted to bite it. "You're not exactly hard to notice."

"We just met," Jen blurted out, then blushed. "Yesterday."

He stopped chewing and regarded her with clear surprise. "I would never have guessed that. You two seem like you've known each other for ages."

"We just both feel ages old," I muttered, but I didn't think he heard me.

Evan leaned back against the plastic bench. The urge to lean against his shoulder was strong.

"So where did you meet yesterday, then?" he asked.

"Our psychiatrists' office," I said enthusiastically, waggling my eyebrows.

He smirked, but looked at Jen. She was definitely the one who was supposed to be answering the questions, but as usual, me first. He made more of a point of ignoring me than most and did it sporadically so that it threw me off. What the fuck.

"You see the same psychiatrist?"

Jen shook her head with the awkward smile, not the nervous one, but didn't break eye contact. Good girl.

Evan picked up on her embarrassment though. "Don't worry, I see one, too. Or did. I used to. Surprise, I'm all cured of Crazy." He clapped his hands together elaborately like a magician with a smile that was, in fact, pretty magical.

Dying to ask what he was seeing a psychiatrist for, I leaned back to give Jen a chance. I was smug about my self-restraint.

"You had to see a psychiatrist?" she asked, disbelief in her voice.

"I didn't have to, I chose to."

"What was bothering you?" Jen asked.

"My chronic perfectionism that made me chronically unhappy." He bit into a new donut, powdered.

Jen nodded like she understood, but I didn't.

"Aren't you supposed to be happy when you're always trying to do better and be better?" I asked.

He scanned my face, his smile gone. "Not if there's nothing better to be had. You have to know when to give in to what you are."

"Well, you'll certainly never be perfect with that attitude," I said.

He cocked his head, eyebrows knitted, and I think he hated me right then. I took a jelly donut and kept smiling, even when jelly dripped onto my cleavage. Evan's eyes darted there, but returned to meet mine without making apologies.

"People weren't meant to be spotless, Charity. People are meant to have scars."

I could feel myself darken. I bit the donut but didn't let the jelly drops touch me.

Jen guzzled the end of her coffee, making Evan and me both smile. It's funny to see someone so clearly inhibited really enjoy the hell out of something.

"I'm glad we bumped into you here again today, Evan," Jen said, given some liquid confidence with that coffee shot.

"Well, you didn't really bump into me, per se. I came hoping you would be here. A little bit."

If you could watch a person melt into a plastic orange bench, I saw that happen to Jen. I soaked my jealousy up with the end of the jelly donut, which I then devoured.

"You came here to see me?" she said breathily, eyes wide.

He only raised his eyebrows in response. They both seemed to forget I was there, eating all those free donuts, watching the show. Evan was hot, sure, but I could get a guy like that. I didn't need to step in on hers.

I elbowed her as I bit into a chocolate donut. I hadn't eaten donuts in forever. I barely ate at all, really, so I made it count when I did. I was satisfied with what I consumed at night.

"Are you busy tonight?" Jen piped up. I was shocked she took my elbow hint. Where did she get off dressing like that and asking out a guy as smoking hot as Evan? It was kind of fantastic.

"I would love to be busy tonight with you," he answered, smoldering. Jen blushed hard.

Leaning across the table, he murmured to her something about Tuscany Tavern, which was a tiny Italian restaurant in the ghetto, making it pretentiously eccentric. She smiled the good smile, and he was done with his short and very interesting visit that quickly.

"Charity, good to see you again," he said, his full attention on me. He had a date planned with Jen who was right there, but he still couldn't turn off the smolder.

"Good to see you, too."

Eyes narrowed, he said quietly, "Don't say it if it isn't true."

"I like lying. It throws people off my trail." But my eyelids fluttered because shit, I wasn't lying. I had been happy to see him.

With a smile, he leaned even closer and I stopped breathing. "You aren't lying. You're not that good at it." And with that, he took his coffee and left. Jen reached into the donut box with a grin and took out the last powdered one. When I caught my breath, I high fived her non-powdered hand.

"Oh. You aren't going anywhere looking like that," I said.

ow the hell did I end up at the godforsaken mall? It became my problem that Jen only owned things that people who "crafted" would wear.

"You can't get me a corset," she said as we walked into a very respectable clothing store I'd never entered before.

"You think they sell corsets here? Anyway, if Evan wanted a corset-type girl, I was sitting right next to him."

"True. I wonder why he picked me, when…I mean, look at you."

I glanced at her but didn't say, "I know," because we both knew. The stares never stopped with me. I could tell Jen lived her entire life *running* from eye contact. I was always playing a part, and she was absolutely real. My mask hid the mythical murderer underneath, before it had even come into being.

"Do you need help?" a not-so-mild-mannered store clerk asked me with disdain.

"More than you can offer, but we could use something with no denim attached for my friend over there," I said, nodding to Jen. She was touching the most boring ivory sweater in the cosmos. I think it was a turtleneck? But the turtle part was too short. I fell into a big puffy chair that had no class whatsoever, no matter how hard they tried.

Jen peered at the salesperson like she was coming to fight her as she approached.

"Jen, this is someone who wants to help you. We only care about you," I said in my best intervention voice, leaning forward.

The sales lady was happy as a pig in shit to get away from me, and to get Jen in the dressing room with a lot of things I would never have picked out. I got comfortable in the chair that lots of kids had probably peed in waiting for their moms, giving thumbs mostly down for different ensembles, all for the same reasons.

"That one!" I said, thrilled to not only be able to leave shortly, but to have found something that was worthy of the girl. A frilly dress with ruffles, the color of a ripe banana. It made her blonde hair and blue eyes shine.

She spun in it, like you'd see in *Pretty in Pink* or something. I couldn't help but laugh. She was so happy, and she deserved it even if it made me feel like shit on someone's shoe. I briefly pictured wearing the *Beauty and the Beast* getup while gnawing on a dead man's finger bones in my apartment.

"This is definitely the one. I feel good in it. I don't remember the last time I felt *good* in clothes."

"That's too sad for me to even discuss right now." She blinked a lot, and I wanted to hug her and tell her how beautiful she was. I winced. "Evan will think you're gorgeous. And he should."

"Thanks, Charity," she said softly. "I know clothes shopping probably isn't your favorite thing to do."

"No, it's not, but what I like to do only happens in a mall sometimes, and never in "Sexified Soccer Moms," or whatever this place is called. Now go get that dress off so you can properly dirty it up later."

"Dirty it up? Oh!" She slapped me on the shoulder. "No, not dirtying anything up just yet."

"Right." I fell back into the chair. "Definitely want that party dress to remain spotless."

STAINED

*H*appy as I was for Jen, if that's what you called smiling at others' good luck, I kept thinking of Evan sitting next to me. The way he smelled, and how he'd leaned back in the booth. I'd wanted to *lean against him*. Like, touch him without punching him. He was classy as hell, my total opposite. He was the kind of knight in shining armor that would run screaming from someone like me, and should. Not that there was anyone else like me. Both of them were just a little better than me in so many ways. They deserved each other.

I deserved what I had coming, and I couldn't wait.

The day was almost gone when I got home. Good. The faster I could shed my pretty skin.

My corset was strangling me. All my clothes were squeezing the life out of me. Part of me welcomed it. Pulling the corset laces, I spotted a big smudge of jelly donut on there that looked like it would never come out, not the way I did laundry; a permanent reminder of Evan Hale and his spotless white shirt.

I stood there, naked but for panties, and closed my eyes. Mounting panic. "Oh, what the actual fuck," I muttered, clenching my fists. I'd become a caricature of myself, like a living lie this time, one thing all day, pretending to be scary, then actually horrifying at night and far happier. Maybe hanging out with good people wasn't so good for me. I didn't want to change my mind about being what I was, doing what I did when I was the Harpy. I *helped* people, girls like I'd been, with every single drop of blood I shed, every bite of flesh. You know, help isn't all Florence Nightingale or smiling-in-the-soup-kitchen happiness, not when you actually *fixed* something. I touched my lips, shivering for the salty thickness of it then.

Hungry.

My kitchen always had meat in it those days. Some nights I couldn't wait for the taste of skin, the discomfort of it catching between my teeth, sucking it off the bone. Dead though it was, it was enough. I pulled a Tupperware bowl of chicken wings out of the fridge. They were a little—a lot—undercooked, but it couldn't hurt me. Without even closing the fridge door, I pulled the cover off and shoved the chicken in my mouth, pulling the bones out with slippery fingers.

"Ugh. Mmmm." Cold, but delicious, the hint of life still under the bumpy skin, the memory of last breaths and a beating heart. My thoughts vanished as my eyes rolled back.

After eating all six pieces, I threw the bowl in the

sink and licked my fingers clean. There had to be meat all over my face, hot pink tendons sticking to my lips. I glowered down at the river of bits and pieces slipping down my chest in pink rivers. It filled me with joy.

I was a fearsome thing, even as a human. Probably more as a human.

I washed the bowl, humming and whistling happily. My singing voice wanted to burst free, for the first time in a long time. Memories of singing made my skin itch, but it didn't if I just whistled. Like a canary.

Then it hit me. "Yes!" I stupidly hoped Robbie heard through the wall. I got a bug up my ass to go out the next day; I wanted a bird. Something to remind me of what it was to be free when daylight came. Something to sing for me when I had no breath left.

Yeah. It would be good to have something to take care of, to protect. To make happy. Of course, I thought all that while I had the remnants of a little dead chicken plastered all over me. Circle of life and shit.

I messed with my thrift store CD player to get it working, and went to get dressed. Iggy Pop blaring to give me strength, I picked up an orange pushup bra off the floor, shook my head and dropped it again, going straight for a white tanktop and throwing it on over my naked torso. I didn't need a pushup bra to boost the B cups when I was murdering a terrified sexual predator.

The thought made my lips curl back and the beginnings of feathers prick at the back of my arms. It was all I could do not to throw my head back and scream with joy. Damn the thin walls of cookie cutter apartments. Who knew what Robbie thought already, what he may have heard?

I went back to the kitchen to crack a beer, knowing full well that I didn't really need to be on my A-game to do the Harpy job well. Like Rob knew I was thinking of him, the knock came from the other side of the wall. I knocked back. The clunking of his boots came next, and we both opened our front doors at the same time.

"Hey," he said with that backstage smile.

"Hey."

"Whatcha doin'?"

"Just hanging out. I'll probably turn in early." It wasn't my favorite, lying to him. He didn't do anything to deserve it, but really, everything he knew of me was a lie.

"Right." He smiled wider, and ran his fingers through his hair. "I was about to make some burgers."

"You're always making burgers. You eat burgers like, every day."

"Yeah, I do. You want one?"

God, I totally did. "Nah, thanks though."

"Come over, you're being dumb. Come in and have a burger."

"I just ate."

"I know you better than that, you'll eat more. That girl in apartment six hates you for how skinny you are, she told me," he said with a grin. "I caught her eating a box of Girl Scout cookies in her car."

"She was probably about to drive to the gym, too."

His laugh was so pure and nice to listen to that it hurt.

"Okay, Rob, I'm going in," I said, nodding back into my crappy apartment.

"All right, beautiful. Talk to you later."

"Night."

Well, it sure did piss me off to have to say no to that invite. And I could be waiting for hours more, alone.

Waiting, waiting, always waiting, had me spending a lot of nights at home alone. I kept putting off our *AHS* date, and I wouldn't be able to do it forever—eventually he'd stop talking to me. This was all *his* fault. If that bastard boyfriend of my mother's hadn't destroyed me, I would never have to be the Harpy. One night I could barely walk home from the townie bar down the street, my feet became claws so fast, I was certain they'd burst out of my steel-cap boots. That'll teach me to hang around dirty middle-aged men avoiding their wives. I had an exciting new sixth sense about what men were thinking since the Harpy showed up, how violent it could be behind the eyes of an average-looking down-on-his-luck guy. As if I hadn't known enough what lurked in mens' hearts, the Harpy was hyper-aware of it. It made me want to rip and tear them all limb from limb, snatch up and chew the falling chunks.

As I sat on the crappy couch watching *The Golden Girls*, I wondered how much of the transformation I could actually control. My tolerance was edging me closer and closer to never wanting to be a person at all; a thought that might have scared some people, but I'd had quite enough of being a person at the tender age of twenty-three.

I was so thankful for a *Golden Girls* marathon. It

made me think of one time, being home on the sofa with a cold, before I'd run away, eating ice cream in my bathrobe, coughing razors and sneezing, but comfortable as hell. Almost happy.

My mother hadn't been home in three days. Absence had not made the heart grow fonder.

And when my mother wasn't home, her men weren't there. *He* wasn't there. But the things he did to me and made me do were always there. They made scabs that would be there until the day I died. I think if I weren't held together by scabs that I wouldn't exist at all.

Every time I thought of my mother, I expected the phone to ring, like she knew I was dreading her finding me, and would never stop wanting me to suffer. Only an idiot would have thought she'd looked for me.

My mouth watered as I wished, wholeheartedly, that she were dead.

I ached for more meat after that, and jumped up, leopard print blanket slipping to the floor. I took long strides to the fridge, pulled it open, growling, a feral need adding to my angry thoughts. I snarled at the naked shelves holding nothing but ketchup, hot sauce, and beer. My eyes fixed on the freezer. There was sausage in there.

Slowly, I pulled it out, skeptical of how it would taste, imagining it rock-hard scraping against my teeth. But the craving soon had me tearing the plastic open and burying my face in the rock-solid meat, scraping the ice off with my teeth for just a taste.

"Sonofabitch!" I threw it in the microwave too hard,

pissed at the fucking delay, like my junkie bitch mother waiting for her next fix.

"Fucking hell!" I smashed a beer glass against the wall at the thought of her, a thousand very satisfying pieces, and I laughed.

The microwave plate spun in slow circles, my brain spun in quick circles. My mother loomed in my head, a needle hanging out of her arm, still walking around like she was June fucking Cleaver, asking me if I wanted a snack.

I didn't want a snack, I wanted fucking dinner. I hadn't had a homemade meal in days.

My stomach twisted with lust for the meat. I leaned down, fixated on the hard package spinning in the microwave, and slammed my hand into the little glass door with fury.

"Fuck it." I whipped open the door, pried the sausages apart, and bit a half-frozen chunk off, hurting my teeth and not giving a shit. I gnawed on it until some parts were small enough to swallow, groaning as the meat inched down my throat, cold though it was. I did it again, wishing I could taste the blood more, feel the slickness, but this would have to do.

Sinking to the kitchen floor, I tore into the sausages until they'd almost gotten warm, until they were gone. My stomach rolled like a rock out of that rock tumbler thing my dad had given me when I was a kid. Before he left.

My stomach was full, a sensation I always appreciated. I remembered how often it had been empty. Everything had been so empty.

"I'll fill you up."

That bastard's voice showed up in my head alongside my mother's, and instantly I was that fucked up kid again. Still. He'd clipped my wings before they'd sprouted.

I threw my head back, jaw working and cracking, and bellowed out an inhuman shriek, the sound of the fucking birds on the National Geographic channel, circling over desert carcasses.

Feathers needled their way out of my arms, just a few at first, then more piled on, and more, slowly until my blood-rusty wings were full. They always had the blood stains on them, before I'd even killed. My feet became the claws, my calves turning scaly and tough, my thighs covered in downy fluff.

The less human I was, the better I felt. I didn't give a shit who heard—I screamed for blood.

DEARLY DEPARTED

*A*nyone could have been looking out their windows, and cars were driving by at the bottom of the hill every night, but if anyone ever spotted me, they didn't say so to anyone who mattered. How could anyone equate *this* with me, whether my face was on it or not? The Harpy was so much more; Charity Blake was just a shirt it wore. Memories of the afternoon coffee date with Jen were distant now, the rest of my life even further away. Time to sate my thirst.

Time to kill.

I took off at a run across the lawn, and spread my wings, flapping my arms like people do in dreams of flying, but my dream was real. Cars drove by in the dark on the street below, and there I was, hiding in plain sight.

I loved the raw, cold rain more than I had ever loved anything in my life. My miserable life. The wind and rain tore through me the higher I went. I left that victim I was behind every night and came back to her soaked in blood. I screamed into the night air.

The world below me looked quiet, but I knew better. I knew for as much peace as I had in the air, there were girls just like me crying into their pillows, praying that if God didn't take the bastard who hurt them that they'd kill themselves before it happened again. Peace came with a price I had paid time and again. With the Harpy, I was reborn. I could save someone.

I flexed my claws, waiting for my sixth sense to kick in and tell me where the night's Big, Bad and Ugly was so I could rip out his beating heart and lick it clean in front of him. Weariness overtook me, as though I traveled more each night, but it was impossible to tell—the sky would be black, then suddenly sunset over a farm, then desert heat… Time wasn't the same as the Harpy. Fine with me, I wanted to get as far away as I could from "home." And I was getting faster. Going for distance meant I wouldn't leave dead bodies, flayed to bits everywhere in my wake, too close to home. That had to lessen my chances of getting caught —though I got the distinct impression there was something keeping me from being found out. Not God or some shit, or even luck, but evil had a way of stretching its fingers and sustaining the thing that fed it. I could rationalize all the dreadful day that I was doing good, but come on. There wasn't a speck of good left in me.

Below me, the sick heat pulsed, that sense of wrongness and dirt. I cocked my head to see who caused it. I could nearly taste the sweat-slicked pulsing of rape. Smelled it. This was my time.

Descending into a thicket of trees in an otherwise open field, I perched high and scanned around for the fucker. I knew in my heart he was in the middle the act, forcing himself on some woman that very moment, and every second I wasted was one she'd never forget. Goddammit did it piss me off that I couldn't shed fear as easily as my human skin.

There were very few houses, shacks really, and barns attached to most of them. The second I could stop shaking, it would be easy to sniff him out.

It was in one of these barns that a dim yellow light glowed. And then came a scream.

With one movement I made it to the dilapidated barn, painted red like every fucking American dream farm, hiding the nightmare inside with a bunch of cows and pigs. I pushed open the big door with little effort, and there it was, right in front of me.

The boy would have been described as a "strapping young man," showing a well-tanned, muscular naked back, and jeans that he was ripping the belt off of. He had no idea what was coming.

But she saw me. A girl of maybe sixteen, laying on her back in a pile of hay, blood trickling from the corner of her mouth, bruises flowering around her neck. Her shirt was ripped, and so was the lacy bra under it. Her eyes were wide with horror, either because of him or me.

In three long strides I was on him.

"Hi."

He turned fast, and fell backward across the girl's legs as he took me in. He was sexy; too bad I was going to eat his flesh until he was nothing and then drop him in the ocean on the way home.

"What the fuck?!"

"Exactly!" I said. "What the fuck is going on here? Oh, it doesn't matter, I can see the rapist on you like a neon fucking sign."

"Jim, what is it?" the girl asked him in a whisper, both of them gaping at me.

"*Jim*? How well do you know this guy, sweet cheeks?"

She turned bright red, and I remember thinking how weird it was that of all things to embarrass her, *that* would do it when she was lying there beaten up and half-raped.

"He's my fiancé," she said quietly. "But, what are you?"

"What am I? Not the real monster here, that's what. Why do you let this piece of shit hit you?"

Jim started to get up, shooting daggers at me like I was just another woman he could slap, but I kicked him back down with my taloned foot.

"I think you should probably sit the fuck still, don't you, Jim?"

All-American boy bared his teeth at me. Damn, Jim got angry fast. He'd taste great.

"She belongs to me, and I'll never let her forget it," he spat.

And fuck me, but the dumb girl actually smiled at him like he'd just handed her a dozen roses! She was as screwed up as he was! It occurred to me she was no older than I was when *he* made me start on his daughter….

I lashed out, grabbing the half-naked rapist by the throat. "You belong to me now." His kicked at the hay underneath, getting it all over the girl. She spluttered and stood up, clothes hanging off her.

"No! Please don't hurt him! Please."

I snarled at her stupidity, still holding Jim. "You don't know what you've gotten yourself into." I bit my lip immediately. *He* had said the same thing to me once.

Rage had me pulsating and shaking, and I threw All-American Jim against a beam, gritting my teeth with joy over the awful *crack* of his back against it before he slid to the ground. I turned to her.

"I'm helping you regain your life, you fucking ninny."

"He is my life," she said, all doe-eyed, stupid farmgirl.

Jim had made it to his feet, cracked his neck like some *X-Men* villain, and came at me. I wanted it. I wanted him to give me a reason, more reason than I already had.

"He's a stain on your soul, you asshat," I said, watching Jim get closer, sweating fury. I smiled. "Sorry, but I think your dearly beloved will be dearly departed momentarily."

"No," she whispered next to me. I remembered whispering that, when I had no energy left to scream.

Jim raised his hand, and I grabbed it, crunching it in

my fist, talons scraping the skin off in shreds. He screamed like a girl, making my mouth water.

"Dearly beloved, we are gathered here today to witness All-American Jim get his ass kicked by a bird bitch!" Still clutching his hand, I threw my body weight into him, knocking him to the ground next to the dumbstruck farmgirl. He grunted with the impact, and tried to roll behind her, pushing her in front of him.

"Big strong man," I spat, getting more disgusted by the second, adrenaline pumping wildly. "You would marry her, spend the rest of both your lives beating the crap out of her and fucking her when she's too weak to fend you off?" The rage built in me at the thought, and more at the realization that the girl thought *I* was the villain in the scenario.

She loved him. She couldn't know any better; a knowledge that brought forth violence from within me. I kicked out at him, avoiding her, and dragged my talons down his chest, flaying him open to the guts. He gurgled blood, and it poured out of his mouth as I did it again, until I could see his spine. My own strength against him was such a high, I could no longer hear or see the girl. I saw nothing but his blood and bones, his dying eyes.

Jim was sprawled on his back, bleeding out, muscles and tendons twitching in the open air. I crouched over him, unfolding my wings to hide him under. He was mine, and if anything tried to take the body, I'd tear through them, too.

Ugly on the inside maybe, but my body glowed with his blood smeared all over me, his finger bones crunching in my mouth, his eyes fading out. The meat of him all that was left.

It could have been hours I was there, pulling his limbs and ligaments apart, but it didn't matter. I relished every bite, wishing dawn would never come. As though there wasn't a girl shivering next to me while I devoured her lover's flesh before her disbelieving eyes.

When I'd eaten the last of his organs, leaving nothing behind but a pile of unrecognizable refuse, I sighed and relaxed my arms, letting my wings curl behind me. Nothing enough to even drop in the ocean.

My talons squished in pools of blood that hadn't dried in the hay as I turned to her. Seeing her eyes was scarier than anything I'd done to Jim.

"Kid, what's your name?" I asked her, leaning close, ignoring her whimpers. This was a kindness I had done for her.

She couldn't answer me, but she tried. She stuttered something unintelligible. I covered her up with a horse blanket, and she managed to nod a thank you.

"Sweetie, what you saw here tonight, you'll forget after it gives you too many nightmares. But what he was making you was the nightmare you'd never wake up from. I don't need you to thank me. Just survive."

With a last look at the remains, I strolled out of the barn. I walked out like I'd delivered a message from God, like it was meant to be. As the barn door shut behind me, I thought of how those two kids thought they were meant to be something, too.

I was a hero. I liked my version of fate better.

*A*ll-American Jim's blood wrapped around me like a blanket, drying hard and unyielding on my wings while I soared back home. I smiled the whole way, through the flickers of different lands and skies. The sun was coming up when I made it back to familiar landscape. I'd taken a particularly long time with him, and I wasn't sure why, but shit, that's what Psychiatrist is for.

Panic ran through me as the sun blazed brighter all the time. I pushed myself as hard as I could to get home. The possibility of looming discovery wasn't what had me freaking out; daylight had frightened me forever. My forever started when my dad left. Anything that happened before then was the beginning of the dream, where nothing really matters. When you get in the thick of it, that's what counts. And my life after he was gone had been thick with nightmares that I was afraid to wake up from.

Facing what I'd become when the sun came up. That's what made me buckle in fear.

It was kill-me hot and bright when I finally made it back to Plymouth. I circled for a long time, high, hoping no one would see me. No one ever really did though, so I swooped down and landed in a thicket of trees at the duck pond. I watched dull people on their ways to work, people who thought they had problems, people who were nobody without their families and nice houses and careers, people who bragged about the pain of their tattoos and childbirths like they could ever know real pain. I cringed from their idiocy. They meant nothing, and there I was, stronger than they'd ever be, hiding from them.

The trees swayed in the early breeze around me, serene, birds chirping in neighboring branches, ready to start the day of simple joy and survival. That's all I wanted. Joy in surviving. I couldn't do that as Hazel Harrington and I'd never be able to do that as Charity. No way that I could ever shed the monster that she was, no matter how far I ran.

A robin landed on the branch beside me, orangey chest puffed out, questioning me with a cocked head. I looked down at myself, a bloody angel with sticky, bloody wings, torn tanktop barely concealing my bony body, matted tendrils of hair on my shoulders. My claws tightened on my perch.

The simplicity of that robin had me gritting my teeth with jealousy. I could crush it and eat it and its entire little nest of chirping babies in a heartbeat. And for once, my own cruelty brought tears to my eyes.

I was powerful in every way and that meek little thing was better than me, still.

Jen was down there somewhere, probably at the bakery, living a robin life. I was a vulture of my own making. I never questioned why I started turning into the Harpy, only why it hadn't happened sooner; the blood-soaked monster was in me all along.

The day wore on, and I grew more exhausted. It occurred to me that as long as I stayed in the tree, I might stay in Harpy form. I just wanted to go to bed, and I could *see* my bedroom window, taunting the fuck out of me. The belly full of flesh and bones was at least keeping me from being hungry. Hunger would turn me into a real bitch.

The door to my apartment building opened, and out came Robbie. Fucking hell, even then I breathed a sigh just to see him. It was our night to watch *American Horror Story* together, and I really wanted to. I'd be pissed if I didn't change back, or if I became the Harpy again before we got to watch the show. It was one of the only things that made me want to be human.

Robbie bounced down the steps without annoying enthusiasm, moppy hair bouncing with him. I could hear his boots through the window when I was in my apartment as he bounced down the outside steps like that. It made me smile then, too.

What would he say if he saw me?

As if he'd heard, he looked up. He stopped dead and gazed up at the sky, turning his head around, searching. My chest constricted. I went cold. Wrapping my arms around myself, my wings slapping against the branches as I moved, I shook with fear.

He can't see me like this. Not him.

I tried to shuffle deeper into the leaves, but only succeeded in disturbing the tree so much that the robin next to me flew off. Then more birds went, and a branch snapped, making me fall a few branches down, swearing. That's when Robbie's eyes met mine, even across the street. It scared me so much I lost my balance, and went down, fast and hard, the tree shaking all around me, stabbing me with a thousand branches, scratching me even bloodier than I was to begin with. I screamed the whole time. It had to be a fucking decade until I hit the ground with a painful *bang*. The landing still hurt less than the fall.

I wouldn't open my eyes. God only knew who was out there, crowding around me on the duck pond lawn, just there to look at some starved ducks they couldn't feed, and there I was.

"Charity?"

My eyes snapped open to see Robbie standing there, looking more unsettled than I'd ever seen him, running his hands through his hair like a madman, shuffling from foot to foot.

"Hey, what's up?" I groaned, trying to roll over. I gave up pretty fast.

"No, don't move. That fall—Jesus Christ."

His hands were on me, warm, and I was so cold.

"Shit, you're cold."

He rolled me over gently onto my back, scrunching up his face at all the blood. I mean there was blood *all over me*, some mine, but mostly All American Jim's. I smelled like Manny, the butcher from the shop up the street that I all but lived in. He always had blood in his beard.

"Okay, Charity, I don't know what the fuck drug makes this happen to you, but we have to get you out of public."

I cleared my throat. "I think I can walk."

"No way," he said, running his fingers through his hair so fast I waited for it to fall out.

"You'd be amazed what I can do."

"That's what she said," he muttered absently, looking around like crazy.

"That's mine, you can't use it."

"Charity, focus; we can't have much time before we're found here. But you can't cross the street like that."

"Like what? Is this because I'm black?"

"Shut the hell up, Whitey Whiterton, time to be serious and get you out of here."

"You're the one *trying* to be funny, I just *am*."

He pulled his black hoodie off and wrapped it around my shoulders. The pond and the Jenny Grist Mill were all but vacant during the day, luckily. The hoodie did nothing to cover the blood, but the wings were a little less conspicuous.

Robbie patted me down like a mom sending her kid off to kindergarten, but with more mind-blown confusion.

Hands on my shoulders, staring hard into my eyes with his fawn brown ones he said, "Okay. I need you to hide. I'm going to get my car. I'll be *right back.* We'll never get you across the street like this."

We both looked around, and found the little wooden bridge that crossed the pond at the same time. We ran to it, me limping like hell and him dragging me along, wincing at my grunts of pain. He pushed me underneath the bridge, pissing off a duck.

"Stay here. I'll be right back, I promise."

"I know you will."

I crouched there, shivering, daytime sounds drowning me. I counted the seconds until Robbie came back: 307.

He tore into the parking lot and jumped out of the car, his door swinging wide. He pulled me under his arm and huddled over me, running, like he was protecting a civilian from falling bombs in a war movie. He shoved me through the passenger door, then ran back to the driver's seat.

Driving right across the street was the best solution, but the stupidity was painful. Quick thinker, that one. He hurried us into the building and into my apartment.

"Why don't you lock your door?" he asked me.

"Nobody wants my shit. And if they want me, they can have me."

He ignored the "that's what she said" potential to give me his finest sad face instead. I rolled my eyes.

He looked me over, trying not to linger on my half naked body, but failing. "You need to get to a hospital, Charity."

"Eh, I'm all right. Nothing's broken. Nothing that isn't usually."

We stood there, a foot apart for an awkward minute. Neither of us was usually awkward, making that moment the king of all awkward moments. I shuffled my bloody bare feet. He just watched me, stock still, serious as hell.

"I've seen you become like this, when you think nobody's looking, you know," he said, pointing at my wings as I shed the hoodie.

My head shot up. "What? When?"

He smiled sideways, really cute. "About a week ago. Through the peephole."

"You didn't say anything?"

"What am I supposed to say?"

"Hey, Freak of Nature, don't claw up the hallway?"

He licked his lips, eyes comforting me, no judgment or fear behind them, only concern.

"How does it happen to you? Did you...do it somehow?"

I pulled at my tanktop nervously. "I think it's just how I'm supposed to be."

"What do you do? Where do you go?" His voice was always so soft, quiet but strong. I wished I could stand behind it, hide from everything.

I ducked my head and turned away, walking toward the bathroom. The blood was crispy on my skin and in my hair, it had to come out. "Robbie, I have to take a shower," I said, but his breath was close on my neck.

"Please answer me," he said gently. His palm covered my shoulder.

"You don't want to know. Forget this ever happened, that's my recommendation to you."

He came around and stood in front of me, in the way of the bathroom I was desperate to lock myself in. "You are such a rock star in my eyes, there's nothing you could do to scare me off. Neighbor." He grinned, and God help me, I believed him. I believed he would stay and that it wouldn't hurt.

"Tell me, Rob, what is it you think I've become?"

His eyes ran over my face. "Scared."

I pushed past him and closed the bathroom door.

THE WATCHED POT

I cried for a while in the shower. It felt so stupid. It felt like one of those movies where girls cry in the shower.

My day had gotten out of control, my entire fucking life had gotten out of control, like control was something I'd ever had. I did not like having my worlds meet. I didn't like Robbie *knowing.* I didn't like how the wings hung around until early afternoon before making their exit the next day, and how I had no idea when I was going to change back to just Charity. If I was changing back at all.

I wouldn't have minded living as the Harpy. That was a creature who knew what she wanted, and dove for it, heat-seeking missile style.

When I got out of the longest shower I ever took, I was shocked to see the sun setting.

"Shit."

My hair dripped down my back, my fingers clenched and unclenched, my wings still lingering and half-formed, a broken bridge between two worlds.

"I'm not ready to change again. It's too soon."

I wanted to watch *American Horror Story* with Robbie. I scarcely remembered the episode from the week before, seeing as I was chanting *don't change 'til it's over* through the whole thing in my head.

Like Robbie would ever want to see me again. I sank to the floor, naked and wet, and tried to breathe normally. Hadn't I just had this panic attack the other day? Get the fuck out, panic attacks. It didn't help my mental state that the floor I was crumpled on might not belong to me much longer if I didn't find a job and pay the rent. Christ knows it's so easy to find a job when you had no social skills or abilities and could turn into a mythical beast at any given time.

I fell asleep, naked on that ugly ass carpet, and was actually happy to wake up still human, even if I was still exhausted, and still Charity Blake.

"Jesus Christ," I muttered, brushing my hair back with my hands, letting it be wild and ugly. I threw on sweatpants and a tank top, swilled a beer, and went to Robbie's.

I stood in front of the door, inspecting the grain, the peephole, my own feet for a couple of minutes.

"Ah, fuck it." I knocked hard and loud. He opened it fast, like he'd been right on the other side the whole time.

"Hey," he said, and turned into his apartment, like he always did. "Tell me again why you knock?"

"Common courtesy. 'Cause you know, I'm full of

that."

Robbie's apartment was a bachelor pad full of guitars and beer signs, "scented" candles that didn't mask a thing, sneakers, magazines, and action movies. An old metal shelf was filled with hardcover books from the library sales; the jackets were ripped, but the pages inside were still good enough for him. He had this really cool vintage pinup artwork all over one wall that he sought long and hard for. The TV was always on. It didn't reek of loneliness. He knew himself too well to be lonely.

"Glad you came over," he said, sprawling on the old leather couch and throwing his leg onto the even older coffee table. "I wasn't sure you would."

"Wasn't sure you'd let me in."

"Hence the knocking?"

"Gives you the option to say 'no,' or hide behind the door with a pitchfork."

"Probably one of those duck hunting guns would make more sense."

I plopped into my spot next to him, with just enough space between us, as usual, ensuring that he could make a move if he wanted, but didn't have to. It bothered me endlessly that I was too nervous to kiss him. Like I actually cared or something.

"It's too hot for pizza tonight. You want to get sushi?" he asked.

"Absolutely," I said, incredulous that I was agreeing to any food after….Jim.

"Excellent." He picked up his cell, ordered a bunch of rolls like he knew exactly what I wanted, put the phone down and smiled at me. The big, toothy one that was so friendly it made me crack.

It was getting dark, and I was getting scared until I realized that even if I changed, I had nothing to hide. Maybe I had an accomplice, though.

"You watch the worst TV sometimes, Rob. Is this The Voice?"

"Uh, yeah, it is, and I'm pretty sure you came over here to watch TV with me, so, what does that say?"

"I said *sometimes*."

He laughed, making his eyes scrunch up the way I loved.

"I like you, Robbie."

"I like you, too," he said nonchalantly. Shit, had I friend-zoned myself? Never done, in history.

His gaze transported me somewhere else, in some book or movie about somebody better than me. Someone who deserved nice things.

"You know, your secret doesn't scare me."

Finally, he brought it up. "If you knew what I did—" *Shut up, shut up.*

"What do you do?" He shocked me by putting his hand on my knee. "You can tell me. You don't have to, but you can."

I glared at him, annoyed by his sheer concern and niceness when I was a fucking killer who wanted nothing to do with anyone nice. I couldn't.

"You can't know what I do."

"That was a lot of blood on you earlier."

I bit my lip, willing myself not to just kiss him to distract him. If I didn't take my chance then, how could

I ever? I think the lip biting distracted him on its own. Red lipstick and lip biting could keep people just far enough away to get them close to you.

"You asking me where the blood came from?"

"Yes."

"I'm not saying. But there will be more. You're better off not knowing why."

His eyes melted, became a sadder brown, and he tilted his head like he was going to say, "poor Charity."

"I'm not a fragile, tender thing."

"Oh, that I already knew."

"Then don't look at me like I'm an orphan scratching at the window."

"I never said that."

"Nothing to say. It was all right there. You *pitied* me."

He took his hand off my knee, and I breathed a sigh of relief. I leaned back, biting my lip again until it hurt.

"Charity, I don't have to feel bad for you. I think you do quite enough of that yourself."

"Fucking excuse me?" He laughed, and fuck me, did that make me mad. My fingernails sunk into the couch arm.

"Whatever it is in your past, or in your head, that you've convinced yourself you're beating, you're not. It's making you into something else, isn't it? You need to let it go, or you're going to lose yourself altogether."

I sucked in my breath, tears springing to my eyes. I wanted to punch him right in the fucking face, but I liked that face and what was behind it. He was so frigging honest. Sonofabitch.

"Well. Look at Robbie, with all his fucking insight. It must be nice to live such a vanilla life where you don't have to run from yourself."

I got up and started pacing, wishing immediately that I was in a corset, and leather pants and combat boots, with more makeup and my hair wild and angry, ready to kick some ass. He didn't try to stop me from raging. It made me like him more, and *that* made me angrier. He just watched me, patient, poker faced.

"You don't know what's happened to me, where I came from. You don't know what I live with," I blurted.

"I don't."

"You haven't done the things I've done." I stopped moving. "And you could never do what I do."

"I'm not trying to compete with you." He sighed, relaxed, one leg up, arm over the back of the couch, but eyes intensely mournful. "I just want this. Us, here, together."

My heart slowed. I stopped thinking. And it wasn't until then that I noticed my toes had turned into the claws I knew. Robbie's eyes cast down. When I looked back at them, they were my toes again, red toenails, normal feet. Robbie raised his eyebrows when I showed my surprise. He smiled a little and stood up.

"Time to get the sushi."

~

I sat in the torn passenger seat of his Audi, tapping my human feet in their flip flops all the way to Sushi Joy. I was waiting for them to turn again, and what the hell would I do? It sucked caring about what people thought. Well, person.

And for the first time that late in the day, I wasn't starving for human flesh. It made me afraid to my core.

We both went in because I didn't want to be alone, and he probably knew it. Robbie took my hand. I clung to it like a life preserver in an ocean of blood.

The pretty Asian girl at the counter blushed and smiled at Robbie. I bared my teeth without even trying, but calmed down when I realized I might trigger the change and turn into Bird Bitch right there. It always seemed to happen when I got keyed up; another reason why I was a monster, no matter what the form.

"Hi," Robbie said with that unintentionally sexy smile. "Number seventy-one?"

"Yes," she said, still that sweet shade of pink. She ducked her head and went into the kitchen. I rolled my eyes at Robbie.

"What?" he said quietly. I just shook my head.

The girl didn't come back out, but the old guy who owned the place did, carrying our brown paper bag.

He took one look at me and dropped it on the floor.

"Demon," he hissed, anger contorting his face. "Out!"

"I just wanted my sushi, for Chrissakes."

"Get out! Out!" He came around the counter, and I had no doubt he'd push me right out the door with all his strength. Robbie stepped in front of me.

Protecting me.

"We're leaving," he told the old man with a curt bow of his head.

I gave the old man the finger on the way out. Robbie pushed me ahead of himself gently.

"Sorry about that," he said.

"Why would you be sorry? I'm the one who's a fucking demon, and he's the ass who pointed it out. Awkward."

We got back in the car and headed toward home. Robbie pulled into the 7-11 parking lot in silence.

"Whatcha doin?"

"I'll be right back," he said, and got out, briefly running his hand over the back of my head. My anger fizzled away.

I watched him through the giant store windows while he was inside, and willed myself not to cry. What the hell did I care what some old sushi guy said to me? But I was embarrassed. Robbie was so pleasant to everyone, nodding with a humble smile to the Middle Eastern guy behind the counter, holding the door for the guy coming in as he left with a small bag.

When he got in the car, I was thankful it was me he was spending his night with. And I couldn't believe it. I was a fucking demon and he knew it.

"What's in the bag?"

"Chunky Monkey and Mountain Dew."

I bit my lip and my throat constricted. He knew what I needed.

And just like that, I knew I wasn't going to become the Harpy that night.

THE NEXT BEST THING

*R*obbie took me by the hand, sending electric tingles up my arm, and led me to the couch, where I envisioned him pushing me down, kneeling on one knee over me, grabbing me by the hair and tilting my face up so he could kiss me with as much brutality as I killed.

Instead he nodded at me to sit. I did it with a serious eye roll. He left for the kitchen, clanking around out there, popping open a can of Mountain Dew, and brought out a huge bowl of ice cream and the soda of the gods.

"You're so nice to me all the time. Even now."

"Maybe I should only be nice to you when I expect something in return."

My eyes glowered, unable to hide my attraction to him, no matter what the consequence. "You can expect something. We both know I'll deliver it."

He didn't smile, only sat next to me, turning so one leg was perched on the couch, and dammit if I wouldn't fit in that space like a glove. He said, "I promise to never expect more than you're willing to give."

I guzzled Mountain Dew, holding back tears. Everything I could give him was ugly.

We watched our TV show, inches from each other. He treated me like one of the guys, but made me feel like the hottest girl on the planet just for sharing the couch with him. He was never too quiet, just quiet enough. He never interrupted the really intense parts with stupid comments. Perfect.

"Charity? Charity." I was being pushed a little and it made me swing out an angry arm.

"What?"

"You fell asleep. On me. I can't move."

My eyes popped open, seeing nothing but men's feet in workboots and a coffee table covered in magazines and empty Mountain Dew cans. I sat up too fast, and got drunk spins though I hadn't drank enough. Warm hands took hold of mine, steadying me.

"It's okay, really. I just felt bad, you just fell over, into my lap. You must be beat, to do that after all that Mountain Dew."

I wiped a line of drool off my chin, glancing at my tanktop that was all twisted around, and winced. "Yeah, I didn't sleep much last night. Or any night."

"Come on," Robbie said softly, pulling me to my feet. "You need to go to bed."

Exhausted as I was, my eyes shot down the hall to his bedroom. I'd never been down there, and I wanted to be, a lot.

He turned me around by my shoulders, and walked me back to my apartment, steps away.

"Good night, Rob," I whispered, the air thick between us with nighttime needs.

"Night," he said back. I thought for a second he was going to kiss me, his lips quivered, and his eyes became so intent, but then I remembered my probable bed head and that I drooled on him, and I was wearing nothing nice—

He snaked his hand into the hair at the nape of my neck, and pulled me to him. My lips parted for his. He was soft and firm, and tasted like creamy vanilla. I always knew he would. He kissed me for only a moment, then rested his forehead on mine, hand still holding my head there like I could leave if I wanted to.

"Good night," he said again, and took the six steps back home.

❦

My eyes hated me the next morning. They could barely open, and my body had been the world's punching bag. I pulled the blanket over my head, unicorn horn in line with my eyes. Gray light streamed in, and it made the colors under the blankets purplish and bruisy, comforting. The color of those big purple flowers old people liked. I wasn't going to move all day.

What day was it, anyway? I'd lost track since I left the last job and not having been the Harpy the night before had thrown my entire life out of whack already it seemed. No matter what, the first of the month would be approaching soon, and I'd have rent to pay. They could wait, or remove me by force. It was the least important thing ever at the time.

I ran over in my head a dozen times all of the reasons why I hadn't changed into the Harpy, but only one seemed plausible, and it was the one that I hated most.

I hadn't wanted to.

It made it all so real, that becoming the Harpy was my choice, and I *was* in control. I'd decided to be that creature, and I decided to be the one that lied under the covers, worked shitty jobs, ran away from her problems and was afraid. I hated that I wanted to be the thing so much. I hated that being with Robbie could make me want to stay human; that anything could replace the pleasure of ripping the limbs from the sick fucks that deserved it. Surges of rage coursed through me. I didn't have to be the Harpy.

It was just more fun that way.

I hated that being with Robbie played second fiddle to the buzz I got when I tasted the sweaty human flesh that I'd grown to love. I never wanted him to be second to anything or anyone. But no one was first in my life. Nobody won. Not even me.

The comfort of my bed began to grate on me; comfort wasn't something I did well. I roared to life, angry already, hating the day, wishing I could kill something or someone. My hands clenched, nails digging into my palms, and I reached for the nearest thing I could—a statue of a little blue fairy, melancholy, perfectly pretty and sweet and sad for no reason.

I threw it with a grunt at the dirty old carpet, so hard that it smashed despite the soft landing. I smiled.

Whistling, I made my coffee, turned on the TV—more Golden Girls was on. It was always on. I sat down, relieved after breaking something small and too sweet.

It was almost ten in the morning. Getting a normal night's sleep was so foreign to me, waking up after having one was like a hangover but without the puking. Changing into the Harpy for almost three weeks, then waking up early to work at the coffee shop, for that dick who was no better than the dicks I killed didn't provide much in the way of normalcy. I wouldn't know a normal night's sleep if it bit me in the ass. Before the Harpy, the nightmares interrupted me too much. Before the nightmares, the reality did.

But I'd slept well, had a weird date-thing in my future, and was looking at a sparkly new day. I wouldn't ruin it for myself. I got my ass off the couch, slugging down coffee as I did, and brought the cup to the kitchen, only once thinking of having a beer before facing the world.

"Jesus!" I jumped back as I heard the knock from the other side of the kitchen wall. I knocked back, smiling. About a minute later the knock came from the other side of my front door.

"Hi," I said, a little embarrassed about the goofy quality of my smile. He just rolled out of bed looking that good, then? And happy. Jesus Christ.

"Good morning." He ran his hand through his hair. I never got tired of it. "Want to get some coffee?"

"Yeah, sure. Come in for a minute."

He shouldered past me, smiling down at me as our bodies brushed against each other. He smelled like men's soap.

He sat on the couch and picked up the remote like he owned it. I went and washed up, brushed my teeth, and tried to avoid the mirror, but couldn't.

A *person* looked back at me. No residual blood, no feral stare, hair only as wild as bed head made it. No blood caked in it, no jungle animal waves. I didn't put on any makeup.

I pulled a pink corset on, a quickie one that I didn't have to lace up, and a short denim skirt. No fishnets. I mean, it was only coffee. Skull and crossbone sandals, ready to roll.

"Okay, let's go."

He gave me a funny look, but didn't get up.

"Pretty," he said.

"Thanks. Ready?"

"But you don't need to wear all that," he said, motioning at my outfit, "to look good. I liked you in sweatpants."

My back straightened. I should have known better than to think he'd like me as is.

"I'm more comfortable like this."

"Do you?" He still didn't get up. "Because I think you were pretty comfortable last night without all that."

"I didn't even put on makeup today."

"Another thing you don't need."

"Look, I know you mean well, but telling me the things I do wrong is just pissing me off a little. So can we go get coffee now?"

He said nothing, but stood up and went to the door, holding it open for me.

I could bet he'd be watching my ass as I walked by.

BIG AND SMALL THINGS

*W*e walked to Dunkin Donuts, the summer air stifling.

"I actually got worried for a second about buying a cup of coffee that costs, what, two bucks? But I have every intention of buying a bird today that could be really expensive, and expensive to keep and probably against my lease, and I don't give much of a fuck about that."

He laughed. His laugh was the most honest thing I ever heard.

"What are you going to do about money, woman?"

"Spend it till it runs out?"

"Ace plan, Charity."

Dunkin Donuts was busy, full of people with jobs to go to.

"Rob, your job is pretty sweet, huh? You seem to come and go as you please. How do I get a gig like that?"

"I go when I'm needed."

Robbie worked at one of the boarding houses, of which Plymouth had many, but he worked at the only one that was dedicated to kids under eighteen. He didn't talk about it much—he didn't talk about anything much—but he cared about his job a lot, more than I'd ever cared about a thing probably. Robbie tended not to do anything that he didn't care about.

It wasn't until that day that the thought unnerved me.

"Hey. Can we get two medium hot coffees, one light, no sugar, one black? Thanks."

"You know how I get my coffee?"

"We've gotten coffee together before."

"But you remember?"

He turned to face me. "I remember important things. I've been waiting to bring you for a cup of coffee for a long time."

My breath caught. The girl handed him a coffee cup, but his eyes didn't leave mine. I broke the hold to take my own cup.

"Thanks," I mumbled.

We took a table in the corner. His eyes bore into my back, waiting for some reaction, but I wasn't capable of more.

"Charity, I like you."

I sipped the coffee, looking down.

"Charity—"

"I heard you."

"I know."

I put the cup down and snapped my eyes up to meet his. "Robbie, you're a nice guy. Really nice. But—"

"You don't want to be with me? You change around me. Obviously you don't want to change."

"You have no idea."

"I know what happens to you, but you don't have to be afraid."

"Don't. Do not talk about it here, like we're talking about some daily life shit that people do."

"You think I would risk you somehow? You know better than that."

I drank the coffee and focused on the table, his hands on it, fingers spread, open to everyone and everything.

"I love that thing I become. You know what that says about me? What you see here—"

"What I see here is someone who's been so hurt they don't know how to be alive anymore." His eyes had searched out my own, his fingers reaching for mine across the table. I put my hands in my lap.

"Please don't use your emotional comradery on me. That may work for boarding house kids, but I'm beyond that. Their wings haven't been clipped yet. Mine have."

He took a sip of his coffee, his eyes falling downward. I was a piece of garbage come to life, moldy and infectious.

The silence was painful and too long. I stared out the window, drinking my coffee, assuming those would be the last moments I'd spend with him. Not knowing what to say sucked.

Then, crossing the street, was Evan. Put together, like some tall, dark and handsome storybook prince in his suit. He was coming right our way. Fucking great.

He walked in with authority, smiling nicely at people. He and Robbie had the same confident ease about them, but couldn't have been more different. Robbie was still looking at his hands, deep in thought while I watched Evan order his coffee.

Evan came over, eyes stuck on mine. "Bumping into each other here has become a thing we do, hasn't it?"

"I may end up living here, if I play my cards right." He shook his head with in confusion, but I didn't explain.

Robbie watched us talk, shooting eyes at Evan, too kind to show his jealousy.

"Robbie, this is Evan. That's my neighbor, Robbie."

They shook hands, but the awkwardness was alive and breathing.

"All right, Evan, spill it. You played nice with Jen, right?"

Evan smiled so wide I thought his face would crack in half. "That friend of yours is something special," he said. "I'm seeing her again tomorrow." He hesitated, a dark glimmer in his eyes appearing.

"Yeah, she's got a way of bringing the light out, doesn't she?"

"Don't discredit yourself, Charity," Evan said, his eyes lingering on my lips in a way that made me think of darkness and moans. "You've got a fair bit of light in you, too. It comes out in a different way."

Robbie cleared his throat, eyes narrowed at Evan

with as much malice as I think he was capable of. Evan's eyes darted to him for a millisecond.

"Good to see you, Charity," Evan said with a funny quirk of his lips. Turning to Robbie, he nodded, and walked—sauntered, more, out the door. He had this Old World sort of grimness about him. It was beautiful. It should have intimidated me, but I don't know how to be intimidated.

Robbie fiddled with his drained coffee cup. His chin was on his chest, and he looked up at me with unintentional puppy dog eyes, waiting for me to say something.

"Rob, I'm really sorry about the things I said, that I probably always say." I gritted my teeth. "I'll lay it out for you. You can do better than me. That's all. I'm a disaster with an active death wish and a real live monster not quite hiding inside. You help troubled kids. Our playing fields are a lot different."

His eyes twinkled, boyish and fearless. He really was fearless, while I just looked like it. He smiled at me, like it was the most pleasant conversation he'd ever had.

"Can you let me worry about the little things, and just be happy with me for a while?"

Tears clouded my eyes. I guzzled the rest of the coffee.

"Wanna come with me to get a canary?"

*W*e went to Petco in his car. My own beater hadn't gotten a lot of action lately, and I was fine with that. My new preferred method of travel grew out of my arms and back.

The pet store smelled like a pet store.

"Is my apartment going to smell like this now?" I asked Robbie loudly, to the annoyance of a cashier.

"Probably."

We walked around before we went to the birds. Robbie might have spent all day tapping the glass to amuse the abandoned cats up for adoption if I hadn't pulled him toward the reptiles.

"Maybe I should bring home this guy," he said, smiling at a fat orange tabby as I tugged on his arm.

"You have enough strays in your life, don't go looking for another."

The snakes and turtles continued their lives, coolly refusing to be interrupted by a couple of staring stupid people. There was this one lizard, a water dragon it was called, that looked back at me as if it sensed my cold blood, too. It was exotic and delicate, but not fragile. A beautiful machine of survival.

"You like him, huh?" Rob said quietly next to me, bent down to look with me. I nodded. The water dragon cocked his head to see me better.

"He's as fascinated by me as I am by him. Look at him."

"I know the feeling," Robbie said, his breath in my ear. I turned my face to his and wondered for a second why I'd considered anything besides him. He kissed me quickly on the lips, long enough for me to taste the heat behind his, to want to bite their fullness.

I swallowed hard. "Fascination wears off," I said, and started moving towards the birds.

There was a big cage filled with probably a hundred parakeets, a sick little zoo of things to own. There was a cockatoo the size of a forty ounce beer that backed away from me, cocking its head like it was seeing something it shouldn't. I sneered when I passed it. It bowed its head to me, queen of small, weak things.

"Don't they have any canaries?" I said, sticking my finger between a blue parrot's cage bars. I yanked it back when the bird lunged at me.

"I'm sure they do, keep looking." Robbie put his finger in the same bars, and the bird nuzzled its head against his finger. Rob winked at me.

"Whatever, bird ass-kisser."

"I wish," he mumbled.

"Hey, there they are!"

They were singing together, it was how I found them. A cage with half a dozen canaries in it, mostly yellow, a couple with brown spots.

"Wow, look at the pink ones," Robbie said. He'd found the beauties when I didn't. He was close enough that his t-shirt sleeve rubbed against my bare arm.

There was a nest attached to the back of the cage filled with baby canaries, the color of watermelon sherbert. They were nestled down, a tiny mass of fruity feathers. But there was one, standing on the edge of the nest alone, neck stretched high, singing strong. On the fringes, but still a part.

"That one," I whispered.

Robbie flagged down a Petco person.

"I need that one," I told the guy.

"You have a cage?"

"No, but I probably should, huh?"

He rolled his eyes at me, and I rolled mine right back. I glanced at his nametag. "Okay, Bert, hook me up with a cage and food, and a canary car or whatever I need."

"My name's Brad."

"Okay, Bert. Let's get this show on the road."

Robbie smiled nervously and ran his hand through his hair.

Tallying the cash as it virtually flew out of my pocket, I ended up with a white cage to put my birdie in, a bag of bird seed, a mirror, and some fake bird thing that frankly, creeped me the hell out.

"You don't want that fake bird, do you?" Robbie whispered to me.

"Do I need it?"

"Do birds have fake birds in nature?"

"Good point." I put it back on the shelf.

Bradbert held a green net and was trying to catch the bird, making all of the others flutter crazy around the cage, and pissing me off.

"Dude, there has to be another way."

"I could do it with my hand," he said.

"Is that any better? And that's what she said."

"Um…"

"Let me do it."

"Ma'am, you can't put your hand in there, I don't think my boss—"

"—is looking. So, get out of my way."

I nudged past him and put my arm in the cage, hoping not to get canary shit on my corset. They stopped singing and scattered, but I didn't close my eyes and cringe like Bradbert had. The nest of pink ones stayed still, and the only one that mattered didn't move, but eyed me with a curiosity that I didn't associate with the intelligence level of a canary. It didn't move as I grasped it and pulled it out. It was resigned to its tiny fate.

It poked its head around, probably happy to see the outside of the cage, and if I knew it like I thought I did, definitely happy to get away from those other birds.

"Can I have that?" I said, nodding to a box with holes poked in it. The guy handed it to me reluctantly. The canary was okay as I eased it inside, but I bit my lip hard enough to see stars. It shouldn't be in there. It shouldn't be confined.

I hated myself for buying a cage for him.

"This is a boy, right?"

"I don't know."

"It's a boy." Bradbert just gaped at me, and I walked away.

Robbie shook the guy's hand.

"That was weird," I said.

"That I shook the guy's hand?"

"Yeah."

"It's weirder that you got your own bird out," Robbie said into my ear.

The cashier rang me up, glaring at me, and I saw Robbie out of the corner of my eye, taking his wallet out.

"Don't even fucking try it."

The cashier looked up, alarmed, because I hadn't looked at Robbie when I said it. I grinned and waggled my eyebrows at the cashier.

Robbie leaned into my ear, but I'm sure the girl overheard. "You don't have a job, Charity."

"Not your concern."

"Let me do this for you."

"No need."

He smoldered at the confused cashier and said in his most seductive, unassuming voice, "Please?"

"One hundred twenty-nine dollars, seventy-five cents, please."

I sighed deep. "We'll go half. That way you're not my boyfriend."

He didn't look at me. "I will pay it all, and I'm still not your boyfriend."

He gave her a stack of twenties, and I clucked to the chattering bird in the box.

"At least you aren't leaving KFC in a box. Things could be worse than going home with me." I held the box to my chest.

Robbie smiled at the box. God, it ate me up to say thank you. I'd rather say sorry. Blame was second nature for me, but being treated extra nicely was a lot harder to cope with. Robbie treated me too well already, without this added thing.

We got in the car, the bird box in my lap, the rest of the bird paraphernalia in the trunk.

"You didn't have to do that."

"I know."

"Thank you."

"You would have done it without me. I didn't do it to be thanked."

We were all quiet, the two of us and the bird.

"What are you naming him?"

"Oh. Right. I don't know."

We pulled onto the street, so Robbie didn't have to look at me when he said, "When I was little, we took in this stray dog. We had that thing for almost a year before I named him."

"Who's 'we'?"

"My brother and me. My parents were there, but not really, you know?"

"No, not really. Tell me."

"They didn't care what we did. They didn't beat us or anything, we were just—"

"Neglected?"

"Yeah. Neglected."

"No wonder those boarding house kids like you so much."

He bit his lip, hard. I'd struck a nerve without even trying. Another testament to why I shouldn't have a boyfriend, or anyone else to unleash my mouth on. My straightforwardness had its perks, I was just hard put to think of a fucking one of them.

We parked and he turned to me. "Some people weren't meant to take care of others. I sorta was. And some people think they're alone in this world, and it's only because they make it that way."

The canary scratched inside his box. Time to let him out.

REVELATIONS

I watched the little bird for a while, swinging on his swing in the pristine cage. He was young, still a baby, really. I think he was happy.

"He's really pretty," Robbie said, his boots clunking on my ugly carpet toward the cage.

"Yeah, he is."

"Any name ideas?"

The bird cocked his head at me, apparently waiting for an answer. In the light, he was the same pink-yellow color as the setting sun. The color of peace when the day had run its course. When the Harpy's day began. I put my finger between the white cage bars. He came right over, pecking at me happily.

"When I was little," I said, "my dad read me a story about a little prince named Keegan. The name means 'small and fiery.' Keegan was wild and free, with energy that never stopped and a smart mouth that ran just as fast. His father, the king, loved the spitfire in him, but the queen feared it would lead him to trouble. So she put him in a golden cage that held his spirit as much as his body. Keegan's father wept every day, afraid his boy's soul would die in that cage before death ever claimed his body. One night, the king finally managed to untie the key the queen kept on her neck. He ran to Keegan in tears, begging his child to hurry out of the cage, they only had a little time before his mother woke. The boy followed his father, running down the long hallways of their palace, until they came to a room Keegan had never seen. 'What is this?' he asked his father. There was another cage. His father said, 'a place I can keep you safe.'"

"That's kind of a terrible story," Robbie said with his grim laugh.

"I know. But I like it. Out of one cage, into another." The quiet in the room was closing in.

"Calling him Keegan, then?"

"Definitely."

*R*obbie stayed almost all day. I was shocked a person could spend all day with me and not lose their mind a little. Maybe he'd already lost it by being there to begin with. While he was with me, I never had an urge toward the change. Things seemed easy, but it was all a façade. Nothing was easy. Nothing.

"Sub?" Robbie said out of the blue.

"Nah, I'd classify myself more as a Dom."

"Do you want to get subs?"

"Yeah. Yeah, I do. I haven't had a good sub in a really

long time." All that sandwich meat…enough to get a girl's juices flowing.

The day was wearing on, and my anxiety about suddenly turning into a cannibalistic bird monster was only secondary to my happiness just hanging with Rob. I was both uncomfortable and comfortable, making me more uncomfortable. He saw something that had gone unnoticed in me. Something I went to great lengths to hide without even trying.

We went to the new sub shop down the street. The cool thing about living in downtown Plymouth was everything that was worth going to was down the street. It was enough to make me never miss Boston.

"You, uh…like meat a lot now, huh?" Robbie said with a smirk. I probably had meat all over my chin right at that moment. He'd given me a sideways glance when I ordered a steak and cheese with ham and pepperoni. My craving for meat was intense, a reminder that the Harpy was never far.

"Ha. Yes. I guess I do." My eyes hung on him, to see how much he meant by all this. It was either a great sexual euphemism, or he knew that I actually ate human flesh. Tough call.

His eyes darted, and he leaned over to me. "It's kinda all over your face. There." He wagged his finger at my whole face.

"Hmmm. Are people looking?" I asked in my coolest voice, knowing for sure people would be. They were always looking at me.

He laughed, not the nervous giggle of a person who's humiliated, but the proud dad kind. "Yeah, people are looking." He scanned the shop, making lots of eye contact while I wiped my face.

We finished our subs, his a lot neater than mine, and took another walk home. These walks with him were another form of quiet that brought out the thinker in me. I hated thinking.

"You know, it happens to me every night."

"Not last night."

"No. Not last night."

"Do you know why it didn't happen?"

"Not really." *Liar.*

"I think I do," he said.

Why did I bring shit like that up?

"Enlighten me."

"You were occupied, and happy about it."

I stopped walking. "You think I didn't turn into a Harpy because I had something better to do?"

"Yep."

"Jesus fucking Christ." I walked again.

"You don't know why it happens exactly, do you?"

"I absolutely do. What makes you think you know why?"

"I just watch."

"That's what she said."

"I think being with me," he smirked, "took your mind off whatever it is that makes you become—you know—and I think maybe that's a good thing?"

"Robbie, if you're implying that being with you is my twelve step program to not becoming Bird Bitch, then I don't know there's a manual for that. So quit while you're ahead."

"Step two. Quit while you're ahead."

We went back to my apartment, a place I'd seen more of in that one day than I had in weeks. I guess daytime had been a blur after the nights I'd been having. Sorta like high school, when I drank too much, went out too much, and hid a lot. Except I wasn't the one being hurt at night anymore.

Keegan greeted us with a song before I opened the door. It was a breath of fresh air to my tired heart, and I was instantly happy to have brought him home. From one cage to another.

"Wow, listen to him in there," Robbie said, close to me, but not touching. Not close enough.

"Happy bird."

"He has better company now," Robbie said, elbowing me.

Keegan was flitting around the cage that was bathed in sunshine from the windows. Alone, free in his confines.

"You did a good thing for both of you by bringing him here."

I put my finger between the bars again, and rubbed his head, our new greeting to each other.

"He'd have given me a new cage if he could."

～

*R*obbie's smartass solution to figuring out whether or not I could banish the Harpy by finding a hobby or whatever, was to take off to his apartment, leaving me to see what happened next.

"I think you're wrong," I told him. "Becoming the Harpy was never something I imagined possible, so how could I decide to do it or not?"

"Haven't you ever wanted something without knowing it? Then it showed up, and you wondered how you dealt so long without it?"

I swallowed a lump in my throat. We both knew what and who he was talking about.

"I am—always afraid to want anything. So, I don't let myself. I'm not built to have nice things."

He rubbed his thumb along my cheek. "I think you're still being built. Don't speak too soon."

That was the thought he was leaving me with? I wanted him to stay. I also wanted to prove him wrong. He had one hand on the door knob.

"Thanks for today, Rob. It was really cool. And for the bird, you know..."

"Don't say I didn't have to do that. I'll talk to you tomorrow?" He was sad to leave and I was happy he was sad about it.

"Yeah, or maybe you'll see me later tonight, you know, flying outside."

He showed no freakout signs. I sighed.

"Bye." He kissed me on the cheek quickly before he walked out the door.

That kiss made me more jittery than any kisses I'd ever had, from any other guy that had been in this apartment or that had hit on me without shame or mercy. Unfamiliarity didn't suit me.

It was getting dark, and I had no idea what was coming. I could only wait.

Keegan whistled, low and peacefully, a little flamingo flame in the failing light.

"Where have you been all my life, birdie?" I whispered.

I texted Jen. *Hey, saw Evan at DD's...he seemed happy.* I realized I was occupying myself because I was scared. That was fucking annoying.

Jen texted me back right away. *He's amazing! Whatcha doin?*

Nothing, just hanging out. I erased that. *Waiting for someone.*

I couldn't risk her inviting herself over and seeing the Harpy first-hand. I couldn't let anyone else know what I was, but letting the Harpy out struck a chord deep down where I was so undeniably *me*, all the complications I knew, was a product of and the cause of. My guts were horrible, but they were familiar. I knew what I was getting.

When the Harpy wanted to burst out of me that night, I'd be ready for the change. I'd decided it.

Except I was wrong. I stayed in the apartment all night, wanting the change to come, but it never happened. My feet never turned into uber vulture talons, I didn't get even a trace of blood-rusted feathers. I didn't grow claws and there was nothing different about me.

I sat in my ordinary gloom, waiting, waiting on something that was never to come.

But something else did.

SHIT GETS REAL

The night was almost gone, and I hadn't become the Harpy, despite not having found anything better to do. The night was empty, full of memories that crushed me with their blackness.

If I wasn't the Harpy, I was worse than nothing.

Robbie was right next door, and Jen was a phone call away, but my desire to be just fucking alone so I could become that Other Thing was overwhelming. Panic flourished at the idea that maybe, just maybe it was all over. No more Harpy.

When I couldn't be fucking confined anymore and my arms itched for the sky, I ran out, leaving Keegan chirping in his cage. My feet pounded up the stairs so hard, I definitely woke half the fucking building. Robbie was probably listening for it all. The front door hit the railing when I whipped it open. Fucking raining.

I hunched over on the lawn/hill, my hands on my knees, panting, anxiety attack rattling my brain, constricting my chest. I was in full view of half the apartments in the building, and half of those had their lights on.

I didn't hurt, only ached. I prayed that Robbie wouldn't come out.

"I can't be me now."

The words fell out. I didn't want to mean them, and absolutely did. But the reality of being me was asphyxiating me more each second. I fell flat back on the grass, soaking in the rain, letting it pelt my eyes and mouth, wishing my banging heart would slow down.

Something moved in the empty sky above me. I squinted into the rain, trying to focus on the dark air. There was definitely a swirling, shimmering spot in the sky. Changing that one spot of the night. Pulsing like heat above hot tar, vibrating with unnatural energy.

I would have done anything to be sucked into it, no matter what it was.

The air exploded like a shattering mirror, and what came out of it was even more shocking.

"Holy shit."

Harpies.

Two of them. Different than me. Hideous, but no less, the same as me. The same as me and I was terrified of them.

The rain seemed to avoid them. Life would have avoided them if it could. To say they were nightmares wouldn't do them justice. One had hair that reminded me of my own, wild and unkempt, but hers was filthy, dirt caked and tangled, dull brown. A haggard monster, she had a witch's nose, broken teeth with gristle between them that I got full view of as she snarled at me. She scratched at the air with black claws. Her wings were enormous; black, huge things filled with holes and rips, like they'd been mauled.

The other one was bigger and clearly stronger, and even more horrifying. Wings like a giant insect, black and slick. Scars covered her face, and her skin was so thin, it was translucent. Huge, shiny dark eyes took up half her face, unblinking. The thing looked like it was in a perpetual state of anger, ready to devour anything that dared to come near it. Nothing had ever scared me so much in my life, not even *him*.

"Little predator," the insecty one hissed, its voice like jabbing needles. The other one laughed a bitter nasty laugh, so it must have seen the disgust on my face.

"What?" I hated talking to them; they made me feel dirty. Dirtier.

"This one is *wrong*," said the first one. It came out like a sentence she couldn't finish, like she was too primitive to use language.

"She isn't wrong, but she's not good enough yet." Insecty's voice was as painful to hear as her face was to look at.

Mother of God, was this what I'd become? They were offensive in every way. I was offensive, but not like that. I could never be like that.

"We scare you, girl?" Its demon bug wings brought it closer to me. I was too afraid to move. I nodded, weakened by their bestiality.

Having them near me made me think of *his* name:

Carl Painter. The wet closeness when he'd even just stood over me, the same lightheaded nausea when he touched me, tortured me. Would make me do the same to his own child.

I brimmed with fury that such helplessness dared to invade me again.

I arched my back, threw back my head and let out a brutal, ripping screech that shook the air. My hands formed into claws, and my mouth twisted and widened. My fear erupted on the outside, making me horrifying, with a Joker smile, mocking life.

Power surged through me. The kind I wished I'd had when my body had been vandalized as a kid, when I was just Hazel. I'd become strong, and not a little evil. My neck cracked when I straightened up with pride.

"There's my girl," Insecty hissed, and suddenly her voice was music to my ears.

"Just take me from this place." It was surreal saying the words, but I sure as hell meant them. Drenched from the rain, my body slipping on the grass, I'd become a giant, bigger and better, but I didn't fit. I floundered in the world; I had to get out of it.

"It's time you came home," Insecty murmured, the soothing sound of a knife breaking skin.

The air buckled and vibrated in a sickening way around me, like the drunken haze right before puking. The fresh rain smelled disgusting, too clean and too new, too full of hope. My body spasmed as the air shimmered, an awful dance as the sky sucked me in. The two dreadful Harpies screamed in the dark.

It was over as fast as it started. I was lying on my back again, on solid ground. Different ground.

"Wasn't expecting this."

I pulled myself to my feet, looking around for the beasts who brought me there. My mind couldn't process the horror of the place. I was going to pass out, static edging in.

"You're home," I heard from the half-wit Harpy behind me.

THE WOOD OF SUICIDES

"*W*ake up!"

A sharp smack across my face shot me up, ready to fight. Nobody woke me like that. Not anymore.

The first Harpy, the one on the stupid side, paced back and forth in front of me. She was soaked in thick, fresh blood, from her gnarly hair to her filthy claws. Stupid carnivore. I was better than her. A better predator.

But I still wanted what she had. I wanted that blood.

"Hungry," I hissed. I didn't recognize my own voice, and that didn't bother me one bit.

"Not time," it said to me, still circus-animal pacing. Pea-brained thing. Who the fuck was she to tell me when I could eat? That place, as little as I'd seen of it, made me vicious.

This was *my* place.

"Now!" I yelled. I'd surprised her, but she recovered herself right away, and inched slowly toward me, trying to corner me. She couldn't beat me, not for a second.

With a hellish screech, I willed every molecule in my body to become the Harpy, and it obeyed. Feathers burst with ferocity from my legs, up over my belly. My hands and feet turned into vulture talons faster than they ever had, with the pleasure of peeling a sunburn; good beyond good. My arms thrust out on their own, and my wings appeared like magic, filling the air around with their bloody splendor. A death angel, ready to deliver. I let out a scream, but my lips didn't move. My cheeks sucked in, my jaw stretched.

I knew I had a beak; sharp and deadly.

The other Harpy backed away, staring at me with fear. God, I loved it.

I lunged at her with my beak, ready to kill and devour the pitiful thing. My new weapon put an evil dollop on my need to kill.

Insecty appeared and descended upon us, black eyes blazing. As her wings cut through the air, whiffs of rotten meat came at me. I would have eaten that, too, if I could have.

With her landing, tortured screams arose all around us, growing like vines from the trees and ground.

"Stop this!" the more powerful Harpy yelled. Pea-brain cowered.

I listened, taking in my surroundings again and actually process the world around me. I was in the woods. It was a terrible place beyond anything I could ever have dreamed up. I knew I was an evil thing for wanting to be there.

The forest floor was covered in clumps of hay, like a barn, and was soaked with huge pools of blood here, there and everywhere. The sky wasn't black and rainy, but blood red, and rippling with the heat of an oven. The only other thing I could see were the trees.

The trees were made of human beings. People trapped inside them, their faces peering out of knots, arms and legs contorted into branches at horrifying angles, skin stretched into tiny twigs, hair wound around dead leaves that dripped blood continuously. Every tree screamed with a pain that I couldn't wrap my mind around.

I wished I was the one inflicting it.

"Don't waste your time fighting each other, there is nothing to fight over," Insecty said, snapping me to attention. "She rules here and she is your Queen everywhere." Her words were full of a primal power that made me bow my head. I didn't question it, even if I had no fucking idea what it meant, and the other Harpy clearly knew better, too.

With lowered eyes, I asked her, "Where are we? What Queen?"

"This," she said in that voice that made the trees cry and my heart leap, "is the Wood of Suicides." She gazed around like she was in Disneyland.

"Hell," spat the other one.

I walked past them both, shying from Insecty as best I could. I didn't hate being afraid of her as much as I hated being afraid of other things. It felt right, the way things should be. She let me by, and I went to the closest tree.

A young woman's face watched me with a knowing terror, though even I didn't know what I was going to do. She was upside down, embedded in the bloody bark completely. Her wrists were twisted backwards, palms up, leaves sprouting from her fingertips, bones eternally broken and held captive. One leg was wrapped around the trunk, the other bent up so her foot was next to her face. Her eyes looked like they'd been weeping thorns.

I bent my head to take in her eyes more closely. She whimpered, no longer screaming. She was afraid to offend me. She should be.

She was beautiful at one time.

Like I had been.

I jabbed my beak into the flesh of her leg where the bark left it exposed. I was offended by its pink newness in that vile place, infuriated by its fresh, inviolate softness that should have been ravaged by the demon heat closing in around it. It stood out like a daisy in a thorn bush, and deserved to be smited down.

The girl screamed in agony. Certainly there was no level of pain she hadn't endured, and yet I could cause more. The joy of it made me dig my beak in deeper, metallic blood bubbling over my nostrils, choking me, and I laughed a wet, messy cackle as she cried. The other tortured souls screamed with her.

My nightmares became dreams come true when I was drenched in another's despair.

When I'd defiled her enough, and I was unrecognizable inside, I stopped, savoring the metallic thickness in my throat before the emptiness washed it away again. I crowed at the red-orange sky in triumph.

It was so clear, why I was the Harpy. I had spent my life being punished for what I was to become.

"No one deserves this more than you."

Carl Painter's words invaded my brain yet again. I cried out, a human cry from a monster's mouth, that he could reach me here. I'd never be free of what he did to me, or what he made me do. My mind was diseased for a reason. I deserved to be this thing. I deserved to be in Hell, and it had happened.

I fell back on the ground, lowly, like I should be. I curled up, burying my face in my knees, nose tickled by feathers. The shaking wouldn't stop. I'd never stopped shaking my entire life.

With a buzzing, the insect Harpy was next to me. I knew it was her without looking up. I knew it like I knew that I'd do anything she said. Not because I wanted to, but because I was too weak not to.

She hummed in my ear, "The Queen can make the memories go away. She can make it so you never know this agony again."

I could only nod. "Take me to her."

ENDING IT ALL

*I*nsecty brought me to my clawed feet. The Wood had gone silent; it was a penetrating, filthy sound. The anticipation dug into me, waiting for the screaming again.

"Come," she said, and I did, with my head hung, I settled right in with my shame in that fucking awful place. Hell was where I belonged. The eyes of the trapped people followed me as we walked. I lifted my head, made myself face them.

"Why are they here?" I asked her, my voice feeble.

"The souls of the damned. Those who rejected the lives given to them."

"Suicides. The Wood of Suicides." Some place underneath my skin knew that name as it had known the word "Harpy." It rang clear through me.

Insecty smiled into the red darkness. "Yessss," she hissed. She delighted in the horror.

"This place is fucked up," I said under my breath.

"It is where they belong. They murdered their

bodies, and now their bodies will live eternally, here, for us to thrive on."

It was then that I saw there were more of us. More Harpies perched in the human trees all around us. They stared as we walked past, a happy court of inmates watching the new prisoner with glee and morbid curiosity. Fresh meat. Some of them were picking chunks of flesh off the trees, the trapped bodies silently weeping blood tears. I shivered with cold in the stagnant heat.

Nests made of limbs and bloody branches held yet more Harpies.

But the Queen's was different.

The monstrosity sat on the ground in a hollow among the trees. I didn't want to think it was beautiful, but it was. Made of glittering black tree branches, with blue jewels embedded between them.

Not jewels.

Eyeballs. Blinking at me, with odd disinterest.

Insecty let go of my hand, and continued on toward the royal nest, all the while transforming from the horrifying bug bitch. Her body became more human with every step, wearing a liquid-slick black gown that rippled as she glided up the branches of the nest as if they were stairs. A crown of silver and blue stones appeared atop her head as she morphed. Her enormous black wings stayed. Some darkness was too real to change.

She turned and folding her legs underneath her, trained her pitch eyes on me with a smile. The air around her crackled with what looked like tiny silver lightning bolts, as if the very atmosphere couldn't believe what she was.

"You may join me," she said.

It wasn't a request, so much as a nicely stated demand. I climbed the huge branches to sit next to her in the nest. Still in Harpy form myself, it was entirely natural. Like jumping into bed, albeit a bed way out of my league. Surrounding Harpies watched, seething with disdain and jealousy.

The Queen shimmied down, as though she were warming a clutch of eggs. The pungent scent of dead roses and rotting fruit wafted from her. She watched me, a content smile on her plum lips.

"That was you that came to get me? But it wasn't you?" I couldn't imagine why the Queen would come and get me herself, or at all.

"It was and it wasn't. I hide in different ways than you do."

"*Why* did you come for me?"

She ignored the question to ask me her own.

"So, my little one. You have much to run from, don't you?"

"I run from nothing," I spat.

She leaned intimately into my ear as she had before. I believed everything she said that way. "Maybe you should. Running may finally make you whole."

"I don't know what you mean," I said, staring straight ahead. I knew exactly what she meant. Fighting my way through the world every day, when nobody could possibly see what I'd been through. It was getting harder, not easier. I knew my demons well, but knowing my enemy hadn't helped me gain on him.

It hadn't occurred to me that I wanted to find Carl Painter when I was running from him.

"You do know," she said, not unkindly. "You have been through terrible things, things you think you have faced. You've only found new ways to hide. You ran from your past, you bury yourself deep. You make yourself untouchable."

"I am perfectly touchable, ask a bunch of guys."

"That is not what I meant. Your heart is a tomb."

The Harpies around us screeched. They shared the stabbing pain when I heard the words; they were my sisters in it.

I risked my heart to look at the Queen. Her eyes were like the moon, if it had been blacked out, a black hole that bit if you dared to go near it. "Do you know what happened to me as a kid?"

"Do you need to tell me?"

"I don't talk about it. Not even to Psychiatrist," I said, but the story was being drawn out of me as if attached to poisonous threads, straight to the Queen. "I was forced to do things as a kid that most women never do their entire lives. And I was forced to do things to another girl, younger than me, by a man my mother let in the house for drugs. Carl Painter." I hadn't spoken his name in so long. It stung like battery acid on my tongue.

The Woods were silent. They were all waiting for me to go on, even the trees. I kept going.

"My mother needed drugs more than she needed

me to be safe. And it wasn't just Painter, it was a few guys that touched me. But he—he destroyed me. And he made me destroy his own kid. He made me just like him."

The Harpies let out the screeches once again, one after another.

The Queen put a dainty hand on my blood-plastered hair, and I wanted the comfort it offered. "You can end all of this misery, all of this fighting. It can be over."

"Yeah, well, that sounds like a dream come true and all, but my dreams aren't that good, and they *do* come true."

"You are complete when you're one of us. Aren't you?"

I nodded.

"And you do the world justice when you feed. You rid it of the vilest creations in life. Monsters that create monsters."

"Yes."

"What if I told you, dear child, that if you let yourself fully become one of us, and left all of those earthly emotions behind, that you would know nothing of pain again?"

Her words oozed through me like a honey drug, relaxing me in a way I never had been since my innocence was taken from me. Since even before that when I knew my life was secondary. I swooned with the elixir of it.

"Yes, please. I don't want to do it anymore."

She took me in her arms and held me against her

chest, the death of her letting my sad soul rest. I went limp against her, and hated myself for it.

"I don't want this pain anymore," I said into her. "I wish I was numb to everything."

"I will be your family now. I can give you what you need."

"I don't need anything except not to need anything." I thought of Keegan, and how he needed me. And I thought of Jen, how she seemed to need me in her life. It hurt worst when I thought of Robbie.

"I know what you need more than you do, dear girl." Her hands on my cheeks, she pulled my face back, and gazed at me like I'd wished my mother would have. "You need power," she said with sugary sweetness.

I moaned.

"You were meant to be one of us, Charity," she cooed into my ear. The Harpies made the most birdlike noises I'd heard them make. Pleasant, if you could forget where we were.

"What are you asking me to do?"

"Nothing you don't know how to do, my darling. Just give in."

THE REALLY REAL HELL

A thundering blackness roiled around me, and I found myself torn from Hell and thrown back into the world that hated me.

I spun my head around fast to see what the world thought of me. It was night still. The grass was soaked. I was clean; the wind between worlds had stripped my filth away. I peeled myself off the grass, and thanked God there were so few stairs into my apartment building. Exhaustion crippled me.

The eviction notice glowed like a neon sign on my door. I'd known it was coming and remarkably gave zero fucks. I had somewhere else to go.

The dripping blood of the self-murderers would keep me warm in the Wood.

Ripping the orange offender off the door, I walked into what was no longer my apartment to find Robbie sitting on my couch. He sprang up, his guilt fading fast. He was too good to be doing anything wrong.

"Jesus Christ," he said, and came at me with a mind-blowing hug.

"Easy, killer. Why are you in my shitty apartment? Squatting already?" I waved the eviction notice.

He ran his fingers through his hair, making it flop around his face in a perfect mess. He looked at the ground, like he always did when he was thinking. "I watched you disappear. Whatever happened outside, when you ran out the other night, I saw it." He swallowed hard. I gritted my teeth at his clear anguish. "I didn't think you'd be coming back. Charity, it felt like you were gone."

"I was."

"You didn't want to come back, did you?" Another swallow.

I just blinked at him like an idiot. How could I tell him that reality was getting more real, and I wanted it to stop? Or that in the Wood of Suicides I could kill things that were already dead, not living, breathing men? How could I tell him that trying to be Charity Blake was clawing me open from the inside?

"How much did you see the…wait, *the other night?* How long was I gone?"

He took my hands in his, coming close to my face. My lips tingled with the need to taste him. "Four days." His eyes searched my face for something I couldn't give him, and he cupped my cheeks in his calloused hands. He kissed me, with a softness I didn't know people were capable of. It hurt worse than a slap to the face, of which I'd had plenty. My shoulders dropped, stomach unclenched as his hands went to the back of my head, fingers curling into my certainly disgusting hair, keeping me from running.

If only he'd known what place it was that I'd run to.

"Just be here," he whispered against my lips, his smooth skin soft on my cheeks, his hands playing in my hair.

"I can't."

He kissed me harder, holding me against him. I wanted him, my body reacting in a way my heart couldn't. I wrapped my arms around him, pressing myself to him. I reeked of blood, but neither of us cared. Keegan sang a couple of feet away. Things to be taken care of, things to overthink, things to do.

"Be here," he whispered again, bringing me back. I kissed him then, bringing him closer.

"For now," I said.

We left the sound of the singing bird behind as he led me to the bedroom.

~

I woke up to the taste of Robbie's lips.

"Good morning," he murmured, leaning on one elbow, well-toned naked bicep level with my face.

"Mmm, hi." I let my lips cover his. I let myself dissolve into it the way I wanted to. He wasn't surprised, but I was. He leaned his chest on mine, and he smelled like *us*. I wanted him again.

In the middle of the night, with whispers and bed sheets wound around each other, both of us holding on for something neither of us could be sure we wanted, I told him I was a Harpy, and I'd been in Hell.

He only took his lips from mine long enough to kiss my throat, my earlobes, to groan into my ear. We moved together like we had a routine, but it was far from ordinary. It was the explodey sex that *Cosmo* tried to convince me was possible, but I always treated sex as a means to an end. It wasn't supposed to be a goddamn team-building experience.

I didn't know it could make me feel like part of something.

I stayed there with him after, close but not snuggling. To think, that a day before I'd been in a circle of Hell, contemplating leaving my life behind to become a Harpy for good. I couldn't let my mind wander to that place, not when I was in his arms. I couldn't stomach a choice like that when I felt so…*happy.*

"Whatcha thinking about?" Robbie asked me, his fingertips chilling my arm.

"Just this. And you. How I can't believe I'm letting myself do this."

He kissed my forehead, his lips lingering enough to make it warm and a little wet. "Just let go."

Nothing you don't know how to do, my darling. Just give in.

The Queen's words made my heart plummet when it was just starting to beat again.

I rolled over, away from him, and tried to disentangle myself from the blankets. He pulled me back against his chest, wrapping us up tighter.

"It's okay. You don't need to run from me."

I gritted my teeth at being held so tight. "I don't run from anyone. I walk away with explosions behind me. Don't be one of my explosions, Robbie."

He kissed my shoulder. "What's an explosion or two in a life of fireworks?"

"You're a helluva poet, there."

"Songwriter."

"Same thing."

He held me, running his calloused fingertips over my skin, and then over the blankets. He let out a little laugh.

"So. You like unicorns a lot."

"Not true."

"Then why do you have them all over—I mean *all over*—your room?"

Nobody ever asked me. The guys who made it in there were hardly interested in my personality enough to wonder about my choice of décor.

"They, um. I guess they make me think some beautiful things can't be destroyed, if for no other reason than that they aren't real."

He went quiet. The kind of quiet I knew in him. He thought too much about what I said sometimes, like I was some Rubik's cube to put together. My world was easier when I scared it away.

"Charity, what's beautiful in you can never be destroyed. Nobody can ruin your perfection."

"Yeah, perfect disaster. It's seriously okay, Rob, you don't need to—"

"I don't say these things just to say them."

"I know. I don't think you know how to say meaningless things."

"Why say anything you don't mean?" he said.

I rolled over and kissed him once, fast, and got out of bed, ready to start whatever day it was. The closeness was all a little too close to me.

Standing there, stark naked, with him staring at me, it would have been really easy to fall back under his spell and into bed, but it wouldn't be smart. Because for as whole as he made me feel, it couldn't last. Imaginary filling in an all too real cavity.

"All right," I said, rubbing my hands over my face. "I have a massive hangover from actual Hell, so let's go get some coffee. I could use the walk."

He folded his arms behind his head, smirking. "I could make a great joke about you not being able to walk today." I laughed, throwing his shirt at him.

"You don't laugh like that enough," he said while I put on yesterday's panties and jeans, grossing myself out.

"Only with you," I said, but it sounded dismal. I couldn't look at him.

"Please, don't put on a corset," he asked. Pleaded, really.

"Why not?"

"I want to see you. Just you. No makeup either. Please?"

Find me the girl that could say no to that face when he said *please.* I reached for a Clash tee shirt instead. Then Rob was next to me, hands under my shirt. My skin instantly sprang to life.

"I have a bird that needs me," I groaned, leaning into him despite myself.

"You have a man that needs you."

"I have a man that's had plenty of me. You want Keegan to starve this morning because you—"

"Because I missed you? He won't, and I did," he said, kissing my neck, working his way down, kneeling at my feet. "Putting this shirt on was a bad idea." He slipped under my shirt, his lips clasping my nipple, and I couldn't hold it in anymore.

"I missed you, too. I missed you while I was there."

He stopped kissing me, and put his arms around my waist, leaning his head on my belly. "We were both in Hell," he said.

~

"Keegan didn't sing like that the whole time you were gone," Rob said, as we left the apartment to a very happy canary. I smiled.

"Really?"

"Really. I went over to feed him the morning after you left, and he seemed so sad, I stayed."

"Did you sleep at my place?" I asked, surprised. Fucking unicorns surrounding him, the probably ten beer bottles crowding the floor near the window.

He blushed. "Yeah, I did. I hope that's okay."

I blushed, too. Foreign girliness. "Yeah, that's cool. Not that it would matter if it wasn't, stalker. Also, no longer my apartment."

He cleared his throat. "Where will you go?"

I couldn't answer him, but that was answer enough. He stopped in his tracks, grabbing me by the arm and making me face him. "Charity, where will you go?" he said slowly.

My cheeks were on fire, but I didn't shy away from his eyes. It melted me to see the fear there. He knew. He knew.

"I'm going with them. The other Harpies."

"No. You can't."

I started walking again, and he caught up. "I will. Robbie, I like what we have here, but it won't keep me from fucking up all over again. It won't give me a place to live, or a job, or take away the shit in my head. *They* can. There's a reason why I'm one of them."

We walked into Dunkin Donuts, where the girl had already started my coffee when she saw me coming. I nodded my thanks at her as Robbie paid, again, and I took my coffee outside. I couldn't be around people, not when I knew I wouldn't be one of them for long. Robbie followed me out.

Shit. Again? "Evan."

I wasn't safe getting a cup of fucking coffee. I had to always bump into the perfect fucking Evan Hale, who I suddenly resented and didn't find attractive anymore.

"Charity," he said. But that was it, no smile. There was a deadness behind his eyes. He looked *wrong*.

"Hey, you all right?" I asked, while Robbie shifted from foot to foot beside me.

Evan looked blankly at me as though we'd never seen each other before, or like he'd come from a place where people didn't talk to him. His perfection dripped away in front of me like candle wax.

"Yeah, I'm fine." His voice sounded thick, like he hadn't slept. His reddened eyes fit the bill, too. He had scruff, and his hair looked less managed than usual.

"Well, you look like shit for doing fine," I said. Robbie snickered. Evan didn't.

"Talk to Jen if you want to know why I look like shit, Charity. I have nothing to say." He pushed past me and went to the counter. He wasn't waiting for me to follow him. He wanted to be alone. In that moment, I knew him.

"Come on," Robbie said, putting his hand on my elbow. "I need to hear more about Hell."

THE INTRUSION OF BEING ALONE

"Your buddy Evan didn't look so hot there," Robbie said with the stank of jealousy.

"Yeah, you're right," I said, ignoring it. I was actually worried about the guy, and I didn't like that one bit. And worse, I was worried that Jen might have something to do with it, so I was worried about two people. Worrying was fucking stupid. She'd texted me dozens of times while I was in the Wood of Suicides. I still hadn't answered her. What was I supposed to say? She sounded rough, too, without even actually hearing her. This bullshit of understanding people was getting on my nerves.

Time to leave it all behind.

We went to the pond with the starving-ass ducks. Would anybody feed them when they weren't supposed to get fed when I left? Robbie would. Robbie would take care of them and Keegan, and hopefully himself. He'd have a better chance of taking care of himself without my blazing fuck-it-upitude in the way.

He sat on the bench overlooking the pond, the bench where nobody saw you unless they were looking for you. A different guy might have patted the seat next to him, but Robbie knew I was going to sit down. That self -assured quiet confidence. I loved it.

"I like this bench because there's no duck shit on it anywhere," I said.

"You like this bench because you don't have to see anybody when you're sitting on it. And nobody pays attention to you."

I sighed. How the fuck did he know those things?

"I *want* to go with the Harpies, Robbie."

"Why?" He was trying hard not to show that he was hurt, but he just didn't have it in him to hide things. I hid pain messily, poorly, and it came out in ugly ways.

"I don't want to be in pain anymore." The hurt never seemed to stop, it was all around me. "They can take it away. Make me free of it."

"There's nothing wrong with letting your pain be heard. With acknowledging it."

I squeezed the Styrofoam coffee cup until its sides caved in a little, droplets of hot liquid seeping between my fingers. "I. *Acknowledge* it. All the time."

He took my hand in his and looked into my eyes. He was always looking in my eyes, letting my monster soul drink him in like he did to me. I felt like I was giving something away, but I was getting more back. My heart was about to seize with all the confused fucking emotions.

"Charity, let me be the one to take the pain away. Please, don't give in to them."

I kissed him, mingling coffee breaths, to the sound of the quacking ducks and lapping water, and I imagined I could be happy. If it would always be like that, maybe I could live with the pain.

It was all or nothing. Try to be normal and deal with shit nobody should have to deal with, or become something that never had to care.

"Tell me about that place," he said, his hand wrapped around mine as he searched my face.

"I can't." Nausea welled in me when I thought of what I did to the girl in the tree. How the hell could I explain that place as the one where I could relax, let my breath out?

"Okay, let's try this. Tell me what you do when you become the Harpy."

"Rob, how are you talking to me about this like it's some normal fucking thing, like *tell me how to make a cake* or some shit? How can you believe this?"

His eyes became deeper somehow, and it struck fear in me.

"Because you're extraordinary, and finding out that you're not exactly human doesn't surprise me."

"What the fuck. Okay. You want to know what I do? I hunt down asshole men and kill them. I eat them, drink their blood, devour their flesh. I love it. I love how uncomfortable it must be making you. Happy now?"

He smiled. Actually fucking smiled.

"Holy shit, Rob, you *are* happy. How does that happen? Oh, because you don't believe me."

"I do. I saw the blood. I saw something take you, or

you go with them, whatever, and after that it's not hard to believe there's a body or two along the way. I've also seen you eat. It's scary."

We watched the ducks and drank our coffee. Neither of us laughed.

"It's the only thing that literally gives me wings, gives me space. But when daylight rolls around, I'm still *this,* a nobody, a victim, worthless, trying so fucking hard to try *not* to be normal…" He let me trail off, didn't fill my head with reassurances of what a wonderful fucking person I was. He let me be myself. I'd never forget that. "I'd never have to deal with normalcy again."

His laugh cut me with its misunderstanding. "Baby, like normalcy ever touches you."

"Baby?"

"Sorry."

"No. No, I liked it." *Fuck.*

"Well, if you like it, maybe you shouldn't take off to become a monster for good."

"I'm a monster now."

He jumped to his feet, facing me, angrier than I had ever seen him; eyes wide, hands flailing. "Charity, for chrissakes, get it through your head. You might do bad things. We all do bad things. You're just a little more efficient at it."

"Efficient. That's one way of looking at it."

"Who you are trumps the damage that you do."

Jaw clenched, I looked at him like something to eat. "I have flayed a man while he was still kicking, and ate his flesh in pieces in front of him. When he died, skinless, staring at me without eyelids to keep my fucking face out of his head, I smiled, and I was more alive than I had in years."

Rob lost a little color. "They all deserved it."

"This unconditional trust you have in me is faulty."

"Only if you abandon me."

Awe is the only word to describe how much I admired the way he could give me so much emotion without worrying if he'd be destroyed because of it. I could never do that. He deserved someone who would.

"Robbie, I don't know how much time I have. To decide."

"If you're going or not?"

I nodded.

"Charity," he said, he pleaded. "I'm asking you not to go."

Swallowing hard, I said, "They can give me something you can't."

"What? Acceptance? I'll do more than accept you. I'll love you. Will they do that?"

Christ. My heart leaped into my throat, choked me. "You...you..."

He sank to a crouch in front of me, and held my hands.

"I love you. Don't take that away from me."

~

I needed to be alone. I kissed Robbie at the door, thanked him for the coffee and the pep talk, and waited to hear his door click shut.

Keegan began to sing. I leaned against the door and closed my eyes to listen.

"You sing the same all the time, happy or sad. Does it ever feel like it's the only thing you do?"

The bird wasn't close enough to hear me, and the words weren't really for him, anyway.

I sat on the couch and listened to the foolish little bird chatter away. Quiet, the apartment smelling like burnt coffee, the fan whirring away. Robbie next door. Not too far. Again the illusion seeped in that I could hack this life, that maybe I'd overcomplicated things. People dealt with the kind of hurts I did all the time. Not all of them ever got justice or revenge. I'd been lucky.

Lucky wasn't the word that came to mind, though.

And when it came to the little luck I did have... Robbie, Jen, the bird...I could only see them as lives I'd do nothing but cannibalize. Devour them before they knew what hit them. There was a reason the things that happened in my life had happened; I was cancerous, and attracted evil like an open wound attracts infection.

"You have an infection, Hazel, but we can take care of it. It just won't be very comfortable."

I shook my head like mad to get rid of the memory. "Infection" was one of those words I tried not to remember hearing. Telling my mom that Carl Painter had given me an STD, and that she probably had it, too.... Good times.

It was harder to be alone after that. Just sitting there, purpose-free, no direction, Hell screamed to me, and invited me back. Once decent vibes showed up in my life I was confused. I couldn't do it for another second. I grabbed my phone and got up for a beer.

"Hello?" Jen's tinkling little voice.

"Hey, Jen, I'm glad you answered. I'm coming over."

"Yeah. Come on over." She let out a long breath. "I really wish you would, actually. I need you."" The nervous laugh was definitely accompanied by that inappropriate smile I hated.

"I'm so the wrong person to be needed. But I need you, too." Rolling nausea.

"I'll put on the coffee. Unless you want something stronger?"

"Suicide pacts don't taste as good. Coffee will do."

My heart was breaking with the hatred of need.

"See you soon."

"Yes, you will."

Keegan was whistling loudly, calling to another beautiful creature like him. I whistled back anyway.

ALL THE WRONG PLACES

*J*en threw her arms around me before I could even get a look at her face.

"Come in," she said when she finally let go. "You smell like beer." She wrinkled her nose.

"Pretty much always. I could use that coffee now, since you drained the life from me with that death grip."

She bounced into the kitchen, she was so happy to see me. It put a smile on my face that I never wanted to let go of, to be wanted like that.

I took over a chair and waited, listening to her whistle in the next room. She hadn't been reading much, I figured. No open book on the coffee table, only tissues, and the remote. A half-eaten donut. Things had been bad for her.

When she came out with two coffee cups and more donuts, I knew we had a talk ahead of us. I was shocked as shit when I realized that I *wanted* to talk. A half hour earlier I'd wanted the taste of blood.

She sat lightly on the couch, like she had it all together, but her internal mess was written all over her. Bloodshot eyes and shaking hands. Taking a deep breath through her nose, she fixated on me.

"I'm sorry that I needed you, and that I texted you so much, but I did need you. I do. I'm a leech, but…"

"Blood sucking things don't scare me anymore. I missed you, too," I said.

We talked about TV and the pollen problem until I almost fucking exploded.

"Small talk is for small people, Jen. Get to it. What's going on? I saw Evan. He looked like shit, and so do you. Tell me what's up."

She gave me that smile again, making my skin itchy with irritation. When she buried her face in her hands, I forgot to be annoyed. Fucking hell, a beer would have been great.

"I can't ever be normal, or have a boyfriend, or anything just *regular*. I don't know how to be a regular girl, Charity. Not anymore."

She sobbed into her hands, crumbling into a little pile of mush on the couch. I held her, because I wasn't normal either.

She cried into my shoulder until it was weird. She sat back, still pretty even though she was ugly-crying, and I became Psychiatrist.

"I can never tell anyone this, but you I can," she said with a wet sniffle, her eyes wide with fear.

"Just say it. Nothing will scare me off."

Big, deep breath. "I have such a connection to Evan. But you know my problem; with the kidnappers, and how all my boyfriends look like him, if you even want to call them boyfriends." Her lip started trembling, so I held her hand. "Evan doesn't look like him. It's been a really long time since I liked anyone that didn't remind me of…you know."

"Yeah, I know. I don't get it at all, but I know that's what your problem is."

She brushed her hair out of her eyes. Her face was splotchy, her nose runny. "It's a bigger problem now. We already slept together, Evan and I."

"Yeah. Okay."

She leaned forward, jaw slack. "Aren't you going to say it was too soon?"

My eyes darted all around as if I could find an answer outside of myself. "What was too soon?"

Shaking her head, she leaned back and laughed. "You just do whatever you want, don't you?"

"What, like have sex? Well, yeah. Why not?"

"I can't believe you aren't judging me for sleeping with him that fast."

"Should I? I don't get it."

"Yes! You should be telling me that if I really liked him, I should wait until we know each other better."

I laughed, but it wasn't meant to be funny. "What if he doesn't like you once he gets to know you? What a waste of potentially very good sex."

Jen shook her head, laughing, unwashed hair falling in her face. I was glad to make her laugh, even if I meant everything I was saying.

She said, "That's not why I did it."

"Why did you do it?"

"I didn't want to lose him, but I'm not good enough for him. He's perfect, and I'm a complete mess."

"You're not a *complete* mess, and that's not what he sees in you anyway. He was totally into you right away, like, I don't know, love at first sight shit."

"I asked him to do something," she whispered, wringing her hands.

"If he has an aversion to oral, he needs to go."

"I asked him to tie me up."

"Okay. Not a big deal."

"And I asked him to hit me."

"Bigger deal. Beer? Got any?"

She got the courage to look at me, but ignored my question. "He was shocked, obviously, and then— Well, then I told him why I wanted him to do it. Why I wanted him—to abuse me."

"Is that what it was?" I sipped my coffee, like any good psychiatrist would do.

She averted her eyes, the shame taking over. Now that was a feeling I understood. "I told him that it reminded me of my abductor. I said if he didn't look like him, he needed to act like him." Her voice cracked, and her hands shook more. She was Denim Dress Sally from the first day we met and it saddened me.

I let out a low whistle. This was a level of screwed up I didn't envy. She totally won this round.

"Did he hurt you?"

She shook her head.

"But you wanted him to? Why?"

"Charity, how am I supposed to know why?"

I took a long sip of my coffee and was so fucking annoyed that it wasn't stronger. I didn't want to hurt her with the wrong questions but what the hell else did I know? I was too aware that I gave a crap about her.

"You talked to your shrink about it?"

She sighed, more comfortable with the mention of the psych. He was a crutch for her. I wished a little that Psychiatrist was a crutch for me, but I was professional at running from him and to him at the same time. To see how much I could hold back, like volunteering for water torture.

"He says that by reliving the abduction over and over one way or another, that I subconsciously hope to change it." She rattled it off like she'd said it a million times. She probably had. I pursed my lips against them quivering as I tried to think of what to say to her. Jen may have looked normal, but on the inside, she was a stagnant pool of acid, never getting any less toxic.

"Kinda sounds logical to me. I mean, I'm not the best person to ask about logic, but I know what it's like. To try to change things, when you can't. "

"I'm tired of never being normal." The venom in her voice shocked me. Fuck, I was wearing off on her. "This is always how it will be for me."

There was heat in her eyes, like she was sizing me up. I didn't know she had it in her. Good girl. "Why doesn't this kind of thing happen to you? I don't want it to, but you know what I mean. You don't need anyone, do you? It's like you know yourself completely."

"Me? Maybe I don't need anyone, but kinda sucky. And I don't know a goddamn thing about myself that I *want* to know, Jen, so save your friend envy for someone else." I chugged the rest of the coffee and got up to find more or stronger. Jen followed me.

"I'm sorry, I'm so sorry, I didn't want to upset you, that's the last thing I want to do."

No fucking beer in that fridge. I slammed the door shut, poured a cup of coffee and added cream before turning to answer her. I wanted to say nothing ever upset me, and I wanted to tell her that she was right about me. I had no right to be offended. I'd worked hard to be the most standoffish person there was, until I wanted something. Clearly, it gave the proper impression.

"Jen, we're both fucked up, and neither one of us knows what to expect of the other. It's more fun this way."

She laughed loud, making more tears appear in her eyes. I laughed with her. That moment was perfect. Standing there, with a friend who didn't judge me, a cup of coffee, hearing my life wasn't the worst one out there. I leaned back against the counter while she poured the rest of the pot, breathing in that second of comfort, a second where my life wasn't a mind fuck.

"All right, so what happened with Evan next? He looked seriously destroyed."

She nodded, like she already knew. "He didn't want to—hurt me. We went out for drinks, ended up going to dinner, then more drinks, and then I brought him back here."

Girls like us always brought the guy back to our apartments, never back to theirs. Safer. Our own turf.

"He was so sweet, telling me how he felt a connection with me right away, how we were both trapped inside ourselves. He's so right. I felt it, too. We kissed, like the first kiss I always wanted, wine-flavored, and gentle. And then it heated up."

"Nice."

"It was. Too nice." She shook like she had the chills.

And I got it. Being abused was fucking horrible, but it was the one thing she knew through and through. New and nice with a man was horrifying, worse than the abuse. It was uncharted, and the brain says it won't last, that every minute of happiness is soon to be a memory. Happiness shouldn't be found in *stolen* moments. I'd fucking steal them and not care, it didn't matter that they weren't meant for me. Having them taken away, the raw edges they left, that was what scared girls like us.

Better to exist with the raw edges by choice.

She told me the rest of the story, sitting at the kitchen table with an endless flow of coffee; how he wanted her so much that he was finally willing to do whatever she wanted, but not just yet. He needed time to absorb what was happening. But when he left, it seemed like she would never see him again.

"I can't call him now, Charity. I'm embarrassed. Embarrassed is an understatement; ashamed. I'm ashamed."

Jen didn't need to hear how it would all work out

okay, and how if he really liked her he'd be willing to look past her baggage.

"I'll talk to him for you. It will be easier that way."

She came around the table and sobbed into my shoulder until she was empty. Just the raw edges forming.

PLACES I DON'T BELONG

I stayed with Jen for a long time. We watched that Bill Murray movie, *What About Bob*, and ate popcorn like two girls at a sleepover. My belly got embarrassing butterflies every now and then over it and I'd have to look away to hide the heat in my cheeks. I'd never had a sleepover, actually, not one where you didn't kick someone out in the morning. You didn't invite girls over the house I lived in, unless you wanted them scarred for life.

"You haven't found a job yet, have you?" she asked me out of the blue.

"Nah. I haven't looked." I threw popcorn in my mouth. "God, why don't you have any beer?"

"I don't drink much. Sorry. How are you going to pay your rent?"

I gave her a sideways glance, hoping it would ward off further pushing of the subject, but it didn't work. I was totally unprepared for what came next.

"Charity, if you want to move in here, you can, even if it's just until you get back on your feet."

Popcorn fell out of my mouth into my lap. "Um, Jen, you've known me for like a matter of seconds. I'm not reliable. I'm a jerk for fun. I drink a lot. I've thrown up in the bathtub a bunch of times. I'm—"

She turned to face me. "You are the only person who wants to understand me. For that, I would do anything to help you."

I looked at the popcorn mess in my lap, registered my knee bouncing nervously and stopped it, thought and thought of a way not to make this life more dense and filled with people that wanted me in it.

"I'll think about it," I said.

"Do more than think about it. Move in here. My bedroom is huge. We can easily fit another bed in it, and your stuff."

"I don't have much stuff. But you don't want to share a room with me; I like unicorns. A lot."

She shook her head, laughing. "Now that I didn't see coming."

We didn't talk about it again until I was leaving. The world was getting to be a little too comfortable for me, and I needed to taste death.

At the door, Jen put her hand on my arm. *Great. Another heart to heart coming my way.* I met her eyes with reluctance.

"I meant it, about moving in here. Think about it."

"Yeah. Yeah, I will. And I mean it, about Evan. Text me his number. Let me handle it."

We hugged again. That anyone had hurt her and

made her so broken made me taste bile and hate. I was dying to sink my claws into some bastard before they could do it again.

"I have business to attend to, Jen. I'll talk to you later."

Confusion was written all over her face. She didn't know what she didn't know.

$\sim$

I got the number and called Evan on the way home.

"Hey, Evan, it's Charity."

"Oh. Oh, hi."

"You picked up. Weird."

"Life is full of weird surprises, I'm seeing. How did you—oh, Jen. Why isn't she calling me?"

"It's easier to let someone else do your dirty work once in a while, know what I mean?"

"So, I'm dirty work now?"

I could make dirty work of a man with that kind of brooding, been-up-too–many-hours voice real quick. I shook the notion off.

"Apparently."

An exhausted sigh came through the phone. I could picture him rubbing his face, trying to wake himself up and escape from me at the same time.

"Well, listen, Jen doesn't know what to say to you, but I do, so you wanna get some coffee tomorrow and talk?"

"Uh. Yeah, sure, Charity. I'll meet you at Dunkin Donuts at noon? I'll be on my lunch hour."

"I will be on my eternal lunch hour, so sure, see you then."

"I hope you can bring me back," I heard him mutter as I hung up.

~

J was getting used to Keegan greeting me with a song as I opened the door. Looking around my apartment that was not to be mine much longer, I knew I wouldn't miss it. I'd miss Robbie being a wall away. Besides that, it was the place I kept myself when I had nowhere else to be, so pretty much all the time. Until I started to become the Harpy.

That first night it happened wasn't really any different from any other night that I'd changed, but something in the air I guess made it a little worse. Something on TV sparked a hazy memory of Carl Painter; an image in the dark of a man doing something he shouldn't be. Then a commercial for that show, *Intervention*, right after. It was a woman with a heroin problem that looked so much like my mother I almost puked. It was a dual punch that brought on an itching all over my body in the worst way. The kind where you scratch and scratch until it bled just to make it better. It started with my feet, and when I scratched, I noticed that barbs were coming out of my insteps. Then my ankles and calves. My curiosity kept me scratching, until the barbs became scaly, like a chicken's, but definitely my own.

All the ugliness emerging, loud and proud.

It hurt like hell and I breathed a sigh of relief to see my body transforming before my eyes, the downy feathers appearing on my thighs next. I took off my corset and skirt, eager to see how far this new thing would go to get rid of the old thing. I looked at the body *he* had touched so many times, and it didn't belong to him; my body was mine. The half-creature I was turning into belonged to me. I could be free of that other me, finally.

That was when the wings sprouted, feather by long, luxurious feather out of the lengths of my arms. Never angel-white, only a dirty sea gull color. Not quite perfect, but perfectly me.

The word sounded in my mind and heart immediately; *Harpy.*

And I had welcomed it with every pained part of me.

This night, I cracked a beer, waiting for night to fall. I'd had enough of quietly forcing myself into people's lives for one day. I was ready to be the thing that did nothing quietly. The Harpy was calling me and I was ready to give in to her.

BREAKING AND BLEEDING

*T*here was no part of me that didn't welcome the change that night. No more thought, or relationships, or trying. Just what came natural to me; ruining a motherfucker who wants to ruin someone else.

It happened fast, too. I was a Harpy almost at once instead of in short stages, like it knew I couldn't wait anymore.

I was a disaster getting out of the apartment. It wasn't lost on me how goddamn hilarious it was that a giant bird monster was busting shit up trying to squeeze out of an apartment building on the sly, like some fat dude in a chicken costume. I laughed, and almost gave myself away to a neighbor who I could hear in their kitchen. The water in the apartment turned off, the dishes stopped clanking, and I just stood still, hoping nobody would look out the peephole. Nowhere to go without making more noise. The walls and doors were paper thin, so it was code to ignore your neighbors unless there was danger, or else you'd never stop looking out the peephole. In that case, the danger would be in paying attention to me.

I made a break for outside, fed up with waiting. I leaped off the landing as soon as I opened the building door, no running start needed. My mind had a running start already. The need was there, hunger of the body and soul that was excruciating, and I had to sate it quick. I wouldn't go far. I was all too happy to destroy close to home, chip away at the all too real world with its false new beginnings.

I shook off the negative thoughts as the cold wind hit my face and rustled my hair and wings. I was happy, and I wouldn't let anything piss me off until I was good and ready.

Quickly, the throbbing, heated sensation that meant I'd found my mark bristled me. I dove down, zeroed in on the spot where I sensed he was. The plain-face monster in plain sight.

As I got closer, I actually could hear a little girl crying. I gagged. I pressed on faster, harder, and crashed through the upstairs bedroom window, landing solidly on my clawed feet amidst the glass shards.

It was always the same with those guys. They stumbled away, dumbstruck with horror until they started cursing at me, then I'd attack them and they'd beg for their lives. The fucker in front of me was no different. An older guy, probably sixty or sixty-five. He was shirtless, in a pair of tailored pants, and reeked of SoCo.

I looked around the huge princess room for the crying girl and found her crouched in a corner behind a giant stuffed teddy bear. Just a pair of scared eyes and a crown of dark brown hair. Her fingers were curled around the bear's paw, and fuck me, they were tiny. She was just a little girl.

Breathing in deep, I tried to get my head on straight and not just rip the motherfucker to shreds because that little girl had seen enough terrible things up close. I folded my wings behind me, making myself smaller for her sake. I was terrifying enough to him, not that it mattered. I didn't have to look scary to be scary.

"You have a nice house here, don't you?" I said not to either of them directly. "Kind of surprises me how ugly things can live in such a lovely home. I guess everything gets dirty sometimes."

"You get out of here, right now. I am an attorney! You can't—"

"Then you'll be familiar with justice when you see it." The chill in my voice got my point across faster than my crash through the window did. He buckled and fell to the floor, eyes wide, mouth jabbering. Because he knew.

I ventured a look to the child. Her eyes were calmer peering at me, her fingers looser on the bear's paw, playing with the tattered fur there. Slowly, I went to her, and bent down on the other side of the teddy bear. She didn't scramble away or try to crouch further down. She already knew there was no real hiding in that room. My heart screamed for her.

"Hi," I said. I put out my hand to touch the bear, too,

and realized that of course I had claws instead. I said sorry to her as I pulled away.

"It's okay," she said in the tiniest voice ever. The pieces of my broken heart stabbed worse than the broken glass under my feet. I smiled through the pain at her.

She began to stand, chin held higher with ever inch she came off the floor. She was little, maybe six, but she had an air of self-preservation that I recognized. She assessed everything, observed details but was still just a baby and didn't know how to make the knowledge work for her yet.

"What's your name?" I asked her. I wanted to see if she knew it was my attempt to calm her down in a situation that there could be no peace to.

"Lily," she said, eyes roaming, stopping on him, huddled in the corner, the way she had been. Afraid, like she had been. When her eyes came back to me, we smiled at each other.

"Lily, do you want this man to go away?"

She nodded without a thought.

"Can you make him go away for good and never come back here?" she asked.

We both watched as a puddle formed underneath him. "I can do that, Lily. I would like to do that very much."

Lily came out from behind the bear with tiny steps. She wasn't afraid of the broken glass. She wasn't afraid to burn the delicate flowery nightgown she wore to the ground with her anger. I wanted to burn all the things that should have been soft and gentle for her and weren't.

She squatted next to me in front of the bear, and looked in my eyes, brushing my feathered head with her fingers. "You're beautiful," she said to me.

"Thank you," I said. I wished she couldn't find something so horrible beautiful, and I knew she would always see beauty in ugly things because of me.

"When it's over, can I climb on your back and fly away with you?"

"Oh, Lily." I choked on her name. Carefully, I put my arm around her, my wing holding her close, my claws protecting her. "I'm not that kind of creature. I don't stay beautiful. I'm only beautiful to some people. And you don't want to be where I'm going."

Another little girl might have cried and not tried to understand. "I'm not always beautiful either," she said. I couldn't hold my tears back. Her pink fingers wiped my tears away. "Don't cry. Now I can be."

A muscle of hate flexed inside me that wasn't there before, hard and cruel. I heard the bastard in the piss puddle try to open the door quietly from where he sat. I glared at him and hissed a long, low terrible noise and he stopped moving.

Lily backed away from me. "Thank you," she said quietly. She kissed me once on the forehead as she walked away with long, proud strides, past him with a blank look, and opened the door he'd wanted to escape through. It clicked shut behind her.

I flexed my claws and became beautiful.

AND SO IT BEGINS

I went to sleep with shards of glass stuck in my feet, blood smeared on my teeth, and a song in my heart. Everything and nothing hurt. That was the most satisfying kill to date, probably the most satisfying thing that had ever happened to me in my life, sex included. Sorry, Robbie, but eating the heart out of that asshole who never deserved to have one didn't come with any mixed emotions.

Sun hit my face, and I smiled as I blinked the crust of blood away. If my nights were always that good, I could face the days after. Lily would wake up with a new life because of me. I recreated her with the special madness I brought to the table; a feast of her attacker's viscera. Fuck, it had been delicious beyond comparison.

Quarter after ten. "Keegan, quiet," I mumbled. I rolled over, not giving a shit that the shades were up and I was naked, covered in dried blood. I walked like the queen of fucking England out to the living room.

"Keegan, baby, keep your melodious singing to a minimum. I'm hungover on the blood of sinners."

Pouring his dish of fruity food and getting him fresh water was so weirdly normal that I had to laugh. Apparently kind of loud, as it turned out, because I got the familiar knock from the other side of the kitchen wall. So unlike the banging on the floor that meant "shut the fuck up" from upstairs. I bit my lip trying not to think of Robbie just rolling out of bed, and knocked back. Maybe I should put some clothes on and get him over here. Or maybe I should just get him over here.

Shit, I was meeting Evan in like an hour and a half, and there was Robbie, knocking at the door. Shit. Double shit. I swung the door open, naked, bowl of bird water in one hand.

"Hey, Rob, what's up?"

"Ummm…."

"You should probably come in, huh?"

I pulled him in by the arm and shut the door without a drop spilled. "I gotta give Keegan water, or you know, dehydration and death."

"Uh. Charity, you're very naked."

I put the water dish in the cage and turned around, smiling. "And you're not. One of us should fix this problem." I licked my lips. Metallic salt. I was a goddess.

He quirked an eyebrow and gave me that sideways grin with the fingers through the hair. "Baby, you're also covered in blood." Quick eye shuffle to the rolled-up shades.

I ran my tongue along the dry blood on my arm like

a murderous cat, and walked to him with as much slinkiness. "It's not mine, but it's part of me, baby." I pressed my tits against him, sucking the more stubborn flecks of blood off my fingertips.

Robbie averted his eyes and did his best not to touch me. I was snarling, I couldn't help it. I tried to kiss him, but he turned away.

"What is it, *baby?*" I spat. "You don't want to fuck me now? Like this, when I'm more me than—"

"Shut the hell up, Charity," he said quietly, toeing the ground. To me it was as loud as thunder.

"I can't believe you told me to shut up."

"I had to! Stop it with all of this 'you don't know who I really am' shit, Charity. You're what you choose to be, not what's been done to you, or even what you've done. Own that, instead of this," he said, motioning to me. Me, naked, bloody and dirty, and more than a little insane with happiness about it.

"Like this, huh?" I backed away. "If you don't want me like this, then you don't want me at all."

"Is this your way of pushing me away? It's just another way for you to hide, Charity! How do you not see it?"

And with that, he left me. He left me exposed.

unkin' Donuts and Evan Hale seemed to come together as a package.

Evan had cleaned himself up to meet me. He stood just in the door frame, smooth-cheeked, straight tie.

His hair had gel in it. His clothes were clean. He looked put together, like he did when we met.

He couldn't hide the lie in his eyes, though.

It wasn't the redness, or the puffiness. It was the dying heat in them. Passionate fire put out before its time. It was scorching his heart.

"What can I get you?" he asked me, without saying hello.

"The huge one. Hot. Black, no sugar. Thanks."

I sat in the booth and watched him order. He slouched. Coffees in hand, watching the floor where he walked, his entire being drooped.

"You look a bit like shit still."

"And you look stunning," he said as he sat down. He wasn't meeting my eyes, but he meant the words. I could hear it from a black hole deep in him; it troubled him.

"Evan."

His head snapped up, like I'd just sat down. "How's your coffee?"

"What, you're the waiter here? Awesome. I don't tip my friends."

He looked away, smiling a little. My mood lightened up.

"So, let's talk," I said, putting my elbows on the table. "Tell me what the hell turned you into a walking autopsy like this."

"I know Jen must have told you."

"Some. But finding out that a girl who spends a lot of time with a shrink has some weird sexual interests is just not enough to send you over the edge like this."

"You think I've gone over the edge?"

I raised my eyebrows. "You don't?"

His eyes dragged to mine, bleary, with a scattered mind behind them. "I think the pool goes a lot deeper than I knew, and I should back away from the edge quickly."

"Evan," I said, my voice in that tone I used with Lily, unrecognizably gentle. "Jen's pool might not have a bottom."

"It wasn't her edge I was talking about."

A shadow fell over him, but it was just him. Just him.

"Do you want to go somewhere else?" I whispered. The pink and orange gaudiness of Dunkin' Donuts regalia in full daylight, littered with passing regulars was the wrong backdrop.

He shook his head, frowning. He glanced around, eyes lingering on a woman in line. I didn't understand where his mind was headed as I watched him watching her, forgetting everything else. His lips quivered with the slightest smile.

"Evan," I hissed. A slow smile spread across his face.

"Sorry," he said. "It's been a while since I've been with a woman. Suddenly, they all came to life for me again." He sipped his coffee, his eyes glued to mine, playfully glinting in their darkness. There was something under the surface there. His eyes reminded me of the cold spot in the pond where all the muck was.

He had a new sex appeal like nothing I'd ever seen before.

"It's all right," I said, snapping myself out of my haze

with him in the middle. "I probably check everyone out, too, and don't even know it."

"You know it," he said with a grin, making us both laugh.

"I'm glad you can still laugh. I was beginning to think you were ready to slit your wrists or something. You know, Jen's all torn up, too."

"Is she?"

"Yeah. Yeah, she really is."

"Well, she's the one who did this to *me*," he growled at me, leaning across the table, instant fury in his eyes.

I refused to be intimidated, no matter how unawares he caught me with the weird anger. "What did she do to you besides ask you to do something different? She isn't perfect, you know. She wants to try to be better with you. You can't just write her off."

"I don't want to write her off! She's a wonderful woman! I've been looking for a woman like her my entire life. But I wasn't looking for—" He cut himself off, squeezing the coffee cup.

"What is it?"

"Nothing. I want to get back to the office now, if that's all right with you. I need to clear my head, focus on something else." He lingered on me for a long moment, keeping his face still, trying not to betray what his thoughts were. He was really difficult to figure out, but he didn't fool me. Suffering takes a lot of forms, and my eyes were wide open to all of them.

"Why don't we meet after you get off work?" I said. *Way to literally ask for trouble, you asshole.* "You can get me something to eat."

His lip quirked just a little. Success. "Oh, I can?"

"Yeah. I can't be out too late, though." Bird to feed, bird to turn into and all.

"I promise I won't let you turn into a pumpkin." He leaned forward and trained his eyes on mine with an intensity that left me brewing inside, naked and wanting.

"You're on."

MIDDLE GROUND

*E*van left in a hurry, and once again, I was faced with the rest of an empty day that threatened to fill up with feelings. I finished that cup of coffee and got another one, not giving a shit that it was more expensive than making a pot at home. Home was where Robbie was, and wouldn't be my home for much longer.

I sat looking out the window at the street. What a fucked up day. Robbie, Jen, Evan. The having friends shit was time consuming, and there were too many ways to do it wrong. Robbie and I were totally not in a good spot, and I found out basically nothing new for Jen. Not to mention it was entirely possible that I actually had a date with Evan, thinking back on it. What a fucking jerk I was.

Well, the Harpies liked me well enough.

"Oh, man." Simultaneously, two terrible things happened. Jen texted me and Robbie was walking down the street toward Dunkin Donuts. For fuck's sake, could I ever just drink a cup of coffee alone?

I tried to huddle over my phone to avoid Robbie as he got closer, but he was gunning right for me. His eyes burned a hole in my head as he got closer. When the door swung open, I looked up from the fake text.

He walked in, that way he does, with this trashy elegance about him that just made want to scream and pull his hair and kiss him as hard as I could. He didn't order a coffee. He came straight to me, never moving his eyes from mine.

"Can I sit down?"

"Do what you want."

"Do you want me to sit down?"

I wanted to slam my head on the table. "Rob, just sit down. For fuck's sake."

He was nervous! I couldn't believe I was making him nervous. Totally a personal achievement. He tapped his fingers, total deer in headlights.

"Charity, I am so sorry about this morning."

To hide my shock, I chugged the way too hot coffee, and dug my fingernails into my thigh to hide the pain. "It's cool."

"No, it's not." He took my hand across the table, not like he was trying to just touch me, but like he was trying to hold onto me. "I'm a hypocrite for saying you aren't terrible for doing what you do, then implying you shouldn't enjoy it. I'm sorry. I was wrong."

He hung his head. Defeat didn't become him. I squeezed his hand, running my other hand over the hair on his bowed head.

"Robbie, I was wrong," I blurted. "Holy hell, coming to you, covered in blood, acting all crazy. I don't know what I was thinking."

"I came to *you*, and you could be covered in, in, I don't know, goat hair, and I'd still want you."

"No, that would be gross."

We laughed and all was forgiven.

Fuck. I suddenly forgave people? What sorcery was this?

"Let's get out of here, Rob. I can't deal with fucking pink and orange anymore."

We walked down to the waterfront. This time of year you could barely see the water over the sea of fucking tourists, but on foot it wasn't so bad. They reeled from me like I was the sluttiest Grim Reaper ever, and they were right. The throng of Hawaiian shirts took over all the public benches and ice cream shops, and everything that had a Mayflower drawing on it.

"These fat tourists are making me hungry," I said, imagining the salt that flowed in their veins.

I didn't expect him to put his arm around me with that statement, like some boyfriend, but he did. I leaned into him, putting my head on his shoulder so that my ear banged into the bone with every step.

"Let me get you some fish and chips."

"YES. Yes, I will let you do this."

Every fish market and restaurant in Plymouth was swamped every minute of every day every summer. It was a fact of life that you had to wait in line if you wanted fresh fish that you could watch them pull off the boat. We stood in line on the stairs outside of Wood's Seafood, the smell of the salt air freshening me, making me more human than I'd been in weeks.

"You're so happy," Rob said.

"Who, me? Yeah, I guess. I mean, I'm going to eat a ton of fish and fries with so much tartar sauce that they could plug up boat holes with my blood when I die." I glanced at him. "And, I'm glad we're good."

He looked at me for a second from the step below me. His eyes melted into me, so capable of filling with emotion in seconds. He stepped up, put his hands in my hair and pulled me to him, kissing me hard, teeth clashing, to the disgruntlement of several nearby tourists. It sent fire through my entire body.

"I love you, Charity," he said, our foreheads resting against each other. "We don't have to be perfect. We're us."

I covered his hands with mine and thanked him with a kiss.

When we finally got our fish platters on their greasy cardboard plates, we took them outside and sat on the wall by the boat dock, feet hanging over as we ate, and watched the fisherman sweating their asses off.

"Goddamn, I love fish and chips."

"Mmmm," he groaned, shoving more fries in his mouth. Chewing, he waved at the ocean with a fry, and with mouth full said, "You'd miss all this if you went with them."

"Yeah, sure."

"You'd miss me," he said, smirking.

I snorted. "Yeah. But I'd just kill a bunch of guys who look like you, then I'd get over it."

He didn't laugh, instead giving me that super serious look again, like he was about to kiss me. But he said something I wasn't expecting.

"Charity, I think you should move in with me."

Holy shit, another offer of residence? This one, though. This one.

"Um, you really think that's a good idea, Rob? I mean, look at the stuff I do."

"You can't talk me out of this. I don't want a wall between us anymore."

I ate fast and watched the guys hauling in the old lobster traps. They were falling apart, but still inescapable.

"I want to go to where the Harpies live, and I don't want to have anything to fall back on here." I said it with clenched jaw and zero fuckery.

Rob put the cardboard container down next to him. A foghorn sounded in the distance. "Tell me about that place. Please? Tell me so if you leave me, I know where you've gone."

My stomach flipped, but I stuck a fry in my mouth. I had to be able to do it with conviction, if I meant it. If it wasn't just some vacation fantasy, I needed to own it.

"Ever read Dante? Yeah, me either but I know a little. Apparently, he wrote about this circle of Hell called the Wood of Suicides. And if you read that, you'll know where I live."

"What? I actually have read Dante, and what? That's not a real place."

"Rob, I'm a fucking bird monster, and you think those things just live under the bridge or something?"

"Jesus Christ." He put his head in his hands, finally exasperated with me. I had to remind myself that I wanted to nail this relationship coffin shut. Robbie was hard to scare off.

I didn't like to think that maybe I wasn't putting my all into it. No level of Hell was more frightening than the prospect of love.

"Yeah, it's this really horrible place where people are stuck in the trees, and the Harpies just kinda live off of them, 'cause they never die. They have to suffer eternally and everything. So, you know, built-in suffering for all."

"I won't let you go to a place like that."

"Already been there."

"You don't have to go back."

"I want to."

"Charity, this broken record of yours is getting old."

"So, stop playing it, Robbie! Let go of me!" People were looking, but fuck them. I was standing, but I wasn't walking away, and goddamn it if that didn't make me want to explode into feathers and talons right the fuck there, and rip apart anyone who had an ounce of sin on their souls.

"You're shaking. Calm down."

"Don't tell me to fucking calm down."

"Charity, how terrible do I have to be to get you to stay with me? Will you only stay if I agree that you're as awful as you think you are? You want me to slum it, too?"

"You'd aspire to be a fucking killer like me? You can't get there on the morality scale, Robbie! Don't try!" Everyone was staring.

"WHAT THE FUCK ARE YOU LOOKING AT?" I screamed at the crowd. "Let me answer that for you! You have no fucking idea! Go look at the useless fucking Plymouth Rock! That's a fucking lie, you know, assholes!"

People scattered in every direction, but Robbie was still there. Fuck, he'd never go away. I started to walk away, but he followed me. My anger was howling in me, ready to let out and I still had a fucking date with Evan that needed cancelling, no matter who it affected.

Robbie yelled at me, really yelled at me then, and his words were too much for me to bear.

"What I'm trying to say to you, you stubborn bitch, is that I would sink as low as I have to in order to make and keep you mine! As low as I fucking have to!"

I spun on him, in the middle of the street, cars screeching to a halt. I wished they'd just pile up all around me, trap me and burst into flames.

"What?" I said, more softly and with more hurt than I wanted to show. "I don't want you to sink at all. Never."

He pulled me by the arm across the street.

"Charity, we don't deal in absolutes, we're just people. Neither one of us is good all the time. I love you for who I know you are."

I kept walking, and so did he. We walked in silence all the way home, or to what was the place I currently lived. The only real home I had, the only one where I wouldn't ruin everything, was with them; with the Harpies. There was a reason they wanted me.

We went to his apartment, past mine with the bird chirping inside. I had no right to infringe on its happy little life, and would just as soon ignore it at the moment. Robbie seemed to know. Of course, didn't he always know fucking everything?

I collapsed on his couch, and looked around at all of the things that made him *him*. Simple, everyday things, stuff you buy at stores and stuff you keep from childhood. My stuff was all stuff I used to cling to a world that didn't want me, and other things that symbolized a peaceful world I'd never find. The Wood was the closest I'd come to peace, and I had to take it. It was the only chance to not be the pile of rubble I was.

Robbie sat down gently next to me, handing me a beer. I took it fast and drank it hard.

"Live here," he said, looking at the TV, sipping the beer.

"I'll think about it."

THE DEATH-TRODDEN GRASS

"*I* gotta go, Rob. I told Evan I'd meet him to talk about Jen and this fucked-up relationship they have."

"You're having like, a date?"

I gave him that incredibly demeaning, 'man, you're an idiot' look, and said slowly, "No. It's a meeting," and repeated, "about Jen, and this fucked-up relationship they have."

He followed me to the door, leaning one arm over it, his bicep flexing. "Okay, well, you said you'd think about moving in, right?" His voice was low, crooning, sexier than anything I could imagine. To wake up to that every day—why would I say no?

Because you're a murder machine that can't do anything right.

"Yeah, baby, I'll think about it," I said, biting my lip, wishing I could throw him to the ugly carpet and do terrible things to him.

He bent down to kiss me slowly, teasing me with his warm tongue and all that I knew it could do. I groaned when he pulled away.

"I love you," he said.

I kissed him, and left.

~

*E*van looked like he'd barely survived the day. His five o'clock shadow was more like midnight shadow. His eyes had rings around them, lack of sleep finally having caught up. He'd taken his tie off, and unbuttoned his shirt at the neck, revealing a tuft of chest hair.

I got into his shiny black BMW with as much finesse as I could in skin tight jeans and a corset. "You look like you've been talking to the devil, Mr. Hale," I said, skimming his slightly maddened face.

"He was talking to me first."

With no more words, he took off fast. It sorta felt like I was in the car with a serial killer. He seemed completely lost in his own mind as he drove, and none too happy about it. If I'd had any sense of self-preservation, I probably wouldn't have thought it was so cool.

He didn't ask me where I wanted to go, and that wasn't okay with me, but whatever. We ended up at East Bay Grille, ironically right across the street from where I'd gotten fish with Robbie hours before.

Evan opened the car door for me, but he didn't pay the meter. We got looked at like a well-to-do gentleman and his hooker should be looked at by the hostess. I sneered at her and grabbed Evan's arm. She didn't look away from my eyes. Her nerve pissed me off a little.

"Your waitress is Stephanie. She'll be right over," she said, and glared at me on her way back to the stupid podium.

"Take it easy, killer, she's just a hostess." I was surprised that Evan spoke or noticed what happened.

"My thoughts exactly. But she better step off, regardless." She was still meeting my eyes from halfway across the restaurant, and I was getting heated.

Evan tapped his fingers on the table, impatience and volatility roaring out of his solemn face. He was watching me, and I wasn't afraid to watch him back, the far more fascinating of the two characters here that could get a rise out of me.

"So, what's up? What has you so….different?"

"I'm not different."

"You are. You aren't yourself."

"What a presumptuous thing to say. You hardly know me."

"And yet, you see me fit to tell your problems to, and take me out to dinner."

"What if *you* are one of my problems?" he said with a sly grin that had no air of joking around its corners. His eyes were dangerous; I couldn't tell what he was thinking, but it was dark.

"What do I have to do with anything? I'm just the messenger. Is this some 'grass is always greener on the other side' deal, because trust me, Jen's grass is far healthier."

"Don't play dumb."

"Not playing."

The waitress came over, a bubbly blonde thing who'd seen too many seafood dinners herself. She didn't have the attitude the hostess with the mostest had.

"I'm Stephanie, your server tonight. What can I get you to drink?"

I opened my mouth, but Evan piped right up that we were ready to order. Clearly, he wasn't looking to prolong this evening, despite having agreed to it so quickly. I was intrigued as hell as to what was going on in his mind, and I'd be lying if I said I wasn't wondering what he was thinking about me.

"I'll have a Sam Adams and steak. A big steak. Rare. So rare it makes you question the rules of cooking."

Evan wrinkled his eyebrows at me like I wasn't supposed to speak or something. He never took his wolfish eyes off me while he ordered a glass of white wine and super expensive swordfish.

Stephanie shuffled her feet back and forth. So, he was weirding her out, too. She couldn't get away from our table fast enough. I watched her go, change direction to the hostess station, and they both glared over at us. I smiled at them, not nicely. We were making all sorts of friends tonight.

"You didn't get seafood," Evan said.

"I need my meat, what can I say? You said that I'm the problem. What's that supposed to mean?"

A shyness came over him, a hint of the man before, but panged with a new unhappiness. "I shouldn't have said that. This isn't about you." He leaned forward, elbows on the table. He was Jekyll and Hyde in a disturbing way, and I was completely at home with it.

He chuckled; a throaty, darkly sensual sound, but with a purity that spoke to me.

"See?" he said. "That look right there, *that's* what I'm talking about. There's something in you that *sees me*," he said more quietly, patting his chest for emphasis.

Not okay. We could not have a connection. That was not what my reason for being there.

"Enough bullshit Evan, spill it. None of this hot-guy-in-a-suit-with-an-edge shit, and your suave talk. Jen really likes you and deserves you, and you look like you've gone belly-up with crazy all of a sudden."

He hardened again, anger smudging his face like black chalk, then wiped off again when he broke up into laughter, but not the scary kind. His kind, I realized. The kind that was so comfortable, you had to laugh with him.

"Shit, I really do look nuts, don't I?" he said, still half-laughing. "I'm sorry, Charity, I just don't know how to deal with this, with her, and with you. How to deal with me."

Sorrow overcame me; I cleared my throat as if I could hack it up. Evan Hale worked hard to keep it all together, and when someone real affected him, he fell apart in bloody bits.

"I can understand a thing or two about not dealing with life." I searched around for the waitress, getting antsy. "If Chubby doesn't get here with my drink soon, I'm going to get it myself."

Evan started, "I thought going to a psychiatrist—"

"Uh, just Psychiatrist. They have names, you know."

"Well, I thought seeing a psychiatrist was supposed to help me deal with my compulsions, and women, and help me find a woman who just wanted me for me."

"What? How do you have a hard time finding a woman?"

"This," he motioned to himself, the suit, the hair, "is just the outside. The inside burns."

"Like a fucking volcano. Where is my beer? Tina!"

"Stephanie."

"Stephanie!"

Every head turned to look at me, just like I wanted. I widened my eyes and made a tipping back beer motion to our lazy ass waitress hanging at the hostess stand.

Evan laughed loud. "Hell, you are trouble!"

"On a good day. Right now, I just want my beer."

The waitress came quick with it, and Evan's glass of wine. He leaned back with a casual smile for her, and sipped. She shuffled her feet, uneasy. Good.

With a beer in my hand I could speak with more and less clarity. I pointed at his chest. "Evan, what's woken up in there?" Something, someone, had gotten to him outside of himself. Not Jen…something foreign that slipped in and out like a knife, jabbing him with ugliness then giving him relief.

"How can you see it?" he asked me, shaking his

head. I was usually more naked when men looked amazed by me.

I chugged my beer. "I can see dirt better like Predator sees heat. That burning, you call it? It can't make you clean. So talk to me."

The food came. I dug in fast. It was the most I'd eaten in one day for a long time. I wasn't dieting or worried about my heroin-chic figure or anything, but the Harpy changed everything.

"You can eat, woman."

He said "woman" in the same joking way Robbie said it. I stopped chewing. I was getting in deeper with this guy, and it only added to my confusion. This was not a date at all. It was about Jen and Evan, not me and Robbie, and sure as hell not about me and Evan.

I sucked back the end of the beer and looked for Stephanie, but caught the eye of the fucking hostess again, still staring. Some girls just didn't know when to stop. I said loudly, "Could you order me up another beer, Girly? It helps me not want to crush the bones of my enemies under underfoot." She rolled her eyes and walked away from the podium.

Again, he wasn't doing much of anything except watching me. "Eat your food, Evan."

"Right." He didn't eat with a lot of gusto. He was a wreck, and I was only touching the tip of the iceberg. What was he hiding?

Chubby Stephanie came to our table with the manager. I knew he was the manager because of his crappy suit and stern look, and his nametag that said "Manager."

"Sir, I'm sorry, but your *girlfriend* has upset the staff, and I believe I will need to ask you to leave."

Evan smirked at me, amused. "My girlfriend was given the evil eye as soon as she walked in the door by your hostess. And our waitress didn't help matters."

The hostess whispered something into the shoulder of The Manager, and *that* pissed me off.

"If you have something to fucking say, just say it, you minimum wage fucking debutante."

She looked at me with horror. My heart grew three sizes that day. "I just don't think you're the right clientele to have here."

Evan made an angry little noise, making me turn his way. He was positively boiling, turning red, and his anger fed my own. I stood up and got right in her fucking face, her bad breath all over me.

"Maybe I'm the right *clientele* to meet you at your shitty car after you get off work. Or maybe I'm the right clientele to remind your boyfriend what it's like to have a girl with a fucking personality."

"Okay, get the hell out," Manager piped up. Now *he* was in my face, and he was bloaty and wanted to put his hands on me. I could smell the fucking need on him to hurt me.

I couldn't stop the grin from spreading across my face, rotten little Alice falling down the rabbit hole.

"What is it, big man? Want me for yourself?"

He turned as red as Evan had, and he was shaking. I laughed loud and hard.

I'd be back for him.

Evan stood up and took me gently by the arm. "Let's go somewhere better."

The hostess had long since run off, her first smart move. I put a finger on the top button of Manager's shirt. "Bye, baby. I'll be seeing you," I said with a snarl.

And I left with Evan Hale with more of an audience than when we walked in.

"*F*UCK YOU, TOO!" I yelled, walking backwards away from stupid East Bay Grille. All the bays were east, we were on the east goddamn coast. Assholes.

Evan was laughing heartily, like a high school kid that just TP'ed the gym teacher's house.

"Man, I'm glad you aren't pissed, because you barely even ate," I said.

"I don't even like swordfish," he said, smiling wide, and ducked his head into the car.

"We got out without paying, too, so a little like a chew and screw, right?"

"I've never chewed and screwed." Shocker.

"Well, today you did. Minimal chewing. All the screwing."

"Would you mind going back to my house?" he asked, starting the car. "I don't want to be in public anymore." Like I said, girls like me always go back to their own places. "I have leftover Chinese food." That won me over, though.

"That sounds fucking great, actually."

"You swear a lot."

"Yes. Yes I do."

Evan lived in this woodsy part of Plymouth on the Kingston line that wasn't far from my apartment, but obviously it was another world. It was called Indian Pond Estates. The houses were enormous, and they all had these copper accents on them, and there was a fountain in somebody's yard. These people sucked.

"The people who live here suck. You don't suck. Why do you live here?"

"I suck a little bit," he said with a laugh.

"We all suck a little bit."

He pulled into a circular driveway in front of a stone monstrosity that looked like it had been built in a medieval village by poor people, but was annoyingly new in reality. It had the copper awning like the other places. No fountain. Bushes pruned by some Mexican guy, for sure.

"You live here?"

"Me, myself and I."

Evan's house could best be described as *rich.* It was enormous, and filled with burnt oranges and chocolate browns; warm, exotic and lush. It felt a little like one of those safari hunters might have lived there, like I wouldn't have been surprised if the next room had a wall covered in the heads of African animals and shelves stacked with leather bound books. Comforting, but with a touch of darkness and danger. Like the man himself.

"Can I sit down in here? I wanna take off my shoes. Can I take off my shoes?" I had every intention of taking off my shoes. Beautiful mosaic tiles covered the floor. I was like something the world coughed up on it.

Evan walked ahead of me, kicking his shoes off under a giant table with a huge plant on it, ripped off his tie, and dropped his jacket on an obviously priceless chair, mahogany with sunset orange silk padding. I wouldn't even touch it, and he used it like a laundry hamper.

"Someone comes to keep me in order," he said with a smile.

"Better job than I have," I mumbled, kicking my shoes off. I placed them nicely under the table next to his.

He went straight to the fridge and pulled out half a dozen Chinese takeout boxes, opening the tops of them all, while chewing on a cold spare rib. I found myself watching him, thinking how cute it was that he was eating like a college kid in a mansion. A box of donuts was laid open on an otherwise spotless counter.

"You want it hot or cold?" he asked me, lifting up a container.

"Cold. Always." I went to him, took half the containers off the counter. The rooms were very open, so it wasn't hard to see that just down a couple of steps was a living room with a huge TV, and a brown leather sofa. I fell onto the couch, my feet landing on the coffee table, and pulled out a Peking ravioli.

Evan sat next to me, holding the other containers, tapping his foot like he was worried about getting in trouble.

"I haven't had a woman here in a while," he said, face reddening.

"Really? A guy like you, I'd think you'd be banging chicks left and right."

"Uh, no. I work a lot, and well, I just don't."

"So, like how many women have you had?"

"What? Oh, I think maybe ten or twelve?"

"EVER?"

"Yeah, ever." He took a ravioli out of my hand and ate it, wiggling his eyebrows.

"How did that happen? I mean, Christ."

"I was shy. Scared."

"Scared?" I laughed, but he didn't. "Of what? Sex is nothing, sex is worth it for that minute when you explode. Nothing to be afraid of."

He shook his head at me, eating lo mein with metal chopsticks. "Didn't sex ever intimidate you?"

Flash of Carl Painter. I almost choked on a chicken wing.

"Are you okay? You need water?" He jumped up, but I shook my head.

"No, no, I'm okay." I shook it off. "No. The answer is no, sex doesn't intimidate me."

"But did it ever? You couldn't always have been so forthcoming."

"How do you know? Maybe I have been." But I couldn't meet his eyes. His gorgeous, piercing blue eyes.

He was looking at me, but not with the kind of unnerving look he gave me earlier. I think having me in his house settled him, made him less dangerous somehow. Maybe there was only so much danger to go around. And I had a bunch of Harpies to share my special brand of danger with.

"What's that painting up there?" I asked, pointing with a chicken wing over the white fireplace. Enormous, but only a picture of a bird; orange and black, but still ordinary, and like no bird I'd ever seen.

"Oh, you like that? It's an amazing bird called a Hooded pitohuis. They're native to New Guinea." He was excited to tell me about it, clearly. "Small, beautiful birds. They feed on beetles that contain the same poison as poison dart frogs. You've heard of them?"

I nodded, and held my breath.

Evan continued, and I began to see more of him as he spoke. "Because of what they live on, their very skin and feathers are poisonous to the touch, an incredible defense mechanism that you would never expect. They even rub the toxins onto their eggs to protect them. Fascinating."

"Yes," I said quietly, oddly uncomfortable. I shook it off. "Now you have to tell me: why did Jen scare you so much with that stuff. With wanting you to hurt her." *And maybe then I can figure out what* else *has happened to send him off the deep end.*

He put down the container he was holding, and rubbed his hair, the way Robbie did all the time. Robbie looked boyish, and sweetly sexy when he did it.

Evan became something wild, waiting to burst out of its cage when he looked back at me; wide eyes and ravaged hair on a man that should be poised and relaxed. He changed so quickly, I had to wonder which one of us was quicker at it.

"I don't think…I don't think you're ready to hear it, Charity," he said, like a man with something to run from.

"You can't scare me. Fucking look at me. Do I look like someone who runs?"

"You look like someone who runs too much."

"I know when to give up. When to stop running," I said. I was tired of the riddles and backspeak. "Tell me what *you're* running from, Evan."

"I'm still afraid." He became so small, then. It was like looking at Lily. Or like looking at myself, the way Carl Painter must have seen me. I reached out and squeezed Evan's hand so hard it hurt my own. He blinked at our hands together, and covered them with his other.

"Evan, don't be afraid of me. I won't do anything to hurt you, no matter what you tell me." My heart broke in places I didn't know I still had.

"I'm not who you think I am, Charity. I'm not a good man."

"Nobody's always good, Evan." I inched closer to him on the couch, as his hands began to shake in mine. "None of us think pure thoughts. And I'm worse than most, so I can pick out the good guys. *You* are a good guy."

His eyes didn't say 'good guy,' but I believed in him. I hated believing in people. People fucked with you, made you less of yourself and more like them. People disappointed, and hurt, and left, and hurt more, and sucked the soul out of you when you'd barely grown one. My hands shook in Evan's then. He noticed.

"How do you do it, Charity? What makes you like this?"

"Like what?" I said through clenched teeth. I knew if I let it, the Harpy would burst forth. The mere thought of the bastard who killed the child in me, and I was the one who was less human.

"You give in to it. There's something that calls you out of yourself, and you give in to it."

"Want to meet her?" I spat.

He shook his head slowly, fear taking over his eyes. "I don't think I do."

I pulled my hands away, letting go in ways I shouldn't. A total absence of rules or even hazy guidelines existed with him.

"Evan, I should go. There's so much you're hiding and I'm not cool with it. Can you—"

He took my hands back. "No, please don't. I—" He laughed nervously, the danger gone. "I feel safe when you're here."

"Just because there's something worse than you when I'm here. That's all."

His hands rubbed mine, making my heart pound. Shit, that was not okay.

"Charity, I want to give in to it, and I can't, I just can't," he pleaded. His voice cracked, and he hung his head, working my hands over and over. It was like watching myself, if I had a choice. If ever there had been a fucking choice for me.

I leaned my head on his, smelled his fear and need. "Tell me what's calling you," I said, my voice quiet. I wanted him calm, I wanted him to give in, I wanted him to be both better and worse than me.

He picked his head up, and for all the times he'd looked at me that night, in all the different ways, that was the first time his eyes lingered, looked harder. I ached to turn into a monster and get as far from his heart as I could.

"Charity, it isn't that Jen wanted me to hurt her. That's not what chilled me, tore me apart like this. It's that once I did what she asked, I wanted to hurt *everyone*."

I didn't want to, but I ran my hand through his mess of perfect hair, and watched his eyes get more tired when he gave a voice to his pain. I let him kiss me, softly, with the pain of creating pain behind it. We kissed like there was nobody else in the world, and goddamn if I didn't wish the world would burn away, leave us both in the chaos we'd found in each other.

He kissed me harder and longer, his hands moving to my sides, up my back. He moaned into my mouth, "Charity," like he'd been so alone. He had been, and so had I. Being terrible made your very being curl up in a ball.

"Stay, Charity, please," he said, winding his hands through my hair, kissing me in quickened bites, his eyebrows furrowing over squeezed tight lids. "I can't make this desire go away. I need you to help me."

I took his stubbly face in my hands and kissed him the way I wanted my own evil kissed away. "Let's try to keep quiet together."

NEED

*E*van wasn't in bed when I woke up. Being alone in his bed felt unnatural, like I broke into a fancy hotel room. I heard the shower running, and I followed the sound across the fluffy carpet.

His bathroom was enormous, with marble everywhere that was probably from Italy or something. There was a huge bathtub up a little flight of useless stairs, giant mirrors, a monstrous shower. That's where he was, his muscular back to me, under streams of water from about a hundred different showerheads.

I'd explored his body every way there was the night before, but seeing his lean muscles, like a runner or something, but stronger, like some god, or perfect killing machine, took my breath away. I wanted to touch him more. No piece of artwork was too precious for me.

I quickly thought of Jen, but what was done was done and who the fuck said I made good choices? I wasn't the type of friend who made good people better.

His eyes were closed when he turned; he was frowning, as if caught in a disturbing dream. I was still there, so maybe he was. I was an intruder there, like I was everywhere. I hoped I'd done something of value, keeping his demons at bay. Then again, maybe I'd just become his newest breed.

I guess I got a little lost in thought myself, because I didn't register Evan staring, one hand with fingers splayed on the man-sized glass door.

"Hi," I mouthed. He smiled, closed lips. His eyes roamed over my bony, naked body.

He didn't invite me into his glass cage, but came out instead, eyes on mine as he wrapped a towel around his waist. His chest hair had little drops stuck to it. He glistened with fresh cleanliness. And I was so dirty.

"Did you sleep well?" he asked me from a distance.

"Always do."

"I wish I could say that."

He dipped his head shyly toward the floor. I was afraid to go to him, like he might take flight.

"Evan, we don't ever have to talk about last night. I'll just go. You know, when you drive me home."

"Charity," he said, and my stomach dropped. He was about to share his feelings. No thank you. "You kept the part of me away that I can never allow to be seen. Jen brings it out, you put it away. Two sides of the same coin." His eyes were cavernous when he looked up. "I need *you* to have *her*."

I reeled back. "Whoa, what the fuck? So you want me to cater to your ugly side so you can what? Fuck Jen and not be remorseful about what you do to her?"

"No! No. Charity, it isn't her I'm worried about. She *wants* my violence." He licked his lips, as if tasting the blood I so wanted. "It's all the others. *They don't.*"

I bit my lip, hard and afraid. The calculation in his stance was something I was a little too familiar with; he was plotting to hurt someone. That was only okay when I did it. It was my job.

"Evan, I'm nobody's savior. Nobody's better for knowing me."

He came to me, taking my hands, his naked body inches from mine. He could have been saying anything, but I was focused on that chest, and that jaw, and those eyes. Sex personified. Mine for the taking. The easy way out of so many things. But so wrong.

"Don't underestimate your worth. You're a good person for staying last night. I couldn't hold in the urge alone."

I ran my hands through his chest hair, my self-control evaporating in tiny explosions. "You didn't hold in the urge at all." I kissed him hard, ripping away the towel and pressing my body against his. I was tired of pretending to give a shit, of pretending I had it in me to help. I wanted Evan because maybe he was worse with me, and I wanted what I had with Robbie, too. I wanted all of it. Evan was on to something. Two sides of the same coin.

Evan pushed me back against the steam-warmed marble sink, his hands grabbing and squeezing. There was no question, no talk of love, or what I was doing with my life. He wanted me and I wanted him. As easy as it should be.

He took me hard and fast on the sink, the steam clinging to me and the mirrors. He was animalistic and needy, and I gave him everything I had. No thinking. Just doing.

When we finished, we held each other close, sweat sticking us together, the steam still fueling us. I loved him, for that moment. I loved him for understanding that I had nothing else to offer.

"She can't see me the way I am," he said into my hair. "Not the way I really am."

"I know."

I held him, and for that time, we were monsters together.

~

I should have been tortured with guilt. I'd betrayed Jen, and Robbie. I hadn't become the Harpy when I was with Evan; I became something worse.

"You understand me in a way nobody else ever would want to, Charity," he'd said over breakfast at his massive kitchen table. He was acting like some fanatical frigging cult leader, like he was in a trance. My mind reeled in the daylight with all the horrible choices I'd made, all the people I hurt.

"Psyched I could help," I said with a mouth full of eggs. I put my fork down and stared at him, my emotions a numb buzzing under the surface. "You know, you can't understand me the way I understand you. You know that, right?"

"How so?" He was completely unruffled by my irritation.

"Because I'm something you can't conceive of."

He grinned. "That sounds a little self- important."

"Too fucking bad." I ate more eggs.

"Charity, I'm not proud of what we've done either, but I know it was the best thing for my relationship with Jen, if there is to be one."

"That's some screwed-up rationalization to make it okay that you fucked her friend."

"No, I didn't *fuck her friend*." His eyes cast down, and I remembered that by sheer numbers, he could hardly be classified a womanizer. "I admire you, for being whatever you want, whenever you want to be. You don't change for anyone. You give in to yourself, but nobody else. You're special."

"You cannot be serious. I'm the least admirable person on the planet. The things I've done, and that I do, actively? You can't imagine."

"Enlighten me."

"Not a snowball's chance in Hell."

"I've told you I want to hurt women, for crying out loud. How much worse can it be than that?"

I slammed my fist on the table, making my plate jump. "You could actually do it! You know what? I do. I'm a killer. A real killer." *Why stop there?* "Wrap your mind around this one; I turn into a Harpy at night, this big bird bitch. Then I murder men, eat their flesh, drink their blood. I do nothing *but* change! I'm not me! And I give in to it for precisely that fucking reason! There's nothing fucking special about me! I want to kill people, and I do it to make my own life go away."

He was shaking his head like a nut, and looked like he was about to start drooling. "You're a what? That's not real. That cannot be real. You can't—"

"I can and do."

"How can you expect me to believe that?"

"I don't care what you believe."

"I was with you all night."

"It's not every night," I said begrudgingly. "I can control it some, when I want to. But I hardly ever want to," I said, and I sounded hard, even to myself.

He stared silently at his plate of eggs. I ate mine, wishing they weren't cooked, and watched.

"What's it like to kill someone?" he finally asked. Not the reaction I was expecting.

"Pleasant. Oddly, wonderfully pleasant."

The world turned bleak, the way he looked at me. "You're not helping me to stay on the clean path right now, are you?" he said with a smirk.

"You don't need me to keep you on the right path. You need me to give you an excuse to do one or the other."

He steepled his fingers on the table, analyzing me for a handful of mental disabilities like Psychiatrist did.

"Charity, you need me as much as I need you."

"Nope."

"I'm on the same side as you. We're killers."

"You are not a fucking killer, Evan. Maybe you have some sick thoughts, but sick thoughts make the world go 'round."

"I'm sick in my heart," he pleaded, voice shaking, hand on his chest, and Jesus, did he appear to be in pain. "Meeting Jen, she unleashed what was in here. It was fate. Fate wants me violent. It's that simple."

I stood up from the table, unable to take any more of his ridiculous shit. "Evan, make up your fucking mind. You begged me to stay with you so you wouldn't give in to your *urges*. Now I'm the justification you need to set them all fucking free? Or is it Jen? I'm confused just looking at you! I think you're crazier than I am!"

He leaned back in his chair, and I swear it was like facing the devil. "Maybe I just need you to understand. I think you want the same from me."

My voice was cold and my heart was colder. "I don't need anyone to tell me what to do. The Harpy does what she needs to, and I need to be the Harpy. You and I are not the same."

He shook his head slowly. "And you think I make excuses."

≈

*E*van drove me back to my apartment building. We sat out front in his car like two high school kids trying to figure out who kisses who first.

"I'm not sorry about this morning," I said.

"I'm not sorry about this morning either."

"I meant the argument."

"Me too."

Quiet.

"And I'm definitely not sorry about last night," he said. "You did keep me calm. You kept me safe. You kept someone safe. Because, Charity, I don't know how much longer I can hold it in, or if I even want to hold back."

"Evan, this is crazy shit to lay on me."

"For that, I am sorry. These are some rough secrets to keep. I can't do it alone."

I glanced at the apartment building on the top of the hill. Secrets from Robbie, from Jen, and now this awful thing, a secret all for me. Becoming the Harpy forever was looking more appealing all the time.

He put his finger on my chin and tilted my face towards him. He put his lips on me with a slow sweetness that couldn't come from a man like him. Not a man that wanted a reason to become a killer.

"Charity," he breathed. I smelled the rich wood scent of him, felt the stubble on his cheeks, his chest move with his breaths. He was just a man. Just a man.

I took his face in my hands. "Evan, you're a good man. Stay a good man. You can do it."

"With you, I can try."

THE OPEN CAGE

*R*obbie wasn't home. Probably got a call to the boarding house to help out some kid. That's the kind of guy Rob was; helped kids. Me? I killed men.

Keegan whistled for me as I walked in.

"Cat calling me, little birdie?"

I lifted the cage door, and Keegan came right over. The fool at the pet store said canaries didn't like a lot of touchiness, but Keegan definitely wanted me to touch him. I pet his bright little head with one finger, the calm easing through me, lulling me near sleep.

"You're the only good decision I've ever made, Keegs." He chirped and nuzzled into me. I wasn't jealous of his happiness, but I was awed that it was because of me. I left his cage door open as I went to get him fresh water. I knew he wouldn't come out. Too uncertain. He may have liked me, but he wasn't going to leave the safety of his cage to hang out with me. Too much can happen to soft little creatures in the world.

I took a long, hot shower, where I did my best thinking. I needed to come up with something to tell Jen. I couldn't avoid her, and she was in such a bad spot, mentally; something I knew too much about. My bad spot was my only spot. She needed to hear answers about Evan, but not the one I had.

I felt like I was washing someone else's body. The thin ankles weren't covered in scales. The slender legs weren't leading up to downy feathers. The toenails were chipped and red, but not with blood. They weren't long and ready to tear something tender apart. The arms were free of wings that could set me free of the world that hated me.

That body was something other people used. All those men my mother brought home, the other guys I'd slept with for no reason, Robbie even, and especially Evan. My body only belonged to me when it was the Harpy. My body worked best when it wasn't trying to survive my life; my body was best at ending it.

Jen had texted me while I was in the shower, asking me to come over. Fuck if I hadn't just barely walked in the door. I threw the phone on the bed and sat down, exhausted of everything. I wanted to crawl under the covers and forget, but that wasn't an option. I had to deal with everyone in my life, if for no other reason than to decide once and for all if I wanted to continue it or become the Harpy for good.

I forced myself up, suddenly irritated by all the stupid unicorns surrounding me. There was no fucking fairytale to aspire to. They mocked me, a shell of what they stood for.

I put on more makeup than I had in a long time. Robbie would have hated it, but I looked killer with red eyeshadow, black liner in thick circles around my eyes, glittery red lips that sparkled as I moved, and china doll cheek stain on my pale skin. My hair had a life of its own. I tucked myself into a ruby red corset and black leather skirt with sky high heels. I was untouchable and beautiful and scary and ready to face the girl I'd wronged.

"Keegan, I'm sorry to close your door, but you weren't coming out anyway," I said to him with more sadness than I wanted to. "You wanted this cage all along."

∼

The Styrofoam coffee cup in my hands shook as I waited for Jen to open the door. I sucked in a breath and straightened my back. I'd dealt with worse, and done worse, and this wouldn't be any different.

"Hi," Jen said before the door was even fully open.

"Hey," I said, maneuvering around her to go in her apartment.

"I'm glad to see you."

"Eh. I'm not that exciting."

I fell onto her couch, spreading out and getting the nerve to look at her. She was so pretty and unhidden. I wanted her to hate me as much as I hated myself.

"I have some chicken pad thai, if you're hungry," she said with a glimmering smile.

"Nah, thanks. I've eaten way too much, and think I'll be having a pretty big meal tonight." Goddamn, I'd make sure of it. My mind wandered to the asshole manager of East Bay Grille.

"Okay." She was still smiling as she sat across from me, expectant.

"You're better today. Not so freaked out," I said, waving my hands around.

"Yeah," she said, turning red. "You just listening to me helped a lot already."

I slugged back the coffee. "Tell me what's been going on." I was stalling. I hated that. I was becoming less and less like myself all the time, and more and more what I expected myself to be.

"I've just been working," Jen said with a halfhearted nod. "Baking helps me keep my mind off of things, you know? I don't know what else to do or think right now."

Dive in, asshole. "Well, I talked to Evan a lot."

Her eyes sparkled with anticipation. Obviously, she hadn't kept her mind off that particular topic at all.

"What did you two talk about?"

How fast I could get my clothes off was the wrong answer, so I went with, "You've affected him in ways he didn't expect."

"Really?" She was breathless, literally on the edge of her seat.

Coffee gulp. I nodded.

"Then why does it seem like I nailed shut a coffin that night with him? Why haven't I heard from him?"

"Have you tried to call him or anything either?"

She blushed. "No. I just got a vibe…"

"I know, I know. Look, it isn't you he's afraid of or whatever."

Her eyes narrowed. I wasn't being clear and that was a good thing. I stood up, pacing the living room floor. I was losing control, and I couldn't. I just couldn't.

"I don't know what you mean." She was so soft-spoken and calm despite her worry that I couldn't handle it anymore. I felt so bad for her, and annoyed by her naivete, I could have puked.

"Jen, it isn't about you. When you asked him to hurt you, it woke something up in him." *Fuck it, just tell her.* "He thinks he might want to do that kind of thing more."

Her pink sweetness went away, leaving her blanched. She became that girl who'd been hurt and knew no other way right before my eyes.

"You mean, he wants to hurt me more?" God, I shivered to hear her say that without disgust in her voice, actually fucking *hopeful*. How had she gone from being destroyed to wanting what would destroy her?

And worse, I had to wonder—if she'd never met me, never gone for coffee with me, would she still have been simply living with failed relationships, safe, and alone? Would she never have explored this level of sickness that would eat her alive?

"Jen, he doesn't want to be a violent guy." Deep breath. "And he's not sure he can stop doing it once he starts."

She nodded. She should be appalled, horrified, Jesus

Christ, did she understand what I was saying? It made *me* squeamish for fuck's sake, and this sweet, kind girl, so full of goodness, *she* wanted it?

I could infect anything, anywhere. Typhoid Charity.

Jen was a beacon of empathy. She came and sat beside me on the couch, ready to comfort me. I deserved nothing of the sort.

"Charity, I shouldn't have let you to talk to him for me. I should have handled it like a big girl."

"You didn't ask, I offered. I don't regret it." I didn't. Because my selfishness was greater than my guilt. I *wanted* to be near Evan. He was the only other lion among all those lambs.

She straightened up a little then, her own guilt dissolving. "How the hell did you get to be so strong? How do you deal with what's happened to you and not let it become who you are?"

I laughed, but she didn't.

"My entire life has been determined by what happened to me."

"No. No way. You've got something that I don't. You're *scary*."

"What every girl wants to hear."

"You know what I mean."

"Not really."

I knew pretty much what she meant. I made damn sure I was scary. But it would never scare off my memories.

"Jen, you aren't in good company with me. You know that, right?"

We studied each other, both of us not unfamiliar

with the process. Everyone was someone we had to measure up, always someone to be wary of. Her jaw set, and she said something to me that I knew she meant, and would never hear me argue.

"You are not the worst company I've kept. And there's something about you that I need to rub off on me."

My voice was soft and sad, and it made me want to crawl into a hole and die. "You've got something I need, too."

"What could I possibly have that you would want?"

"You're still human."

She bit her lip, like she was afraid to say the wrong thing. "I am. But the beast is coming out of its cage."

PARTS TOO WELL KNOWN

here was too much emotion in me, too much anger and desire and sadness. People were fucking draining. I totally lost control of anything, and all I wanted was to have the world in my grasp again, completely separate from me.

It was getting dark by the time I got home. I ripped off everything below the waist as soon as I opened the door. The corset could stay when I changed.

And goddamn, was I ready for it. I wanted to change like nothing I'd ever wanted. I wanted something that couldn't hurt my heart and make me doubt myself. I wanted to grind the bones between my teeth.

I waited a long time, pacing, staring at the clock. Ten forty at night. I realized Robbie hadn't been home yet, and was glad as hell.

I felt it come on in my stomach first. The energy rolled up and out of me in a growl that sent Keegan fluttering to the back of his cage. The wings burst from my arms, painfully that time, all at once with no warning. My feet and legs transformed, but I didn't notice until after, so intense was the pain in my arms.

But I was whole again.

I looked out the peephole. Nothing and no one. I tucked my wings down, and moved with more ease than usual through the door, up the stairs, out to the lawn on the top of the hill. The Harpy was my natural state, far more than being a person. I just wanted to feel natural somewhere.

Unlike other days, I knew right where I wanted to go. I had a certain restaurant manager to surprise.

The waterfront was crowded with tourists, so I flew high. If anyone noticed, they were too drunk, stumbling from one of the many bars, to make much of a scene about it.

I went straight to East Bay Grille, to the back where the boat docks were. None of the fisherman were out that late, and nobody from the bar would go back there. I hid in the shadows of a stack of lobster traps, and rested. I was still exhausted, as energized by the imminent kill as I was.

I got comfortable listening to the ocean's calm and the laughter of people walking to their cars or out onto the jetty. Close enough for me to hear, but too self-involved to know I was there. It made me smile that I could take them by surprise if I wanted to, but I mostly just wanted to fade away.

Until he came out. I heard him first, sounding almost professional, and looking anything but, as he pulled a cigarette out from behind his ear like the frigging high school dropout he definitely was.

"No, tell them the kitchen is closed, but be pleasant, Armando. Yeah, pleasant, like nice," he was yelling to some employee inside as he backed out the door, letting it slam. He sat on a pile of crates and lit the cigarette, making a tiny speck of brightness in the dark.

Were they expecting him back inside? Of course they were, but they also wouldn't be sad if he never showed up again. Who wants their boss to come back when you worked some shitty restaurant job? My claws dug into the pavement, long scratches that would mark my place forever.

I knew he was a terrible person. It was written all over his fat face, even if my Harpy senses didn't scream it to me. He had the air of a man with thoughts dirtier than your average bear's.

His eyes narrowed in the darkness, I could see them as if he were right in front of me. I'd been spotted.

"What the fuck?"

I was enormous; the shadow of me must have been terrifying. Good. I walked out, the world's largest vulture, and stared at him with my human eyes. A real monster, right in his own backyard. The face and hair, tits and attitude he remembered from our little spat the day before, now attached to a nightmare creature. He knew nothing good would come of it.

"Hi," I said casually as I inched up on him. "Remember me?"

"What the fuck?" he repeated, scrambling back, knocking over crates and boxes. The reaction never got old. I laughed, and scared myself with how demonic it sounded. Briefly, only briefly, I doubted that I was the good guy in the scenario.

Images of the Wood of Suicides, and what I'd done there. Images of Carl Painter's daughter, shaking and naked in front of me, with Painter behind me, panting and pushing me to her. With a banshee scream, I flapped my wings once and was an inch from the manager's cigarette breath.

"You shouldn't have treated me the way you did yesterday, should you?"

"What the hell are you?"

"Someone not to be fucked with, clearly. Your shitty life is over. You can thank me later. Oh, wait, no you can't." I raised my hands, claws extended, ready to tear into him.

"Don't do this!"

And for a second, I didn't.

"Fuck you. Why not?" My wings covered him in darkness. I was ready to cover him in darkness. He deserved it.

"I have kids, for Chrissakes, please."

"That's the best you got? They'll be better off without your filthy fat ass hovering over them, helping them with their homework." I descended on him, and he screamed wildly.

"Shut the fuck up!" I yelled over him. It wasn't going well. I needed to finish him fast, but something felt wrong.

"Why are you doing this?" he shouted at me through a sob, pushing me off. I let him push me, he wasn't stronger than me.

"I know what kind of man you are!" I yelled. But it was me. It was me who said it, Charity, not the beast I became.

He shook his head stupidly, and I could hear footsteps coming toward us from the kitchen. Time to go.

"I never did anything to deserve this!" he cried.

I got up really close to him, and stuck my claw under his chin, drawing blood fast.

"And you goddamn well had better keep it that way."

I opened my dirty wings and let the black sky suck me in.

~

*T*ears streamed down my face in the darkness, pissing me off and driving me forward. I didn't know where I was going, but I had to get out of there. Fingers pointed at me from the ground as I rose higher out of sight. I was pissed not to have finished him, and even angrier that maybe, just maybe, I had been wrong.

I screamed loud and wished for once that there was someone there to stop me, to just fucking stop me before I ripped the world apart to match the shreds of my heart.

The air cracked ahead of me, like a lightning streak that had exploded. I knew what it was, and I wanted to fly at it, into it, disappear and die. Like a dream come true, the sky cracked again, closer, and I was sucked into the void, as dark and nothing as I was, the tidal wave of pain no worse than anything else I lived with. I relished it, writhing in the grasp of torture as every bone and ligament twisted while I hurtled through the emptiness.

My longing to be in the Wood of Suicides threatened to squeeze my shriveled heart right out of my chest. There was no need of a heart where I was headed anyway.

The blood-soaked hay scent hit me first, while the world was still black. I hit the ground hard, splayed out, even though I tried to land on my feet. The story of my fucking life.

A lot of things cracked as I pulled myself to my feet, and looked around at the death-red world as it slowly lit up. The Wood of Suicides never changed. Alive, but not full of life. As if I were sloshing around in the disgusting gut of some animal. Enough quiet noise to let you forget who you really were. Whimpers, moans, the sound of sucking flesh. No screaming. There was nothing left to scream for.

The Harpies were too engrossed in tormenting the suicides to notice me. I got my footing back, and started walking.

I wondered if the Harpies were all there for the same reason I was; had they all been hurt so badly that it was the only place their souls could thrive? I'd ask the Queen. Big ol' black beauty Queen wouldn't wait long to find me.

I was there for a reason; because she wanted me to be. I was pretty sure the only other way to get to the Wood was as one of those poor suckers in the trees.

The Queen had a reason to have me there. Jesus, I'd never stop being used, even in Hell.

A screech echoed around me, bouncing off the invisible gut walls of the place, and a Harpy landed in front of me, growling. She looked like a witch doctor or something, insanely primitive, with bones woven into her dreadlocks, white skull features painted on her face, and a gold hoop through the middle of her nose. She grunted in my face, exposing dead teeth and gristle.

"What the fuck do you want?" I said, sizing up her black feathers and wings. I could take her.

She pushed me fast, her claws scratching my arms. I stumbled, but came back at her faster, swiping claws across her chest, my wings taking me over her. I brought my fist down on the top of her head, knocking her to the ground.

"Don't mess with me," I said, and stared at her until she got up and ran away. A thing with no sense of dignity, only self-preservation. I recognized it.

I kept walking, heading towards the Queen's nest. No fuckery, straight to the source to get some questions answered.

All the Harpies were watching me, some hissing and spitting, screeching, but none of their shit would get to me. I killed just like they did. They weren't better.

"You've come," the Queen said to me as I approached the nest.

"Yup. That fucking hurt. Maybe we could come up with a better mode of transport?"

She smiled at me. I could almost warm up to her if she clearly wasn't a fucking monster in charge of a bunch more monsters, ruling over a nightmare land.

I didn't wait to be asked, I climbed up into the nest like it was my job, the embedded blue eyes blinking at me. I sat down next to her without a word. I'd make her speak first. I smiled inside at my little victory when she did just that.

"Did you want to come here tonight, Hazel?"

I hated when she called me that. "Yeah, I did."

"And why is that?"

"I think you know why, and I think it's why you brought me here."

She raised her human hand to her chest in dramatic surprise. "Oh, sweetheart, I didn't bring you here tonight. You wanted to be here, so you are."

I wasn't really expecting that, but I didn't let her see it.

"Like when I don't want to become the Harpy, and I don't. I do have some control here, don't I?"

She gently touched my hair, her scent of dead flowers and moldy fruit wafting over me. "You have all the control here," she said, looking around at her world. "In this place, as one of us, everyone will bow to you."

I recognized her sales pitch, but I didn't know what she was pitching.

"Not you," I said with a smirk. "You won't be bowing to me."

Her warm smile disappeared. "Oh, certainly not. Not to you or anyone." I was far more comfortable with this Queen. The one who came to get me that rainy night with her disgusting Harpy sidekick. I wanted to see her scary face, the real one.

She unfolded her great insectile wings slowly, stretching them, as if to show me how beautiful they were, and then put them away after the glorious show. Her face was cruel.

"I want to know why the Harpies are here, and I want to know why you want me here."

The Queen made no attempt to look more pleasant. She was regal and needed no excuses. "This is where we belong. This is where legend places us, where we can feed eternally, and where these souls nourish us. The Wood is where we get what we want; revenge. Justification. To be good somewhere, at something."

We both contemplated the Harpies, roosting peacefully among the tortured souls in blood covered trees.

"Are they all here for the same…? Did they all get raped and…" I didn't really want the answer.

"There are infinite ways to be wronged, and my Harpies are the hellish representations of them all. All of these creatures have suffered like you. Your sisters."

"Witch Bitch back there sure didn't treat me like a sister. What do they know about me?"

Her dark eyes twinkled, and I could tell she'd been waiting for that question, that moment. "If there's one thing that powerful beings know, it's when someone is more powerful than they are. They know you can take this place by storm. The Harpies despise change."

"Why me? Why are you even talking to me? I don't see you letting the rest of the Uglies in your nest thing."

She laughed, a real laugh. I tried not to relax. "Dear girl. You are blinded by your own loathing. You do not see what I do. Or what they do. Your utter hatred for your world makes you a very strong Harpy. The more powerful you are, the stronger we are together. And while they may envy you, they know that we thrive on strength as any predator does. You can bring it to us. It is that simple."

"Don't lie to me, your Highness." I grinned. "I know there's more to it than that."

"My child, I have no reason to lie to you. But I do have something for you."

"What, like a present? Cool."

"In a manner of speaking. What I can give you, Hazel, when you choose to become one of us forever. I will sever all of your human ties. You will no longer struggle with love and how to make it work. There will be no worry of hatred and sadness, as it will be what you live off of. You will lose all the pain you have now, and the memory of the pain as well. I can free you of all sentiment."

Everything around me went death still, my mind the same, and it sunk in; my suffering could be over.

"Those tears could be the last you ever shed," she hissed into my ear. I moved to wipe my face, muttering that I could still have tears to shed. She gently held my hand. The Queen brought her face to mine, as if to kiss me on the cheek, and licked a tear from my skin. She closed her eyes, long lashes brushing her cheek and moaned. The Harpies moaned with her, but we were all so alone together.

"You can make it all go away," I said, eyes focused on my hands twisting in my lap. A nervous tick that didn't belong to me. I didn't ever want to be nervous again. I wanted to be the me that never doubted herself. I wanted to be the one that never felt broken and stripped.

I swallowed a lump in my throat and nodded at the flying Harpies. "Do any of them…make mistakes? Like I did tonight?" I knew the stupid manager of that restaurant wasn't the caliber of the men I killed, but I went to him anyway. More ways emotion was ruining my life.

She put her arm around me, sheltering me with her wing. "You were angry. You saw what you wanted to see, like so many do. It doesn't make you wrong."

"I almost killed that man, and he wasn't what I thought he was. I was seen, I almost gave myself up."

"We don't play by their rules."

"It doesn't make killing right."

"According to who?" The Queen was becoming frustrated with me, and I pushed more. "Was what Carl Painter did to you *right*? Is what you go through every minute of your life any more right, or justified than what you did to that man? When someone fights as much as you do, the pain will get in the way now and again. It will cloud your vision. It doesn't make you wrong."

I wanted to believe her.

"Did you tell all of them this? Did all of the Harpies go through this?" I asked her quietly.

"No. These you see around you," she said, gesturing

at the countless beasts of revenge, "never questioned leaving their pain behind. They had no fight in them to begin with."

So I *was* better than them. There, I could be as strong as I needed to be. I would own them. I glimpsed the Queen out of the corner of my eye. If I was stronger than them, maybe I could be stronger than her, too. Maybe I could make her afraid. If I wanted to. Maybe Hell was where everything could make sense.

"I have loose ends to tie up."

She smiled, taking her wing from around me, and left me open.

"*I*t is daylight," the Queen told me. "And you have not eaten."

I knew what she was getting at. I also knew she wasn't overly concerned about my health. She wanted to see what I would do. An initiation.

Well, nobody was going to get the best of me in a challenge.

"I'm starved," I said, and got to my feet. My stomach turned with its emptiness. If only I hadn't been wrong about the fat manager.

I climbed down out of the nest, heart pounding, and considered my options.

Harpies watched me from the trees, and some on the ground. They knew a hazing when they saw one. Prison yard mentality.

One tree, its trunk dripping crimson, had the emaciated limbs of a bald man wrapped around it. His face studied me without the insanity of the others'. He had to be new there, or he'd been there too long to care anymore. His steady, hard gaze challenged me. I went to him.

His eyes didn't waver as I approached. When I was inches from him, salivating, I did something I wished later I hadn't.

"Who are you?" I asked him.

"Nobody," he answered.

"How long have you been here, Nobody?"

"Long enough to know that I'm in Hell, and that I should be."

I reached out my hand, shocked that it was indeed a hand and not a claw. I was in human form, not Harpy. My rolling stomach was trying to tell me how disgusting the situation was, but I had to behave like the Harpy then no matter what. That much I knew.

"You killed yourself. Why?"

"There was no life left in me."

The other Harpies watched in silence. I don't know if any of them ever spoke, let alone to one of the suicides. It was my moment of truth.

"You know you've been sent here to suffer for eternity, don't you?" I said, dreamily, touching the man's head.

He just stared back at me.

"I'm here to help you."

He continued to stare.

One of his arms was covered in welts from Harpy claws, continuously bleeding. I don't think he felt a thing. I stuck my finger into one of the wounds, covering it in blood and gristle like I'd dipped into the peanut butter jar. My eyes never leaving his, I sucked it, disgusted with myself beyond anything I ever knew, but physically and emotionally craving it. The Harpy was alive in me.

I made a show of it for the Harpies and the Queen. There was purpose to what I was doing. Keeping my eyes fixed to the nearest Harpy's, I put all ten of my fingertips into Nobody's open scratches, and traced them down, gathering fingerfuls of red-black gore. Sucking one at a time, I got lost in the flavor, and couldn't help but curl my other hand up and put all the fingers in my mouth at once, moaning with pleasure, breaking my gaze from the Harpy as I closed my eyes.

When I tasted only my own skin, my eyes popped open, ready for more, and I zeroed in on the man's wounds. I fastened my mouth on his twisted, naked torso, my hands clinging to his slippery, hot arms, desperately trying to pull him to me as close as I could. The air pulsed with blood and heat and sound. The man barely wrestled, his limbs so wound in the tree, but I wanted the fight and I thrashed my head when he went still, ripping the flesh more.

My belly was full and warm, and I was getting sluggish. I pulled back, and observed the damage I'd done. Nobody lied limp, staring as if dead, but that would never happen. He'd resigned to being where he was, resigned to what I was doing to him. There could be no greater despair; not even my own.

Maybe that was what the appeal was in the Wood of Suicides; I could watch people suffer more than I had. Then I could show them how much worse it could be.

I was the only human being there, and I was more

horrifying than any one of the creatures that mind-lessly ravaged and destroyed. Harpies stared dumbly at me, fear in their eyes. I didn't need to look down to know blood was coursing over me, pooling at my feet, dripping from my human teeth.

Nobody can hurt me here, I thought.

I raised my arms to the sky and smiled at my future kingdom.

~

*I*t was daylight when I burst out of the sky and landed again face-down on the soft grass outside my apartment building. I stood up quick, and immediately crouched back down. I was only wearing a corset, and I was coated in blood. People were out and around. Thank God I lived in the building up on a hill, so I went unnoticed from the ground. I scuttled behind a bush in front of my base-ment apartment window, hoping I could sneak up to the doorbell buzzers and get Robbie to let me in. Shit, I hoped he was home.

I figured that it was just after nine in the morning. I could see the late sleepers taking off as fast as they could to work. So teenagers were still asleep, kids were watching cartoons. I could get to the buzzer if I went quick.

No more waiting. I ran out from behind the bush, around the banister and up half the stairs when the front door opened. I didn't even have underwear on.

My neighbors didn't like me already, but shit, no need to give them more reason.

I crouched again, as low as I could, like I was picking something up. My ass was certainly gleaming white in the sunshine, but for the blood streaks.

"Charity!" Robbie said in an aggravated whisper. "Get in here!"

"Thank fucking God. How did you know I was out here?"

"I was in your apartment, saw you from the window."

"Weird."

"Why didn't you try to open the win—"

"Fucking hell, Robbie, get me inside!"

We pounded down the stairs and into my apartment. Robbie slammed the door behind us.

"Holy shit, I thought you were just going to dinner," he said.

"Sorry to piss you off, but I'm also a mythical beast in my spare time."

"Charity, why didn't you tell me?"

"Tell you what? You already know what I do at night."

"You don't do it all the time. You don't. So I didn't know where you were—"

"You don't need to worry about me."

He was pacing and running his hands through his hair so much he was going to make a bald spot in that mane of brown beauty.

"You can't make me not worry about you. You disappeared when you just said you were going out to dinner. I don't know this Evan guy, and neither do you."

Fucking reality, right back in my face. The reality I created. "You might be surprised," I said under my breath.

He stopped, mouth hanging. "Oh my God."

"Oh, Robbie, I didn't mean—" I bumbled, trying to brush it off. My big goddamn mouth.

"Please don't joke about this," he said, defeated, and fell on the couch, head hung. Fuck.

I sat next to him. Another guy would have lashed out, would have called me a whore and told me to get the hell away from him, but not Robbie. He forgave me everything before he even knew what I'd done.

"I'm sorry, Rob."

"Don't say that. It isn't true."

"It is! I don't know why I...did it...exactly, except Evan and I are alike."

"Spare me the gory details, Charity. I could take you telling me about your latest kill easier."

So close to me, his warmth was everything safe and strong and home should be. Things I was never supposed to have.

"Rob, I am sorry. I'm sorry you ever met me."

"Stop."

"I'm not being self-loathing, Robbie. I can't give you anything good. There's nothing good in me to give, it's been gone a long time."

He still wouldn't look at me. Maybe he was listening this time. I wished he would, and I could never survive if he did. I knew what the squishy, airy fucking bubbles in my guts were that ate at the core of me when I thought of him. It couldn't turn out well, not for someone like me, a human wasteland.

When he did look at me, it wasn't to say he didn't care that I was trash, or to tell me he never wanted to see me again.

"Tell me why you're so broken."

I was doing that stupid nervous shaking of the head I did when I was really scared. Didn't happen often. "You don't want to know."

He pierced me with his eyes, and said, "If you want me to stay. If you want me to understand why this is so complicated between us when I just want to be in love with you, you need to tell me why. I deserve that."

How impossible that I could feel more exposed, sitting there wrapped in a freshly bloody blanket, naked and filthy. But the idea of telling him *why* was too terrible for me to deal with.

I could almost hear Psychiatrist in my ear. *You have to let it go if you want to escape it. It's your choice.* And I could hear the Queen telling me I would never have to remember it again.

Through gritted teeth, I told Robbie about my mother, my dad leaving, and the drugs. I told him about the men. I talked about going hungry, missing school because I had to hide my bruises, all the holidays that were the same as every other dirty day. None of that was so bad, and not the first time I'd told it.

He listened, but didn't try to comfort me, and didn't interrupt to ask questions. He was so good that way, never making things harder than they should be.

"That isn't it," he finally said.

My heart stopped. "No. No, that isn't it, I guess."

Robbie got up, went to the kitchen and came back with a glass of water for me. Still being nice to me after I betrayed him. I nodded my thanks, wrapped the blanket tighter around me, and sucked the water down. It didn't make me any more ready to continue, but I did.

"Carl Painter was the one who made me like I am. He wasn't the first or the last one to abuse me, but he was the worst. He did it when he was sober, and I swear I think he didn't even come to the house for the drugs, or my mother. He came for me."

I was shivering, and Robbie pulled the blanket closer, but didn't tell me to stop.

"At first, he'd pin me down and use his hands on me. Then he raped me. I was plenty old enough and had too much experience by then to know not to let men touch me in the private places, so he did it by force. It'd been done before, that wasn't any different from what I knew. But the look in his eyes—he hated me. He hated me and he knew what he was doing to me. He wasn't some addict with issues. He was a monster who wanted to hurt me as much and as hard as I could be hurt."

Robbie grimaced, swallowing back bile, I think. "Why didn't you ever go to the police?"

"I was humiliated. And if they ever came to where I lived—ugh. I guess, maybe even then, I thought I had it coming. I lived like an animal, was treated like one. I was still young enough to think it was all my fault."

Robbie took my hand then, and my entire soul breathed a sigh of relief. It was still so hard to believe he loved me. Harder after that, of course.

"Carl raped me more often than any of the others, and got more and more violent all the time. He burned me with a cigarette while penetrating me. He hit me, always, pinched me, cut me with a steak knife once. And then other kinds of torture." I made myself breathe. "He tied me up for a day when my mother was out cold. He force-fed me cat food while I was tied up, until I was puking all over myself, and he laughed the whole time. The whole fucking time."

"Jesus Christ." Robbie's hands were shaking in mine. It gave me the strength to keep going.

"There was more, always new, always creative. But it was when he brought his daughter over that I cracked."

"Charity, you don't have to keep going. I get it."

I looked in his beautiful, soft eyes. The kind of eyes that said so much more than most words. Talking about it didn't help me. It came alive in my head even more, became an entity in the room with us. Hey, healing hurts, right?

"I can do this, Robbie. You're right. You deserve to know, and I deserve to tell it."

He pulled me to him, holding me so tight I could barely breathe. I couldn't believe I'd slept with someone else.

"His daughter was a year younger than me. I'd seen her in school, but never talked to her. She was quiet, I wasn't, and I was a sophomore, and didn't associate with freshmen.

"When he brought her over, she was already scared. My stomach fucking turned, like when he made me eat all that shit, and I had to puke, but I couldn't. If I let her see how afraid I was, she'd be even more terrified. I couldn't let her keep her waiting for the worst anymore, and I knew it wasn't going to get any better."

"Your mom? Where the fuck was your mom? Where was she?"

"Where she usually was, right under our fucking noses."

Funny how the mind remembers the light in the room, how it was daytime, but so dark. And how dirty the wooden kitchen table was. I remembered the girl's shoes, and how they had holes where the big toes were. But I couldn't remember her clothes, or her voice.

"Charity?"

"Oh, sorry. Zoned out. Where was I? Oh, yeah, the most horrible thing ever."

"Please, don't, if you can't."

"I can. I can because you're here."

"Okay."

Of all the horrors that I'd witnessed and created, telling the story was the scariest thing I had ever done. To admit out loud what I did to that girl was an atrocity in itself that I could never match with countless killings as the Harpy.

My voice was shattered and small. "He introduced us like we were at some fucking birthday party or something. 'This is Maggie. Maggie, this is Hazel.'" Robbie shook his head, not knowing about Hazel, or what Hazel had turned me into. "You girls play together, and I have a special game in mind for later.' Twisted fuck."

"Oh my God."

"I sat with Maggie at the kitchen table. We talked like two inmates on death row. No point in going into small talk. It wouldn't matter for long. She'd given up, it was all over her. I could see it because I had the look too, but in a different way. It made her look small; it made me look like a wild animal.

"I will never forget the last question I asked her before it started. I wish I never opened my stupid fucking mouth."

"What did you ask her?"

I couldn't help but laugh at my stupidity and the fucking irony of it all. "I asked her if she thought we could get away. She said 'never again.'"

The sob broke from my throat before I could stop it. I was powerless all over again. Robbie rocked me and shushed me like a screaming baby. I didn't know if I could go on, but I had to. I had a responsibility to.

Sitting up straight, I backed slightly away from him. I think if I had any more kindness shown to me I would have died.

"I'm going to tell you what happened, Rob," I said, my voice thick with unshed tears. "And I understand that you won't want me anymore. I get it. Thanks for listening. I've never told anybody any of this. Hell, I never even said her name until today."

He didn't say anything, didn't try to offer me comforting words that meant nothing. I appreciated it.

"He came for us, and we just went. We just went with him. Lambs to the slaughter. We went to my bedroom. Neither of us talked. I can remember more than anything the big, nasty grin on his face. I think I was waiting for Maggie to say we didn't have to do it, that we stood a chance. But there were no more chances for us. We'd never had chances.

"As soon as we went in, he hit me hard in the back of the head. I fell on the bed, and he did what he always did, but this time, Maggie was there, watching. I wasn't crying or moving. She didn't make a sound, or maybe she did, but I couldn't hear over him. He was really rough on me that day, made sure I knew there was no getting away. He'd punch me in the back of the head now and again, until I blacked out eventually. When I woke up, Maggie was tied up, naked. I still remember pissing myself a little looking at her; she was covered in fucking scars. I mean they were all over her body, and all different ones. He'd done some bad things to her, worse than to me.

"He slapped me, to wake me up more, I guess, and he gave me—" I coughed, almost gagged. Fuck. "He gave me a, um, a toy. I guess it was a toy. It was a vibrator, but it was-- worse. I don't know who the fuck would make something like that, but I guess there's more screwed-up people out there than just me."

"Charity—"

"No, there isn't much more. He made me use it on her, of course, and whenever I looked at him, to beg him to let me stop, he'd hit me, until Maggie asked me to just do it. I think that pissed him off because he made me—he made me do it harder, and she was bleeding and crying, and when I cried he hit me and then her—"

I couldn't speak anymore, but my mouth was moving, and Robbie rocked me and held me, saying it wasn't my fault over and over. "You couldn't have done anything," he said. I pulled back and looked at him, his face blurry.

"We didn't even try to save ourselves," I choked out, barely able to speak, wishing I never had to speak again. "I couldn't help her. I didn't."

"Oh God, baby," Robbie said, rocking me, crying with me. It made me stronger. I thought *whoever said getting this shit off your chest is helpful is a fucking imbecile*, it didn't. I felt worse for having said it out loud. But it brought me closer to Robbie than I had ever been to anyone in my life by choice. And goddamn if I wasn't actually grateful that he was still near me, after knowing what I really was underneath.

"Thank you," I mumbled.

Robbie pulled back to look at my face, his own streaked with tears. He kissed my cheeks softly, taking away the blackness that threatened to eat me alive.

"I wish I could have been there, to save you. I would have saved you then, and I'll save you forever."

I crumpled into him, smiling like I never had before.

WHEN YOUR INSIDES LIE

*R*obbie stayed. He stayed even though he knew what I did with Evan, and knew what I did to Carl Painter's daughter. He stayed though he knew I was a murderer. He stayed though he knew I wasn't completely human.

I was totally devoid of energy when I finished telling him the story. I could have told him more, but he got the picture. He probably had enough of a picture to keep him awake at night forever.

Sitting next to me on the couch, he took my head in both his hands, smoothing my tangled, clotted hair, and looked in my eyes. "I'll get a hot shower going for you. I'm not going anywhere." I nodded, and fell in on myself when he stood up.

Tears dripped on my still bloody hands, turning them pink. My mind, myself, blank. Robbie came back, slowly removed the blanket from my shoulders, and began to take off my corset for me. I let him. He took me by the hand to the bathroom, and helped me into the shower.

"I should have started a bath. I don't know if you can stand up."

"I know for sure I can't sit in a steaming pool of my own filth, so shower was the way to go."

He laughed, more from relief that I was still funny than anything probably, and kissed me with the softness of a child on the cheek. I thought of Lily.

He was still there when I got out of the shower a long time later, with clean hair, clean skin, and a fresher mind. I didn't have a towel on when I walked into the bedroom. He was in there, just taking in all the unicorns. The stupid fucking unicorns.

When he turned around, I sucked in a breath at how drawn his cheeks were, like the guy who'd been in Iraq that lived upstairs. I guess Robbie had a reason for post-traumatic stress, if I wanted to believe he loved me like he said he did. He certainly showed it enough.

His eyes ran over my body, and he licked his lips. "I never wanted to ask where those scars came from before. You never seemed to notice them, and I didn't want to be the one to bring them up." He was looking at the white marks on my stomach and thighs that I ignored.

"My scars show plenty from the inside, without having to talk about the ones on the outside."

Robbie wasn't shy about my nakedness. I loved that. Showing so much skin all the time distracted people, made them think of me sexually, and not care about me any other way. Not him. Not him.

He came to me and put his arms around me slowly, as if trying not to scare me off.

"I understand why you slept with Evan, I think. It's not okay, but I do understand."

"I wasn't asking for understanding."

"Well, you got it anyway."

He backed away, picking up a unicorn figurine. "Do you think you'll become the Harpy tonight?"

"I don't know. I'm exhausted." I swallowed. "But hungry. And last night, I went to the Harpies' place again. The Wood of Suicides."

"You did?"

I nodded.

"I guess we'll just wait and see, then."

I sighed, beyond happy that he was willing to live through this with me. Amazed at it.

"You know what?" I said. "I want to wear sweatpants." That made him smile.

I put on the one pair of sweatpants I owned. They were these old gray things, I think they were men's but they had no tag, and I had no idea where they'd come from, or more accurately, who'd left them. A white tanktop, and I was ready to sit my ass on the couch and not get up for the rest of the day.

When night came, I didn't know what I'd be in for. Or we would be in for, I guess.

"Come on, you must be hungry."

"I don't want to move off the couch until I absolutely have to."

"That's fine," he said, running his fingers over my collarbone, and down my arm, leaving a tingling in their path. "But my couch. Our couch. Move in with me. I'm not taking no for an answer."

I was vulnerable as hell but I really wanted to just be with him, safe, comforted. I wanted it to never end.

"I'll start moving my things tomorrow."

He hugged me, and actually *thanked* me. And we went to his/our apartment.

I brought the caged bird.

~

*R*obbie made me mac and cheese with hot dogs, and we had a Quentin Tarantino-thon. I wrapped up in a black blanket that smelled like his laundry detergent, and did not move, as promised. We cuddled—actually cuddled—something I'd never done with another guy. We talked about his band that practiced too little to be any good, and he played guitar for me. It was a Zen paradise for a day. The good old guilt that I loved resurged because he was treating me so sweetly. Better than I'd ever been treated by anyone in my life. I didn't want to be treated like a queen, I just wanted to be treated like I had a place no matter who I was.

So when he asked me why I said "Hazel" and not "Charity" when I'd told my story, I didn't have any trouble saying it.

"My name was Hazel Harrington. When I ran away from Boston, I didn't have enough money to go anywhere far, and wasn't about to change it legally. So here I am, hiding, with a different name."

"But your mom is still—around?"

"I'd be shocked if she wasn't dead yet."

"You wish she would die, don't you?" he asked, with zero judgment.

I nodded. "Yeah, I do. She doesn't deserve the worthless fucking mess that she calls a life."

"You're right."

I snapped my head up from his shoulder. "I'm right? About wishing my mother dead?" I laughed. "You help troubled kids forgive the people who hurt them and you think I should wish my mother dead?"

His jaw set. "Look what she did to you."

Keegan chirped for me across the room. I got up and opened his cage door.

SCREAMING

*I*t was getting dark. The mac and cheese tasted good, but it didn't bring the comfort I needed. It didn't fill me. The Harpy was still in there, starving now that it had been woken. It wanted me to take my memories and crush them. I was too weak not to give in.

Robbie was twirling my mess of hair in his fingers. I hadn't even brushed it when I got out of the shower, and it was grossly dreadlocked.

"You want a beer?" he asked.

"Yeah, that would be excellent."

He got up, leaving me alone. Whenever he left me on a couch, I wanted him back fast. I watched the sun going down out the window, and gnashed my teeth. I was so content, and so restless and hungry, and dissatisfied with the lack of kill as the Harpy the other night, and disgusted by what I'd done in the Wood, and proud of becoming stronger there. And terrified. And confused. And crying.

Rob came back with two beers cracked.

"You're crying, baby."

"Something I do now, I guess," I said, wiping my cheeks. I drank half the beer in one gulp.

He stroked my hair, and kissed my forehead. "What can I do?"

"Nothing else, please. You've made me…you've given me a home here."

"You're home," he whispered, nuzzling his nose into my hair. I wanted him to take me and kiss every part of me the way I never wanted anyone to.

"Robbie."

"Yes?" Nose circling in my hair.

"I love you."

He froze, finally taking his lips from my hair, and tilted my chin up. "I love you, Charity. Hazel. Harpy. Whoever you are, whatever you need to be. Your heart is always the same. I want to give it a home always."

I don't care who you are, a man like Robbie says something like that, you melt. You melt like a schoolgirl and would do anything for him.

I pulled his face to me and kissed him as tenderly as I knew how, trying my hardest to show him that I wanted to keep him safe too, be his home, even if I didn't know how. I loved him for everything he was and wanted to be to me.

"I love you, Robbie," I whispered into his lips.

"Perfect," he whispered back.

*H*e fell asleep in my arms on the couch, even though *Reservoir Dogs* was the loudest thing imaginable right then. It was after ten, and the urge for the Harpy to take me lay dormant. The confusion of being bloodthirsty and still so thrown by the mistake I'd made with the manager made me too afraid to change. And then—Robbie's olive cheeks, hair flopping onto his eyelids, lips parted in a half-snore—that moment was too much to give up. Not to mention that I needed a break from the Wood to think. I had a bad feeling I'd end up there again if I left the couch.

It hadn't been so long ago that I was treated like royalty in that Hell. I told the Queen that I was going to settle some things and be there, be a Harpy for good.

I was a complete dick about decision making, clearly.

I'd committed to living in two different places; one where my heart exploded and one where my heart died, taking all of its torment with it. I looked at Robbie's head in my lap, and ran my fingers through his hair as he'd done so many times to mine. I was going to fuck him up, and I was going to do it hard without even trying.

As if on cue, my phone buzzed from the coffee table. I tried not to squeeze Rob to death as I reached for it.

"Oh, lord."

It was Evan. Sonofabitch.

Three words, and three words only:

I need you.

I thunked my head on the wall behind me. Night-time brought Hell with it in so many forms. My already spinning head then had Evan Hale shooting through it like a pinball, remembering his hands on me and how it felt like he was combing through the scattered ashes of my soul, looking for something to hold on to. Looking for a voice to tell him he wasn't as bad as he wanted to be.

We both were.

How could I turn my back on him when we were so alike?

A mass of guns went off on TV, just like the mass of guns going off in my head. Robbie slept soundly as a purring kitten, oblivious to it all. As he should have been. He shouldn't ever have touched the life I led.

The night was closing in on me, and I had some insane choices to make. I'd have to be stupid to even consider leaving the man in my lap after what we shared. After telling him I would pack my things, and telling him the story of my life that I ran from in my own head. He was good for me, but good wasn't for me. Because he made me believe that it wasn't my fault, but he couldn't make me believe that all the good hadn't been erased from me and replaced with the black gunk of my past.

There was a chance I could do something fucking worthwhile; keep Evan from doing something terrible. It wouldn't put me on the heavy side of the dignity scale, but hey, anything that might help keep me out of Hell.

Hell, where I was supposed to be moving to. Fuck me.

Tears clung to my eyelashes as I texted Evan back.

I'll give you the help you don't want. Be there soon.

ALL AT ONCE

"*R*obbie?" I whispered in his ear, and he smiled a little in his sleep. My chest tightened. I tried to wake him again, but he was out cold. I turned off the TV, picked up his head and laid it on an old Grandma throw pillow. He was warm, but I covered him up with a matching Grandma afghan. I wanted to hide under it with him for the rest of my life. I took off his boots, and his socks. He always wore the damn things, like he was going to have to run out all the time. If one of the boarding house kids needed him, he would run out and help, no matter when it was. Maybe he'd understand, that for what it was worth, I just wanted to help, too. I just wanted to help someone with what Hell I could offer.

I found a piece of paper with lyrics scribbled on it. I'd never read his lyrics. I should have. I should have known so much more about him. It shouldn't always have been about me, but it always was.

Robbie,

I had to go. I won't lie to you, not now or ever. I'm going to Evan. He needs my help, and I have to try. I might be able to keep him from doing something terrible. He thinks I'm the only person who can. I hope this doesn't hurt you, and I won't ask you to trust me. You have no reason to. But I'll be back.

Love,

Charity

I checked on my canary before I left. I needed something pure for just a second. Keegan came to the open cage door. He didn't come out, but chirped at me. I pet his soft head with my finger.

"I love you, little bird."

And he sang for me, loud, bright and clear. My ears hurt to hear it.

∼

I hadn't bothered to change out of sweats and the men's white tanktop, no bra. What for? What did I have to hide from? What did I have to get pretty for? There was nothing pretty about me or what I did, or was going to do.

Evan was standing outside his house when I pulled up. On the doorstep, waiting like some axe murderer in the woods.

His face was stone, eyes cold in the night. The scruff on his face had become more of a beard and his hair was a disheveled mess. He was wearing an outfit just like mine.

"Murder twins. Awesome."

"Come in, please," he said without the energy of life behind him.

The silence in his house wasn't quiet. It was like having huge walls close in on you that you could never climb over. I wished it was darker.

"All right, spill it," I said, not getting comfortable. "What are you on the verge of doing, Evan? Don't waste my time, I waste it enough."

He didn't sit either, and we stared at each other in the kitchen, where I'd thought how cute he was eating cold Chinese food. I wanted him so much to be that guy, not this one.

"I saw Jen today. As beautiful as she is in my dreams. Perfect in every way. With that crack in her that's just dying for me to open it more." His voice trailed off, but his eyes were still focused on mine. Unnerving.

I kept my cool. "So, how are you doing now? 'Cause you seem a little more off your rocker, frankly."

His voice was cool and low, like he'd already made a decision. "I'm ready to do what I should have done. I have a place in this world, and I shouldn't fight it. For what? Because the world I live in tells me it's wrong? I am not wrong, and there are other worlds beyond this one."

Other worlds... "What are you saying?"

"I'm ready to give in. I've found a girl. I have you to thank."

Bile filled my mouth. "No fucking way." I was in his face, ready to shake the shit out of him. "I wasn't saying to do…whatever you've done, Evan! Where the hell were you during our little talk?"

"You *said* nothing of the sort." His calm was horrible. "It's in your every gesture, in your voice, the set of your jaw." His eyes roamed over my face, my body. "You have no dark side, you're whole, complete." His lip was trembling, a bead of sweat forming on his forehead. "You give in every minute of your life to the dark, and that's what I must do. Lose my inhibitions."

No. No. No. "No. Evan, where is she?" I was spinning around, but I wasn't going to find her, not without him wanting me to. That wasn't how a predator worked. I remembered. I'd been on both sides of the disgusting fence.

"I'll show her what being hurt really is, and tomorrow she'll be able to overcome anything."

"Holy shit, Evan, listen to yourself! This is crazy-man shit. Like really fucking crazy, I should know. This isn't the guy I met in the coffee shop that had his shit together. Don't lose your fucking mind! You were lucky to have one."

His calm was gone too fast. "I thought you'd see. I thought you would understand! I watched you, you know. When you went back to the restaurant that night, I saw the thing you become! It's only a shadow of the monster I see here in front of me!" He looked me up and down, grimacing. It hurt. I didn't want it to, but after sleeping with me, asking for my help… "My shadow begs to come to life, and you're the one who let it out! Don't you dare turn on me now, Charity! Don't you fucking dare!"

The rage had him shaking and sweating. A sick determination had grown in him, hard, fast, and wild. I had to find that girl, and, get her out. I could do that one good thing.

"Evan, cut the shit! This is not cool! There's a reason you had this sick need suppressed all this time; Don't give into it, Evan! I'm taking that girl out of here, and we'll forget this ever happened." Evan had to think I was on his terms, or saving her was a lost cause.

"You're better than them. She said so. You're different from everyone else. You have to believe that or you're a hypocrite like no one I've ever seen before."

"Don't you make this about me. There's justice in what *I* do! What you're doing... Wait, who said so?"

"She visits me, too, Charity. We're alike." *The Queen. Shit. Super shit.* My body buzzed in fear, knees weak, at the thought that she'd influenced him anywhere near what she'd done to me. Evan continued his fanatical speech, one that the man in the coffee shop I knew wouldn't be capable of: "What I'm doing is not even killing, it's awakening. So fuck off and leave if you plan on talking me out of it, because it won't happen, Charity. Go back to denying what you really are."

A *thud* sounded from the second floor. My eyes gave me away, and Evan came at me. I ran for the big spiral staircase in the foyer, but he had longer legs. He tackled me to the floor, my teeth cracking against the marble, blood spurting across the pristine white.

That was all I needed. The Harpy burst into being, my wings spread wide, dirty white in the dark foyer. My claws clicked and scraped at the marble. Evan just stared, unsurprised and angry as I towered over him, bloodthirsty and horrifying. My sweatpants had exploded in ash gray tatters all over the floor, revealing the legs of a bird of prey underneath. Stronger than his, no longer running.

My image reflected back at me from an enormous mirror. Tanktop spattered with blood from my busted mouth, the color of my nipples showing under it, platinum hair in electric waves around my head, mouth a vicious beak as it had been in the Wood. Half Hellwhore, half hurt hero. Neither clean, neither good.

"Magnificent," Evan whispered.

My own voice came through the clacking beak. "Evan, give me the girl, or I'll finish you."

His mouth gaped. He actually looked hurt, like I'd insulted him.

"You'd do that to me? After what I've shown you?"

"Your dick? Lots of people have shown me those."

"Don't joke about this! I let you see *me*!" he yelped, pounding his chest with one fist.

A dagger of sadness pierced me. "I can't unsee what you are now."

He sneered. "Does it look too familiar?"

I screeched high at the ceiling that was so close to my head in my Harpy form, furious revulsion overcoming me. She screamed upstairs with me, and I remembered what I needed to do.

Twisting as only a bird can, my wings propelled me up the stairs, brushing the white walls with their everyfilthy tips. I let out a call to her, as she screamed for help.

Evan tackled me from behind, but barely budged me. I threw him off, and he tumbled down the stairs with sickening thuds and grunts. I didn't spare him another glance. He wasn't the Evan who wanted to be good, he was running from being good as fast as his legs would take him. He wasn't anything like me. Couldn't be, not really. If the Queen had touched him at all, she'd tip the scales to her favor. She was a monster of the worst kind—the kind who gave you a reason behind your worst aches, turned them into a manifesto.

"Evan!" I screeched as he scratched at me, chased me. "You're stronger than this! Don't change who you are because that bitch fed you a line of crap!"

He screamed at me incoherently, a disheveled animal accepting no commands.

The upstairs was big enough for me to walk through in my monster form. It didn't take me long to find the woman. She wasn't young, or especially pretty, not the abducted girl you see in movies. She was real. So real it made me sick. He had already gotten to her.

She was naked and soft all over. Not fat, but with rolls and curves like a mom, probably. Her hair was still clean and pretty, so she hadn't been tied up and played with for too long. Her feet were bound to expensive kitchen chair legs, her wrists behind it. She knocked the chair over and was sprawled partly under it, looking at me with raccoon-like mascara eyes. She'd wiggled out of her gag, possibly just to scream at the sight of me.

"Good Christ, stop screaming. I'm here to help," I

said. Jesus, people would never figure out to look past the outside layer.

I swiped through the thick ropes on her feet with one claw, silently pleased with myself at my accuracy. Getting the ones behind her back undone was harder, more time consuming, and every second counted as I listened for Evan. Sneering at myself, I couldn't help but worry what condition he was in. How much blood there would be. If he was even alive. If he should be.

"What did he do to you?" I asked Soft Lady while I struggled with the knots.

"What are you?" was her answer.

"Really? You want to answer my question with a question? I should fucking gag you again."

"No! No, sorry. He….he…raped me."

Heat wave, lead lump in the gut, images of a hundred girls saying the same thing, every one waiting for me to avenge them. "Well, I could have guessed that. Are you hurt?"

She shook her head. "What are you? Why are you helping me?"

I stopped. She wriggled the rest of the way out of her ropes.

My eyes met hers but only one of us was scared. "Why wouldn't I help you? I'm no different than you."

There was noise from downstairs, like Evan was trying to get up. So he wasn't dead. I glanced at the woman when she choke-gasped.

"Is he coming up here?" she moaned, naked body shaking. The fool was still trying to cover herself up, despite the dire circumstances. What the hell did she have to hide at that point?

"I won't let him hurt you again." I grabbed a blanket off the bed to wrap around her. I was so glad it was a spare room and not the one I had had sex with Evan in.

"The things he said—"

"Can you walk?"

Her legs buckled under her once, but I grabbed her. "Ow!"

"Really? I have fucking claws, obviously I scratched you. Come on."

She was limping and crying. I squeezed my eyes shut at my misplaced resentment, my superiority. *Imagine if she'd endured what I had, for the years I had. She'd never fucking make it,* I thought.

Evan wasn't at the bottom of the stairs; only thin trail of blood among my own smears across the floor. I'd forgotten about my smashed teeth until then. Maybe some magical fucking healing power would fix them when I lost the beak.

"Where is he?" she whimpered.

"Don't worry. I'm faster than him."

"I'm not," she whined. I couldn't take this self-defeat bit much longer. *I was a child when I got away,* I thought, and so help me, fucking *tears* clouded my vision. Perfect timing for PTSD.

"Get on my back."

"What?"

"You fucking heard me, get on my back, put your arms around my neck. I can carry you."

The woman made a mess of climbing onto my back,

stupid blanket falling all over the place, and I had to fold my wings down to try and wiggle her onto me. She was weak. I pitied her, and deemed myself better than her all at once. I'd begun to think the same of Evan Hale.

Her tears dripped onto my neck as I carefully glided down the stairs, the front door close. I didn't know where I was going with her, I sure as shit didn't want to be any more familiar with her than I was already. But I had to get her away from him. I could save at least one of them.

"I need you to open the door," I said.

She twisted, reaching for the knob, and I glimpsed movement in the dark room adjacent to us, a big room with a stupid piano in it.

"Wait," I whispered to the woman, and slid her off my back.

"No," she whimpered.

"Shhh, it's okay," I said, and I went into the dark room, trying to keep one eye on her as I did.

"Evan?"

Someone was lying on the huge sofa, and as I got closer, it wasn't Evan I saw.

It was Jen.

"*J*en!"

Kneeling at her side, I did my best in the dark to figure out what condition she was in. *If Evan had hurt her, too...*

She appeared to be unscathed, but she was out cold. It was more than just a nap; she'd been drugged.

"She's fine."

I spun to see the faint outline of Evan in the darkness, sitting casually in a chair. He should have had a smoking jacket on or something, so relaxed he was.

"Evan, stop fucking surprising me."

"We were on a date," he said with a snort. "I had no business going out with her again. She's too good for me."

"Jen would have said the same of you."

"I never had value, and I never will."

I swallowed, trying to figure out his new twist of mood, understanding that it was the Queen's doing. Hating him for what he'd done, aware of the victim's muttered prayers just feet away, knowing who Jen had been, who he had been, the worst of them all exposed, exploited…

The Queen would get what was coming to her. But not yet.

"Did you drug her?" I asked him.

"She drank too much wine. She's fine. She asked me to hurt her again. I couldn't, Charity. I couldn't do it, but I had to do it to someone, do you understand?"

"That woman out there doesn't understand, Evan."

Shadows within the dark swallowed him. I wished he could fight harder. I wished that man I'd met over coffee was still in there, and I had to think he was.

From the corner of my eye, Naked Woman In A Blanket fell against the door in exhaustion.

"What you did to her will scar her for the rest of her life, Evan."

"Misery loves company."

Jen grumbled and moaned. Her hangover was going to be horrific.

Shit, she couldn't see me as the Harpy.

"Evan, I'm leaving and I'm taking that woman with me."

"We weren't finished, Charity."

"Fuck you, you weren't. I won't let this get worse."

He rose from his chair, but he wasn't trying to intimidate me. He couldn't. He was the saddest case of giving in I had ever seen.

"Holy shit!" Jen screeched in painful morning voice.

She'd sprung to life, knocked over a lamp with a

crash trying to get away from *me*. When I turned at the noise, she saw my eyes.

"Ch-Ch—"

"Yeah, surprise, it's me, Charity."

"What the fuck—"

"Right, right, what the fuck am I. I'm a Harpy. And I'm not taking questions at this time."

"Evan? Evan, what's going on?" Jen was panicking fast, I mean, what a thing to wake up to. Just like that, my plans to take off were fucked. As if they would have worked anyway.

"Jesus Christ." I went and flipped on the light switch, lighting up the room harshly. We all looked like shit.

Jen was partly hungover, or still drunk, shaking in shock, but I didn't have time for that. Head swiveling back and forth between me and Evan, climbing up the back of the sofa, she hyperventilated, and still had no idea about the surprise in the hallway.

"Jen, take it easy. Nobody's going to hurt you, especially not me."

The woman in the hallway crawled into the room with us. Perfect. She and Jen stared at each other, mouths hanging open.

"Yeah, about that…" I started.

Evan piped in. "Jen, I can explain."

"Explain what?!" the woman yelled. "That you abducted me? *Raped* me?"

Jen rose to her feet. "Oh my God."

The woman spoke to Jen when she said, "He tied me to a chair. He told me—" her voice broke, she drew the blanket tighter around her shoulders. "He told me he was going to—"

"—hold you down until your arms were bruised and hit you until you were barely conscious. Just awake enough to know what he was doing next," Jen said, trancelike, fixated on the woman.

Jen approached her slowly, as if in a dream, as if afraid the woman would disappear. Soft Lady's confusion twisted her face.

"He said that to you, too?" she asked Jen.

Evan had come to stand next to me, like I could save him.

Jen reached out and touched the woman's cheek, looking through her more than at her, tears in her own eyes. Her lip that always curved to one side when she spoke, trembled. "He didn't say that to me. I asked him for it."

The woman's bruised eye twitched as she looked back at Jen, who did sound insane. Maybe she was. Because if the Queen had gotten to Evan, zero luck that she wasn't poaching whoever else was nearby for her freak Hell party. Pretty rough going that I was the one of all of us who could help this shivering, violated woman. What if I couldn't help any of them? I couldn't even help myself.

I took Evan's hand in my talons one without looking at him. I don't think he could have handled my eyes on his as much as my claws on his skin.

"Evan, this ends now," I said. We watched the two women in front of us go through stages of anger and denial at lightning speed. "I'm taking that woman out of here." My jaw tightened. "I'll leave Jen with you. Do you understand?"

"Please, Charity," he begged, sounding like a small, scared boy. "I don't know what to do."

"I will tell you what to do, Evan. I repeat: I'm taking the woman. I'll leave Jen with you. I know you won't hurt her even if she asks. Neither one of you is to leave until I get back. Got it?"

"What if she hurts me first?"

I spun on Evan, my patience totally obliterated. "You listen to me. Jen is *broken*, and she cares about you. You can either make this about your sick needs, or you can help fix her. Your choice."

"I want to see you do it to her," Jen said just loud enough for us to hear, while the woman shook her head madly back and forth.

Both Evan and I whipped around, stunned. "What? Jen." I was speechless. This room was a ticking time bomb of nothing good. Jen stared at the woman like she was seeing a movie replay in her head, and I was more terrified than I had been all night.

"Time for choices, Evan," I said, and I left him there.

Jen could barely pull her eyes off the woman to look at me, like I wasn't the most fascinating thing in the room.

"Jen," I whispered into her almond-scented waves. Tears coursed down her cheeks, and the hurt in her was alive in them. "This will condemn you. It's time to take control of your battle wounds. Pick the person you want to be."

Her green eyes glistened like marbles when she tore

them away from Evan's victim. "I'm not like you, Charity. You're a different kind of monster." Her voice was cracked and small. I would have done anything to stop her pain.

"You're better than me. Be better than me, Jen."

I took the woman by the hand. She shuddered with my touch. "Really? Still? I'm getting you out of here, you want that, don't you?"

"You want it," Jen mumbled to herself. Her breakdown was imminent; I didn't want to leave her, but I had to. I couldn't carry them both.

"You can walk now, right?" I asked the woman. She nodded, and I had to believe her. She would have crawled to get out of there.

And we walked out the front door, monster escorting the degraded, and left the broken behind us.

TAKING THE HARPY OUT OF THE GIRL

"You ou probably should go to the police, huh?"

We were still on Evan's football field lawn, the night thankfully starless and pitch black. It would help us hide in plain sight. She was shivering, blank-faced, mouth working. I didn't have time for it.

I grabbed her to put her on my back, and she screamed.

"What the fuck?! Shut up!"

"You scared me, sorry."

"Yeah, I'm scary, I get it. Sorry, though. I shouldn't have come at you like that after what you've been through." With that, I got her onto my back like a rag doll. "I'm taking you to the police."

"No, no you can't, please!"

I took off down the driveway. It was like a runway, for fuck's sake. The whole time she's crying, tears falling on my back as she begged me not to take her to the police.

I'd have given anything for someone to take me to the police once.

Once in the sky, I told her what she needed to hear over the wind. I knew how cold I was being, kept telling myself I didn't owe her anything more, that letting people affect me only brought me trouble. But at this point, either I accepted that trouble, or gunned for a different kind where revenge and heartlessness and zero salvation awaited me.

"Hey," I said, more softly. "It's not your fault. There's nothing to be embarrassed about. The police will take care of it. Of you. Of him." *You're not my problem, Evan.*

"No! My husband will know! I was at a bar, and I shouldn't have been. It's where I met…Evan."

She was shouting over the wind, but it was meant to be a whisper. Her shame rang true with me—at her choices, not just at what Evan had done. "I get that you think this was your fault, and your husband won't be thrilled about where you went and why. I get it." Did I though? Because I couldn't erase the thought, *At least you had a life to ruin.*

I'd been so young. Maggie Painter, Lily, so young.

My mind flitted to Robbie, asleep on the couch, and my heart fell. What was left of it.

"Fine, we'll do it your way. I'm good at hiding things and people."

She lived on the nice street with the big houses that held a bunch of fucked-up people. Good families that produced a bunch of junkies, whores and sadists. We got along just fine.

"Over there," she said, pointing to a stunningly

landscaped yard. I dug my talons into it with a little extra *oomph*.

She climbed off my back more gracefully than she'd gotten on. She'd needed to get a hold of herself, and her little ride had given her that. She was tougher than I originally gave her credit for. "Time to get ready to lie and cover up your mistakes and the stuff that's not your fault."

The blanket hung from her, and she stared at me like we were saying goodbye after a first date.

"Don't kiss me."

"What?"

"Joke."

"Well, thank you. I mean truly, thank you."

"Yeah, well. I still think you should go to the police."

She was a mess, but gawked at me like I was out of my mind. Of course I was, but she was worse, at least for the time being.

"You know Evan," she said plainly, eyes darkening as if she knew a secret.

"I do."

"Did he ever—"

"No, he never raped me." My stomach lurched. I hadn't helped Evan the way he needed, and I'd caused a tragedy. I should have tried harder, should have taken some responsibility…and the Queen stepped in where I didn't. There's a life lesson for you: Do good fast, or bad will be faster. "I couldn't…I *didn't*…stop him from hurting you. I'm not that good. I'm sorry. Really, really sorry."

He head cocked at me, knotted hair brushing her cheek. "You want to help him, too."

"Doesn't mean I can."

"Or that you should," she said bitterly.

Somehow, on the surface of my nasty brain, the layer of guilt for shit that I didn't do grew thicker. "Look, I just wanted to get you out of there. I don't need to debate shit with you. This is your pain to deal with, not mine. If you want to see him suffer, I'm not the one to make it happen. I did what I could."

Shaking her head slowly, eyes wide, she said, "You're no better than he is."

"Never said I was. I'm probably a fuck of a lot worse."

"You can make him pay for what he did to me."

"Or you can. In a better way, a way becoming of your nice house and your nice lawn and your nice life. The right way. This isn't my battle to fight."

She started to walk toward her house, the blanket dragging on the grass. At the door she turned, her eyes like steel. "I guess we all lost this one."

~

*D*awn was cornering me. Almost time to turn into a pumpkin, but there were still loose ends to tie up.

Evan's victim pissed me off with her self-righteous talk. I get it, she'd been damaged and afraid to seek justice the right way, and she was all fucked up, not thinking straight. But I was nobody's fucking loaded weapon. I wouldn't be used by anyone.

Mission: Get Victim Lady Home was accomplished, and I was going back to the literal scene of the crime to save more people whether they had it coming or not. I was bone fucking tired of the whole thing.

I could just go home, to Robbie, leave Jen and Evan to sort out their misery together. What could I do as *me*, fucked-up Charity with as many problems as Evan could fit in his well-tailored suit pockets and as much fear as Jen could hide in her mom jeans. No, I needed to go home and try to be normal. Try to be.

As the dawn came faster, I wanted nothing more than to be in Robbie's—my—apartment, just being the person he loved, and nothing else. A fantasy of him playing his guitar while I sang along flitted through my mind. It had been such a long time since I'd sung at all, my voice was under lock and key. Robbie could break in.

After that night, I didn't want my wings anymore. I couldn't fly away from who I was, the same tragic mess no matter what form I was in. The Queen could be dealt with another time, or by someone else for what she'd done, whispering into Evan's ear all the wrong things, causing the downfall of so many. But I deserved a break. I needed to rest my soul, for fuck's sake.

And yet, I found myself in Evan's front yard, the sun coming over the horizon. Everything was still, but madness lived inside.

"No. Screw this."

The Harpy's night was over. I'd done enough. I had a life to lead for as long as I was able to hold onto it.

~

I became me again outside the apartment building, after I slipped a talon into the lock to pop open the door.

"Why the hell didn't I think of that when I was goddamn naked?" I huffed.

It was early. Nobody was out. It was almost peaceful. I had to get the rage out of my brain before I ruined it all.

After the night I'd had, I didn't belong there, in an apartment building with people who walked their dogs, and didn't drink all day, and had Sunday dinners, and didn't destroy everything in their paths. Going down the stairs, my jaw sore, my teeth busted up, what was left of my clothing a wreck, I knew I couldn't pull this off much longer. From one minute to the next I was in a completely different camp about where I belonged; Earth or Hell. I wasn't leading a double life; I was hiding from one under the mask of another.

I crept into Robbie's apartment, but he wasn't on the couch where I'd left him. I tiptoed down the hallway toward the bedroom. He met me halfway.

"Whoa there, handsome. You're up early." His hair was a mess, eyes glazed over. That faint, warm scent of sleep emanated from him. I was happy he was able to sleep.

"Heard the door. I tried waiting up for you…" He

rubbed his eyes with his fists like a little kid. I couldn't take it, I had to throw my arms around him.

"Hey, hey," he laughed, wrapping his arms around me. He had a way of holding me closer than I thought could be done, like he wanted to absorb me into himself. His sleep smell overcame me. Being with him was all I could want. There was no choice in the matter.

Rubbing his nose in my hair, he asked, "So what happened last night?"

"Long, fucked-up story. It isn't over yet, but I don't know if I can do anything to help the situation now."

"You mean to help Evan. He's not a situation, he's a grown man. You don't have to solve the world's problems, Charity."

"Good thing, because I'm awesome at making them worse."

He pulled me away from himself, and I reluctantly allowed him to.

"Let's go to bed. You need some sleep."

"But you don't want answers about what I was up to all night?"

He smiled and ruffled my hair. "Maybe after more sleep and a pot of coffee. Or not."

∽

*B*anging. The door shut quietly when Carl Painter came in, but the click was a shotgun blast that never stopped echoing.

His hands on my arms, fingers pinching to leave

just the right amount of marks, and I kicked, hard, but it did nothing. It never did anything. He was unfazed. "Charity."

I sat bolt upright in bed so fast my vision went black. "Get the fuck out of here!" When I saw Robbie, the memory of Carl was as real as he was. "Where is he?"

"Who? Charity, you were dreaming."

"What's that banging?" No Carl, just Robbie, and I was safe in his bed. I'd wanted to bolt like scared rabbit.

"I think someone's banging on your apartment door," he said.

"Well, that can't be good."

I got up quick, threw on a pair of Robbie's jeans from the floor that didn't come close to fitting, and a Ramones shirt that almost did. With Robbie behind me, zipping up another pair of his jeans, I ran into the hallway.

Jen was there, banging on the door. She swung around when we came out, but had no sweet Jen smile for me. She didn't look like the girl I'd come to know, that was a little too eager to please. She was on the edge of something, and I didn't want to know what she wanted me for.

"Jen, what are you doing here?" Tears rolled down her cheeks with painful silence at the sight of me. How much worse could it get than what already burdened her brain? The things she'd wanted to do at Evan's, I didn't think there could be anything harder. "You know what," I ran my hand through my matted frizzball, "I'm glad you're away from him. Jen, you've got to stay clear of Evan, like him, or love, or whatever, it doesn't matter."

She ran into my arms. I was shocked she'd touch me after seeing me as the bloodied-up Harpy, but I guess we were accustomed to becoming worse and more frightening all the time.

I took her by the hand into Robbie's apartment. He went without a word to make coffee. I sat with Jen on the couch, remnants of the early part of my night with Robbie still inhabiting the coffee table. She took a deep breath, resting her gaze on Keegan. I'd brought him to Robbie's, unwilling to part from him anymore. He was too small to be alone.

"Hmph. Ironic."

"What? That I'm a giant bird freak of destruction and I have a tiny pet bird that only lives to make life beautiful? Yeah, it isn't lost on me."

She laughed loud, like she'd been waiting for something to laugh about for years.

"Jen, where's Evan?"

"He's home."

"Alone?"

She nodded.

First sigh of relief I'd had in a while "What are you doing here?" I asked, grimacing.

"I needed you."

"Yeah, there's a lot of that going around."

Keegan sang sweetly, his throat moving up and down, and stretched his wings.

"Jen, you wanted something awful last night, like what had been done to you."

"I know," she said coldly.

"I want to help you, but I don't know how," I said, willing myself not to crack and cry at the thought of her losing her mind even more. I'd been down that path, and the end hurt to see. "You have to call your psychiatrist, stay away from Evan, maybe go away for a while."

"Are you an angel?" she whispered.

"Definitely not. I'm a Harpy," I whispered back.

"Wha—what. I don't even know what that is. How?"

"It, uh, just happened one day. Or night, actually. I guess my hostility needed somewhere to go, and boom, Harpy. It's my deconstructive outlet."

She gazed at me, as if seeing someone else. "You were so strong, and you took care of that woman. You would have done whatever you had to. I almost hurt her more, and you protected her. You were more in control than I've ever been. Like some kind of goddess."

"Oh, that is beyond unlikely."

Robbie brought out two mugs of black coffee.

"Black for my girl," he said, smiling deliciously at me, and handing me a Sovereign Bank mug. I smiled like a teenager who wasn't discussing the black hole of the soul. He handed Jen the other, and left again, coming back with stolen sugar packets and a container of cream.

He patted my hair, not caring that Jen watched. I didn't care either. His affection didn't embarrass me.

"Baby, I'm going to go back to bed for a while. This is all way too early for me," he said in a soft voice meant only for me. "You guys talk, I'll see you later." He kissed the top of my head, and with a smile for Jen, walked down the hall.

Jen took a long sip of coffee, and when the bedroom door clicked shut, leaving me picturing Robbie's naked chest, she turned to me fast.

"Make me like you."

"Whoa, what?! I'm not a fucking vampire or some shit! And I'm horrible, truly fucking horrible! You don't even know what I do!"

"I don't care. I want to do it, too." She pulled my hands into her lap. "You make things happen. If you wanted to turn me into a Harpy, you'd figure out how. It's who you are."

"You fucking fool, you don't know what you're saying. You've seen the other one like me. The Queen? We're evil."

I had to get up, move, she was pissing me off so badly. What kind of fucking moron had I gotten mixed up with, that she would blindly wish such actual Hell on herself? Jen followed me, and I let out a crazy cat growl in my frustration.

"I've never seen anyone like you, what are you talking about?" she was saying.

I spun on her. "You haven't?" She'd sunken into this black hole of abuse and horror on her own?

"Charity, please," she pleaded, trying to calm me with her usual soft-spoken, annoying voice. "I can't be weak like this anymore. I don't want to live—" Her eyes darted to mine before she finished, "—like this."

Angry, venomous bile surged up. "Jen, you couldn't

handle being what I am. You couldn't lead two lives, a fucking murderer in both. When I'm not ripping the fucking bloody limbs off men and sucking the marrow out of their fingers, I'm thinking about it. Believe me, you ain't seen nothing yet."

I had to hand it to her, through my furious confession, she didn't even flinch.

"Charity," she said, running her fingers down my arm, with a sweet smile on her lips. "I like to keep my murderous rage close to my heart."

I swallowed my nerves.

"Jen," my voice cracked, "You don't want this."

"Don't tell me what I want."

Our voices had become soothing, gentle, but we spoke of horror movie shit. It was one thing to be the Harpy, but to consider wishing it on someone as good as Jen? Because she *was* good, all the way through. The terrible turn she'd taken was a by-product, and not her fault. But it made me doubt everything I knew. It made me fear her.

A harsh whisper was all I could manage. "I cannot make you a Harpy."

"Maybe not you, but you know who can. Don't you?"

My stomach turned, and I coughed into my hand. "No fucking way are you going to that place. No motherfucking way can you ask me that! I'd never bring you or anyone there! You have no idea what I've seen and done in that place!"

My head swam, waves of boiling heat pushing and pulling me in and out of consciousness. I passed out all the time with Carl. It was the only peace I knew then. That she would hold me down like this, *force* me— I wouldn't let her. But the Queen would find a use for her quickly.

Gritted teeth and shaking fingers showed my rage, and I wouldn't try to hold it back. The sun was shining, but it didn't stop me. My wings spread wide, scaring Keegan into a flapping frenzy in his cage. Jen stepped back slowly, mouth hanging. No talons, no feathers, just the dirty wings, tipped in dry blood.

"Do. Not. Push me any further."

"Charity, help me out of this life. You do good things for people like us. People who have been—taken apart."

I reminded myself that she was trying to manipulate me, and straightened my spine. "I don't need to help everybody. I'm no fucking angel."

I'd never hurt her, but my angry switch had been flipped. All at the wrong time, my claws formed and dug into the carpet. I wasn't all that surprised when the air became a hole around me, sucking me into the void that led to the Wood of Suicides.

SHINY LITTLE BUTTONS

I was accustomed to landing hard on the hay in the Wood. Jen was not.

"Oh shit, how are you here right now?!"

I looked around like I'd just stolen a fifth of vodka and was waiting for security to come get me. The eyes of the other Harpies were on us, and a few of them were a little too interested in the fresh meat I was toting. I wrapped my winged arm around her shoulders. Jen was shuddering and mumbling, eyes wild as her head whipped back and forth. That place wasn't meant to be seen by your average human.

So what was she doing there?

Jen shivered against me, her sweat drenching my arm. The heat had to be intolerable, obviously, but it never bothered me. More proof that I was from Hell.

"Come on, Jen, we need to get you somewhere safer."

"No one is safe here," she sobbed.

On cue, a Harpy drenched in fresh blood from head to wingtips to vicious claws landed in front of us, scowling and screeching like the demon she was. Jen fell to the ground, blubbering incoherently.

I screamed an awful sound in the demon's face, spreading my wings as wide as the red sky. I was bigger than her, but she was muscular, and clearly wanted what I had.

Nobody took from me.

She maneuvered around me to lunge at Jen, but I clotheslined her and knocked her backwards, throwing her off balance. She flapped her bony, batlike wings to regain her balance, and I surged forward, grabbing part of the filmy wing in my claws and shredding it fast.

The creature made a noise I couldn't manufacture in my nightmares, and hobbled away flapping the one wing, half crying. I grinned like a kid with a new puppy.

I put my hands under Jen's arms and pulled her up. I wiped the line of drool running down her chin. I was watching her go insane. I had to get to the Queen. The Queen orchestrated everything in the Wood. She was the reason Jen was there to begin with. I also knew the Queen didn't care if I knew what she was up to.

Hissing at all the Harpies salivating over the human who didn't belong, I walked confidently through the Wood, keeping Jen under my arm, sheltering her from the cries of the suicides and the glaring eyes of the beasts who tortured them. All she could see was the bloody hay underfoot and the red glow of the sky. I could only imagine what it sounded like to her, but hey, she was the one who wanted to become one of *us*, so she'd better get used to it.

The Queen sat in her glittering, black nest, a fairy tale beauty intent on destruction, a sinister smile playing on her lips. She didn't need to invite me to sit with her, I was going anyway.

"Climb, Jen. It's cooler and darker up there, you'll be okay."

I unfolded her from my arms at the edge of the nest and gave her a push up onto the branches. She climbed, and I did the same, my claws made for it. I helped her into the nest while the Queen watched. It was only then that Jen got a glimpse of the ruler of the Wood of Suicides. I'm sure she thought she was beautiful. Horrible things were sometimes.

"Welcome back, Hazel," the Queen said. She knew I didn't want to be called that, but my discomfort over it was just more fuel to be the best Harpy I could be.

"Thanks. Sorry if I screwed up back there, turning at daytime and all."

"Yes. Meaning threatening a human woman that you care for in a moment of passion?"

I was sick of the propaganda bullshit. I sighed, tired and annoyed. "You don't care about one human over another, and definitely don't care who I kill as long as I'm killing. So, why bring Jen here, why try to use her against me?"

"I did not bring—"

"Oh, wait, I know this one. You didn't bring Jen

here, she wanted to be here, so here she is. Super Confuciusy."

Her smile was condescendingly pleasant. "It is the truth." She leaned forward to look around me and see Jen. She waved like she would to a little kid. Jen waved back, slow, mesmerized.

"Jen doesn't belong here and you know it," I hissed. "I don't know what you're playing at, but I want out right now if it means she has to be subjected to this place."

"Well, well. I like this heroic twist on you, Hazel. But I think Jen is grown up enough to make her own choice."

"What choice?" I hissed, but I knew exactly what she was talking about.

"I know what choice she's talking about," Jen said in a small but strong voice.

My head snapped to look at her, mortified that she was getting comfortable enough already to speak to the Queen. "Jen, you can't be serious."

"I want to be a Harpy."

I spun on the Queen, trying to hold in my panic.

"You heard her," the Queen said with a grin.

"Fuck off, she doesn't know what she's saying. You want to *collect* us now, you fucking magpie of a thing?"

The Queen straightened up, looming over us. "I would watch my tone, were I you, little Harpy, before your own invitation to the Wood is revoked. And I do not take traitors lightly." I cowered, despite myself.

"No, this can't be happening. She's too good for this.

Jen, you aren't—evil—like I know how to be. This isn't you, don't let yourself fall."

"You think I can't do it," Jen said, her lip tilting to the side in that soft way she had. My heart burned to know what that mouth would do to a person if she kept this up. "Or you're afraid I'll do it better."

The Queen snickered next to me, and I couldn't help it. I couldn't help the idiot pride that flooded me. "You think you can out-torture me, do you? You think you can give in to being a fucking monster better than I can? See how long you can split your life in half. You think you can become something worse than what I have? Be my guest, Jen. Be my fucking guest. But remember this; I was chosen first." I swept my gaze across the Harpies. "And they all fear me."

I stood in the nest, while the Queen sat back smugly.

"You hear me, you vile fucking wastes?" I yelled to the onlooking Harpies. "You can't out-do me here. Don't fucking challenge me and don't try to throw another surprise at me. I'm the crown jewel and don't you forget it."

It was so easy to forget the other world when I was in the Wood. It was too easy to let Hell take me over and become what I wanted deep down, to give in to what came to me so easily. To *win* at something. The submission I'd been forced into my whole life, that I tried to master in the real world, was under my clawed foot there, ready for me to grind it into dust and death and blood. Nothing mattered more. Not Jen, not Robbie, not ridding the world of evil men, not anything except giving into the demon I'd been made to be. It didn't hurt for a second.

The Harpies shrunk back on their branches, leaving the living corpses they'd been plucking flesh from. I sat back down, glancing at the Queen out of the corner of my eye. She was pleased.

"I didn't do that for you."

"You don't do anything for anyone else, dear. You do it all for you, one way or another. You were meant to be by my side." The Queen brushed my wild hair back, motherly and sensually all at once. "I know you don't entirely want to leave your half life on earth." Her lips brushed my ear as she breathed sweetness into it and whispered, "Perhaps a friend along could sweeten the pot." She hissed the words, pronouncing each, savouring the flavor of them.

I didn't look at her or Jen, just out at the Hell that could become my home. No rules, only my own. No memories of the evils done to me. No memories of the unthinkable touching and prodding and violence and images that had shaped my life.

"What a lovely Harpy you would be, Jen," the Queen said, snapping me back. "So full of innocence and degradation."

"Another shiny button for your collection," I muttered.

"The things I'm willing to do now…" Jen said. "I can't live that way for another second. I think I could do something sick to a person, and I know I want those things done to me." She hung her head for a second, and looked back up at me with glassy eyes, the Jen I knew that was soft and hurt, but perfect. "I loved Evan from the minute I saw him, and I've turned him into… And you think I can't become a monster?" Her chin trembled. I took her under my wing.

"Jen," I whispered to her, the way the Queen had to me. "You didn't do this to Evan, *she* did. But it was in there already. I don't want to think it, but she drew on something.. It was a horrible thing, what you two have done to each other, but he's in a totally different world of hurt and I won't let you in there. You're my friend. I might be able to help him, but you need to *stay away*."

She snarled at me, pulling away. "You want him for yourself."

"No. No, I really don't. But you need to leave him behind you all the same."

"She doesn't have to," the Queen said. Her voice pounded through my brain like a walking headache as I tried to figure out what awful thing she could mean.

Jen let out a scream that tore my ear drums with its misery, and brought the cringing Harpies back out to play. And that's when I saw what hurt her so much.

A young tree sprouted from the bloody hay, reaching for the red-hot sky. The trunk was small, with but a few leafless branches sprouting from it. Nothing really grew in the Wood. Its size didn't mean it was weak. It's two thickest branches formed a V, and impaled the feet of a naked man, making him stand upright in the air. His arms were spread to the sky, held in place with branches that weaved in and out of his skin in an intricate braid. His head was twisted at an odd angle, thorny twigs piercing it from all sides, but his eyes were visible to us, tortured with memories that were too fresh from his recent life. I could only hope they would fade in the forever he would endure.

"Evan," I whispered. His name was poison on my lips.

NEVER SAFE

*J*en took one look at her gutted fairy tale prince and passed out on the bottom of the nest.

"Don't touch her," I spat at the Queen.

The flap of my wings to get to Evan rustled up a scent of rotten meat. The second it took me to get there was too long, but I dreaded finally reaching him.

"Evan!" It came out like a swear as I landed, my hands human again, to hold his hand as best I could with the tree jabbing through his palm. "Shit, Evan, oh my God."

That first time I met him flashed through my mind soundlessly, the majesty of him, so very much himself, and elegant, smart, and kind. I'd been jealous of how perfect he seemed, that anyone should have that as their natural state. The way he looked at Jen; how I'd wanted him to look at me. But that wasn't how he looked at me at all. I'd become some warped reflection of himself. That "perfect" person? That man was too much for him to be and it destroyed him.

I rested my forehead on his bare chest, slick with sweat and dirt, bleeding with punctures. He grunted.

"Jesus, Evan, why did you do it?"

He tried to clear his throat to speak.

"No, not a real question, don't speak, it will hurt so much, you must be so dry—"

That was when I noticed the rope still dangling from his neck, twisting around the tree limbs, a part of him now. He'd always had a noose around his neck, invisible to everyone else. The rope dug into his throat brutally. I reached up and tried to pull it away, but he screamed like a wild animal, and I gave up with a sob-scream.

"Charity," he croaked.

"No, please don't, please."

He actually smiled at me. I howled so loud that my throat hurt, and when it was done, I howled again. When I didn't think it could be worse than that moment, Jen appeared at my side, and I crumbled to the ground at their feet, wishing I were dead more than I ever had before.

"I did this to you," she said to him. She sounded so composed, like she was acting out a part in a play.

"Sweetheart," he said, the sentiment and the bubbling blood of his throat wounds making me choke back vomit. "I did this to myself. I'm sorry I couldn't be what you needed. Or maybe I was too much of what you needed." His brittle voice cracked, and he sucked in a harsh, dry breath. The heat of the place bubbled his skin. "I didn't deserve you, or the life I had. There was always violence under my skin." He coughed, and went silent. I knew it wouldn't be the end of him, ever.

Jen sat next to me like we were having a picnic in the park, cross-legged, almost a bounce in her movement. Shock, of course. She would never come out of it.

"This decides some things," Jen said, lip dipping on one side like always. She drew her knees up to her chin like a kid, hair falling over them.

"Jen, please don't make any decisions right now. You're in Hell for fuck's sake. And Evan. Oh my God." I leaned back against the tree, and it gave under my weight. I hoped I didn't hurt him, and knew that I had.

My heart wanted to tell Jen about what Evan and I had done, but it was no use. She was irreparable as it was. The Queen was right to want me as a Harpy. I was human venom, waiting to be spilled on anyone who came near me.

"I think I've made a choice, too," I said.

She chuckled. She was crying at the same time, tears streaming over her cheeks endlessly. "I thought you said now was a bad time to make choices."

"All of my choices are bad anyway. Just out of curiosity, what choice were you talking about?" I regretted asking her immediately.

"I have to be a Harpy now, whether I want to or not."

"Not much of a choice then. Also I won't let you. Whatever you're thinking, it isn't true."

"It is, and you know it. Evan's here, and he's here

because of what I did to him. I went to you, when *he* needed me, and he did *this.* We were meant to be together."

I was too drained to argue the maniacal logic. Fuck me if it didn't make sense in my diseased mind, if I didn't see how she blamed herself, how she wanted to help him then even though they were both beyond help in one way or another. Their tales had become too twisted to be unwound, and I was at the heart of them. How could I fight her happy ending? What the fuck could someone like me do to fix it?

Jen loved him. Senseless, black love. How could she go back to the timid thing she was, dreaming of normalcy while banging guys who reminded her of her rapist, knowing Evan was—

I knew a lost cause when I saw one. I looked in the mirror often enough.

The screams of the suicides began. The Harpies had lost interest in us to ravage their victims again. Jen's attention roved from one trapped soul after another, all making horrible sounds when crying wasn't enough. One of the Harpies was fool enough to fly near Evan, and I leaped at her, pulling her down to the ground. It didn't matter that I was in human form; not one of those fuckers would ever touch Evan Hale. Jen was right there next to me, swatting at the Harpy, and even gave her a good kick to the belly. Jen cocked her head triumphantly. She looked strong. For maybe the first time in forever, she felt that way.

"I have to stay here, you see it now. I have to protect him. He's mine," Jen said. Her eyes were hard and bright. I knew the face of a person who couldn't turn back.

Evan was stirring in and out of consciousness with all the racket of the Harpies and screaming trees. Jen's hands wrapped around the tree branches that held his arms, whispering soft words to him. He smiled, eyes closed.

He'd never smile again if he opened them and she was gone.

Would I not have done anything to be with the man I loved forever, no matter what forever turned out to be? And no mater what kind of man he was? If it were me, would Robbie do the same?

I couldn't destroy Robbie like I did everyone else, but the fucking tragedy of all the loss disgusted me. I wouldn't be defeated anymore.

THROUGH THE CRACKS

*E*van may have made the noose himself, but the Queen supplied the rope. She didn't get to be the overlord of a circle of Hell without having some tricks up her sleeve. No way had all of these terrible coincidences occurred without being constructed by someone with something to gain. One conniver could always spot another.

"Jen," I said, tugging on her sleeve, hating that I was distracting her from Evan. "We have to go to the Queen. I need to find out what she's up to." I forced myself to glance at Evan. "This stinks of her."

Jen shook her head in a panic. "I won't leave Evan alone. I can't ever again."

The Harpies circled, scrutinizing Jen as eagerly as they were the fresh suicide to pick apart. I couldn't leave either of them there, but I sure couldn't stay.

"Jen, please come with me. They'll rip you to shreds."

"And what exactly will they do to Evan?"

I took her hand in mine. I had to talk some sense into her. "Jen, this isn't easy, but please listen. Evan killed himself. This is the Wood of Suicides. It's his fate to be preyed upon by the Harpies, one of the things you're trying your damndest to become, for the fucking record. But you can't protect him if you don't live long enough to become a Harpy yourself." Gotta speak the same language as her, even if it sickens me to say it. I took her by the shoulders, burned my eyes into hers. "If you've learned anything in life you know that you *just need to survive the next few minutes.*"

She went pale under her hot pink, sweat-drenched face. "I understand." Her eyes darted to a Harpy pulling at the intestines of a woman suspended from several branches. Jen retched. I questioned my sanity, and stopped as soon as I started.

Jen turned to me with excitement in her eyes, and I was more afraid than ever.

"I know what we need," she said.

"What?" I said, staring down an approaching Harpy. I raised an eyebrow at her, hoping she took the hint to stay away.

"We need an ally. Someone to protect him while I'm gone." Jen pointed at a Harpy crouched on the ground, watching us from a thicket of trees. Limbs were piled all around her. "Her."

"Why her?"

"She's been watching us, curious, not just waiting to attack. And she likes the remnants of people that fall off the trees; she doesn't rip them apart herself."

My jaw just about hit the fucking ground. "When the hell did you become so tactical?"

She smiled wryly, eyes glinting. "I'm a survivor, Charity, I just look different than you."

"Well, okay then." I turned to the Harpy Jen wanted. "You. Yeah, you. Come here."

The crouching Harpy's expression didn't change. I raised my eyebrows to give her my *hurry the fuck up* face. A second later, she got up, never taking her eyes off of me. She was tall and waiflike, with full, black lips and darker eyes. A headdress covered her hair and framed her doll-like face. The flapper of Harpies. Elegant, mysterious, and apart. Apart from the rest of them. She was the star of an old gangster-slash-horror movie, a captivating mix of picturesque glamour and spine-chilling terror.

Awed, I stared as she silently approached us. Jen stepped in front of me. Man, she was a fearless bitch when she wanted to be.

"You're different than them," Jen said, nodding at the treetops.

The Harpy merely shook her head *no.*

Jen smiled at her. Not that nervous smile that pissed me off, but one that exuded confidence. She was different in the Wood. I wished she weren't in her element, but she was.

"Yes, you are. I'm different, too."

"Human." The Harpy's voice sounded like a tomb opening. She hadn't spoken in years.

"Not for long. And when I'm one of you, I'll need some help. I'll help you, too."

"No."

"You don't like to touch the humans. I bet you go hungry. I'm betting much meat doesn't hit the ground. Looks like those limbs you've got over there are rotting. I'll bring fresh ones to you."

Jen was goddamn amazing. I underestimated her, the whole world probably did. But not Evan.

"What do you want?" The other Harpy was cold, but not unfriendly, not compared to the rest of them. She'd lost something in the Wood. She was hiding.

Jen's smile faded. All business. I was proud of her like a mom, a theoretical mom, would be for handling the whole thing the way she did.

Jen turned her back on the Harpy to cast her sight up at Evan in the tree, but I didn't take my eyes off Betty Boop for a second. Jen needed to give her a subtle show of trust, but I sure as shit didn't. With her back still turned, Jen told the Harpy, "This man here is very important to me. He's hurt himself enough already, and I've hurt him plenty, too." She turned back, eyes burning with determination. "Nobody hurts him now. Nobody touches him. Ever."

The Harpy turned to Evan, hanging there, half-conscious, forever tortured.

"It will not be easy."

"Nothing ever is," Jen said.

The Harpy turned her head to view her own hollow among the trees; a miserable flattened area of hay that had to smell worse than the rest of Hell for the decay in it.

Turning back she said, "I'll do it."

She held out her pale, oddly elegant arm, a gray, lacy wing unfolding beneath. Jen took the claw in her little hand and shook it as firmly as any businessman.

"I'm Jen," she said.

"Loretta. Pleased to meet you." Her voice was becoming more human. Jen's was becoming less.

"Well, as long as you two are making nice, I have a Queen to talk to." I started back toward the nest when Loretta wrapped her claw around my arm.

"Take it off me—"

"The Queen does not miss a thing," Loretta interrupted. "You may think you've got her all figured out, but you never will." Her dark eyes spoke truth and goodness to me, no matter what she was.

"Thanks."

She nodded and let me go. Jen said nothing.

The Queen waited in her nest, turning a blue eye covered in mucus over and over in her claw, cocking her head at it hungrily. Her collections were pissing me off.

I didn't climb into the nest, I circled the top of it to let the heat of the red air flow through and under my wings, to see the chaos below me with its rise and fall of awful cries. She sat, knowing I was there, but paying me no mind. She was the Queen, and nothing took her by surprise.

I came down next to her like I belonged there.

"Nice little prize you've got yourself there."

"They do seem to find their way into my hands," she said, rolling the staring eye over and over.

"No more bullshit. None of this happened by chance. Jen ending up here, Evan committing suicide. It takes a deviant bastard to know one. You used me to get to them."

She stopped, and smiled cordially, like the royalty

she was. "Oh, sweetheart, no. Not at all. You are the kingpin, darling girl. They were lovely surprises that came along with you, ones too delectable to resist."

"You played me."

"I did nothing of the sort. There is a web around you, and you ensnare people in it, Hazel, people that belong here. Those two knew it. Look at the power your little friend bristles with when she is here. She was meant to be one of us. But she will always pale next to you, my flower."

"Nobody makes me theirs. Everything you made me *feel* here was a fucking lie, the control, all of it. I might have to leave Jen with you, you won that round. But you won't win me."

I stood up, and wanted to kick the fucking eyeball out of her claw, punch her beautiful bitch face in, rip the gorgeous dress off her half-beast body, but I held back. Holding back made me boil like the red Hell that surrounded me. That place loved my violence, but it didn't have to be *my* place. I had to believe that.

"My Hazel—"

"Stop calling me that. It's not who I am."

"As you wish, Charity. I prefer Hazel. That persona is the one that created you, hardened you."

My mind snapped to Robbie, a thought that pulsed like an infected sore in the Wood. The docile softness, the vulnerability Robbie brought out in me didn't make me less *me,* take away my control.

As if I had control of anything. My life was a wild top spinning like mad, but at least it was my own lie. In the Wood, the lies weren't my own.

"I don't want to be consumed by what was done to me anymore."

"You already have been. But I can bring you peace again," she cooed, standing up next to me, soothing me with her very nearness. A fraud of a feeling. "I can give you the justice you deserve."

"It's not enough for me to forget everything about my life. My life is more than just what *he* did to me."

She was the hiss in my ear that wanted the world tar black, that wanted blood caked under my fingernails and the taste of rot in my teeth. In my ear she said the words even I didn't know I wanted to hear.

"Behold what we can do."

I screamed, as a hurricane of horror battered me. The Queen created an image in front of me, shifting in and out of reality, pulsing fast like a sick heart, shaking in the heatwaved air in time to the silent screams within it.

Deformed into the roots of a dead tree, being crushed by the weight of it, was Carl Painter, roaring soundlessly. He was soaked in sweat, curling hair of his chest and overgrown beard and hair dripping it, mixing with the sweat that I remembered in my waking nightmares that dripped onto my body. He gnashed his teeth and strained his neck until every vein was exposed, and I screamed and screamed. The hologram assaulted me like a thousand electric shocks.

It burned my throat in a way that touched my heart. His suffering was a blanket on my cold soul.

"You know you want it," the Queen whispered in my ear.

My body burst into the Harpy painfully, completely, beak screaming for his blood with the primitive instinct of a starved vulture. I screeched until my monster body shook and the lights behind my eyes flashed in sync with the throbbing hologram.

In a flash I was upon it, trying in vain to rip my claws through the dead bark and his thick leg muscles, covered in itchy hair, but I couldn't touch it; he wasn't real. He wasn't fucking real. I screamed so loud my ears popped, and Harpies screeched with alarm. The only satisfaction I could get.

I spun on the Queen, ready to puncture what skin I could see. She didn't budge, and my sanity returned a bit with her coolness.

"What do I have to do to make it real?" I growled, barely able to focus, I was shaking so hard.

"You already know. Give in. Give in and become what you were meant to be. This is your natural state. This is what you want, to make him pay eternally for how he ruined you. He will live in fear of your power forever. You can make him suffer in ways even he could never imagine with his treacherous mind. Just leave the rest of the world behind. It holds nothing for you."

I abhorred the tears rolling down my cheeks.

"How would you get him here?"

"A man as weak as Carl Painter listens when the devil whispers in his ear."

More rage filled me. "How many of these people met the devil, then? How many of them did you *whisper* to?"

Anger flitted across her face. So, I'd struck a nerve.

"I didn't become Queen without the power of persuasion. Don't question me."

"Seems to me if you were as powerful as you say you are, my questions wouldn't bother you."

"Don't make more trouble than you're worth, Charity."

"Wow! That's a milestone! I cause too much trouble in Hell? Heavy metal bands will kill each other to meet me!"

Her screech hurt my ears, but I wouldn't let on.

"You dare to make a joke of me? I created this place! You will bow to me as your Queen! You will serve me as I see fit!"

I smiled an ugly smile that made me happy to my very core.

"This really is Hell. Living eternity in servitude. You can't have me. I'm no prize anyway. I've caused enough pain, I won't do it in your name."

"When you do something well, girl, you can never do it enough."

"We are finished," I spat.

She spread her wings fast and threw her head back, making Harpies bow down all around us. She was majestic and formidable, and right about one thing; I was there because I'd wanted to be. I no longer wanted to be.

She pointed one wing tip at me, the other blocking out the blood red sky behind her. "You are not finished until I say you are."

I buried my nerves like I always did, a thing that

Charity always did well, and I tucked my wings behind me, envisioned my own cherry red mouth back until the beak disappeared. I was as strong without all the extras. Those things weren't real.

"I don't want to be terrible. No devil in my ear will change that."

She grinned, showing pointed teeth I hadn't noticed before. "Are you so sure about that? My powers of persuasion work in a multitude of ways." Saliva dripped from her lovely mouth. "I have ruled long enough to know when my plans need back up."

My blood ran cold.

*T*he Queen's elegant body shook with laughter. It was deplorable to watch her enjoy things.

"What's so fucking funny?"

"When happiness comes to you so infrequently, you tend to relish it, drink it in, and hold it close to you. But now it is time to release it."

"You really are just a demon."

"Bite your tongue," she said. She stepped down the branches of the nest like she was gliding down a spiral staircase, the sophisticated bitch. "Your fiery stubbornness and determination, Hazel, told me you could never be a team player. And I had to have some insurance against losing you to yourself. Do you understand?"

"Tell me," I growled.

"I will make this choice easier for you," she said.

"There is no choice anymore. I made it. I'm going home." *To Robbie.*

"Well," she said, running a talon along the edge of the nest, the glistening eyes nestled in the black branches blinking at her, "you may find *home* is a bit occupied at the moment."

Again, I burst into the Harpy, from the frustration of it all. I couldn't take it anymore, her fucking riddles were killing me. She loved every second I struggled. The constant shifting of form was exhausting.

"Hell may not offer much, but what it lacks in creature comforts it makes up for in simplicity and truth." She strode up next to me, chin up, an air about her like she'd already won. "I would love to show you what kind of—incentive—I have for you to stay with us."

And I knew. I just knew. "Please. Not Robbie. Don't, please."

The Queen stared into the distance, and another bubble of an image appeared again, clearer than the image of Carl, but shimmering around the edges like it could pop into nothingness any second.

It was a vision of the beach, and the sky was dark. So serene and completely opposite of the Wood, it brought tears to my eyes. I was shifting in and out of Harpy form so fast my knees buckled by the second.

Then, beings came into view.

Two Harpies pacing back and forth on the sand. They were both stunning to look at, with enormous white wings and golden ringlets tumbling over their shoulders. The angels of dreams.

"She's made her choice," one of them said, voice otherworldly, unreal.

"No. I don't believe you."

Robbie. Oh my God.

"Her love for you is the only thing good in her life. It's not enough to keep her here."

"She sent us to tell you goodbye."

They paced around him, heavenly, predatory wretches.

"No," he said, shaking his head, running his hands through his hair. I whimpered to see the familiar sweetness of it. "No way. Charity wouldn't let someone do her dirty work for her." His breath was short, confusion and anger furrowing his brow. My heart pounded to watch him struggle, over me.

"Don't be angry with her, my sweet," the second one said, reaching a hand, not claw, out to him. I wanted to rip her entire arm off. *"She knew she could never measure up to what you deserve."*

"I only want her, I don't care what I deserve. She knows that." He paced in the circle the Harpies made around him.

I clenched my teeth and screamed at the Queen, "You let me go to him right now! RIGHT NOW!"

"Oh, do watch the show first."

All the power the Queen claimed I had, the power rush as I walked through Hell, was lost to me then, as much of a lie as everything else.

Time to put my fucking thinking cap on, and fast. How could I get *out* of the Wood if I wasn't a Harpy? But to become one meant I would have to stay. One look at the Queen and it was clear as day that if I chose Harpy form in that moment, she'd be damn sure I was never able to change back. Tears fell from my eyes, as hot as the Hell I was trapped in.

The angelic Harpies continued goading Robbie.

"There may be a way—"

He stopped moving. "What? What is it, I'll do anything to be with her."

I vomited on the bloody hay. I saw it coming.

They both went to his side, running their fingers through his hair, comforting and cooing to him. He was too lost in desperate thoughts to see what they really were. Monsters worse than I was.

"You can be with her forever, watching her do what she was meant to do."

"Robbie, you'll never be whole again if she isn't yours."

"How?" he said, lightly leaning his head into the palm of the creature, resting with the comfort she offered. I'd sucked at giving it to him.

"We can show you. But it won't be easy, sweetheart."

"Nothing about Charity is easy. I don't need easy, I need to be wherever she is."

I couldn't take it anymore. I had to do something fast, fast! Pulling myself away from the horror, I turned to the Queen.

"I won't be a Harpy. I don't want it. I can deal with the fucking pain of my memories, I can let Painter live, I can do whatever it takes to be a real person, just a person. But I can't let this happen to him."

"This is Robbie's choice to make now."

"You aren't giving him a choice, you're lying to him! They told him I left him behind, that he wasn't enough!"

"You cannot unmake your choices, Hazel. You cannot simply resume your *life*, and be the person you were. The wheels are in motion to make this your eternity. When Painter took you, your hatred became you, and you became the Harpy. The rest of your life was planned for you."

"No one controls me now. Get the fuck out of my way, or I will get you out of my way."

"You don't know the depth of this mistake, girl!"

I laughed. "I never do, but I make them anyway. One of my bigger fuckups was listening to you. Now I'll say this one more time. You get out of my way, or I will break you into pieces that can never be put back together." I cracked my bony knuckles.

The red sky swam in circles around her in a magical haze, and she looked even bigger. She stretched her wings and whirled at me in a flurry of deathly wind and smoke, choking me and subduing me in a fog. Blows rained on me, all over my body, all at once, knocking me to the ground. I could hear the cackles of the Harpies through the din of the Queen's storm and the throbbing in my boxed ears. The rest of me buzzed with numbness and it happened so fast.

That made me mad.

I threw my body up hard and fast, every muscle screaming from the beating. Fury flooded me with a darkness that even I didn't recognize. Before I could prevent it, I rose with Harpy wings, hovering over the Queen who stared at me, horrified. My wings cast a shadow over her, putting her in the dark for once. I wanted to cover her with as much blackness as was in my soul, take back everything that had ever made me the vicious monster I was. I wanted to forget everything, but on my terms, not hers. I wanted to destroy her, because it was easy for me to believe she was the source of every evil that had taken my life away.

I roared, more dragon than bird, and when I did, a black oily thickness erupted from my mouth. It steamed where it hit her, bubbling all over the ground like black lava. The Queen's wails drowned out the relentless screams. The bile pinned her down like living tar.

Spinning in the air, I surveyed all the monsters around me. They stared at me in awe and fear. I loved it, wanted it, but not forever. Only for that moment.

"I want out!" I yelled at the Harpies, black bile pouring out of my human mouth onto the ground below.

The Harpies eyeballed each other, glued to their spots in the trees. Their world had been silenced and turned upside down with what I'd done. Their Queen still struggled underneath me. She'd live. If that's what you called it.

"I want out now," I said again. Some Harpies moved, but their fear kept them from moving far.

One was not afraid. The flapper, Loretta, with her calm reservation, got up, eyes on mine. She was resolute, and ready for revolution. She walked slowly past me, never letting me out of her sight. If there was any fear in her, she wasn't about to show it.

She reached a clearing and raised her claw at face level. Forming a fist, she punched the sky in front of her. It offered resistance, like she'd hit a piece of heavy plastic. The air vibrated, then opened up in a human size, warped circle.

We exchanged glances, and without a second's hesitation, I dove through.

LETTING GO

*T*hat cavernous void between worlds was the same as always, but I had new perspective. No ending up where the black hole threw me; I had a place to be.

I righted myself in the chaotic pitch, and didn't let the travel throw me around as usual. I found my way and I faced it, even though I couldn't see a goddamn thing. When the end of the abyss was in sight, I put my feet in front of me, and when I hurtled through the hole in the sky, I landed with my clawed toes in the sand.

On the beach. Right where I needed to be.

My claws hit the ground with a dull sound, and the twin fake-angel Harpies turned around fast.

"You can go now," I said.

"Go back where you came from, little girl," one said, her voice like a shadow.

"I suggest you do what I say. I'm not really in the mood to be fucked with."

"Vulgar beast, you don't belong here. Hell owns you."

"I can't be owned."

Robbie stepped out from behind them, the sea at his back, a low moon hanging over it. A bonfire burned not far off, and shadows of us all danced on the sand. It would have been a perfect night without the addition of the Harpies. Fuck them, their time was up.

"Charity?" Robbie whispered. He blinked like he'd just woken up. It was easy to see that he didn't think I was coming back. My stomach curdled to think that he might believe he wasn't reason enough. Once again, I'd done a shitty job showing him he was. "You're here?"

"I'm not going anywhere," I said, my smile reaching deep into every part of me. My cold voice cut through it. "But they are." The Harpies faced me. Clearly they weren't taking a hint without some ass kicking.

They started towards me at the same time, identical, beautiful nightmares.

"Get away from her!" Robbie yelled, but I held up my hand to him, and winked.

A flash in the darkness blinded me.

"Cheap trick," I muttered, and they were both on me. One held me while the other raked her talons across my face three times, before I could even gather my wits to move. Shit, they were fast, and me, still beaten up from the fucking Queen.

I kicked behind me, catching Number One in the groin, and swung my leg back out in front of me, catching the other in the gut with my talons. I pushed off the ground high into the air, and came back down fast, landing a punch on the skull of the one who'd scratched me. The other came at me with an ugly battle cry. I kicked the bitch hard in the knee, scratching her leg to shreds and making her fall to kneeling. But in an instant they were on me again, like I'd barely touched them.

Time to bring out the big guns.

I backed off from them, and they came at me slowly, moving closer together. They were getting comfortable. They thought they could take me. I let anger take me over, using it like a weapon, with more focus than I'd ever had in my life, thinking of how they would have taken another good man to that awful place. *My* good man.

I leaned forward, and shot my slick black bile from my mouth like dragonfire, covering them in it from head to foot. Only their stunning white wings remained pristine. They didn't look like angels anymore.

The gunk did the same as it had in the Wood, boiling and bubbling on them, clinging to them like a living thing. I loved to hear them screaming.

I looked over them at Robbie, his jaw jabbering, disbelief all over his face. I didn't want to be a monster for him.

Stepping over the writhing Harpies, I went to the spot I'd landed when I burst from the dark. I studied the air, found the shimmering place where I'd emerged, and punched it, hard like Loretta had. With all the strength I had left, as if I could throat punch the very Hell it led to. It opened up, and like it called to them, the Harpies rolled across the ground, over each other, clawing at the sand, finally managing to sloppily fly into the void.

"Charity?"

How did he still sound strong, so composed, after what he'd seen?

I couldn't have looked any further down if my eyelids were held to the sand with rope. I saw the black goo bleeding down my chest, soaking my legs and feet. My folded wings were filthier than usual. I ran a clawed hand through my hair, and it stuck. It was matted with blood and other gross liquids I didn't want to think about.

"Robbie, I'm so sorry. I so fucking wish you weren't seeing me this way."

He lifted my dripping chin with a finger and smiled at me. The same love was in his eyes. It never changed. "You look gross," he said.

"Yeah, I know. Hey, ocean, though."

I soared over it, and dove down, letting the salt water hug me all over. I twisted and rolled under the waves, the darkness of the ocean mirroring the darkness up above. The quietest my life had ever been was that moment, and the clearest. I could have stayed there forever if Robbie could be there with me. The ache for him made my lungs begin to hurt, and up I went.

I burst out of the ocean, jetting into the sky, with the sound a gunshot. I sailed through the summer night, stars lighting my way back to shore. Back to him.

Robbie gazed up at me, hands in his jeans pockets. His olive skin wasn't ghostly like mine in the moonlight. Lithe arm muscles were bare. He was never hidden from me.

I descended lightly in front of him. Robbie touched my salt-cooled skin, and pulled a tendril of hair over my shoulder, without thought.

"What is it, Rob?" Asking questions I didn't want to know the answer to was new to me.

He didn't meet my eyes, and it killed me. Their chocolate warmth was focused on anything but my face, twirling his fingers in my wet waves. Harpy or not, I was bad, and he saw it. I was finally too ugly for him. I'd never be clean.

"The things they said, Charity. They were true. It doesn't matter who said them."

"You can't listen to those fuckers. They all lie." And I was one of them.

He smiled sadly, his fingers tracing droplets down my arm, over the feathers that poked through the skin. "They spoke some truth."

Tears ran down my cheeks, hot and hated.

"I'm working too hard to be something you want," Robbie said.

I shook my head. "What? No, you don't have to do any work at all, Robbie. Change nothing."

"Evan, the Harpies, they offer you something I don't have. I'm sorry."

I threw my arms around him, the wings enveloping us both. My stomach clenched, and I prayed for the first time since I was a teenager, for him to please, please see it my way. Let him see how being without him rendered me something horrible.

"Robbie, listen," I sobbed into his ear. "You're the only thing that makes me want to be human. The Harpies, and doing what I did with Evan, those were choices that *I* made. They didn't happen to me, and they weren't because of you. I own my mistakes. And now I'm letting them go." I pulled back, stiffened up, and calmed down. I needed him to listen to me. "I need to be someone that's worth it for you. I won't run from you anymore. I've seen my past, what I did and didn't have control over, and I won't let that be my future. *You* are my future. Please be my future." I was running my hands anxiously through his hair, like he did when he was nervous. We could be the same, we could both be good. I could be new.

"I love you, Charity. There is no future without you. I would have drowned myself like the Harpies wanted if it meant I could be with you forever. I don't care what Hell looks like. It couldn't be as awful as living without the mess you bring to my life."

My body buckled with the sob that broke out of me, and I couldn't see past my tears. "I love you, Robbie. I can't believe I've put you through all this. Nobody else would have ever fucking bothered."

He squeezed me, his arms wrapping around me without any reservation, his nose nuzzled into my neck. "Don't ever leave me again. That's all I ask."

How could I ever? How could I let go of the only thing that made me human? I knew what he said was true—he would have actually killed himself to go to Hell for *me.* The most disturbing fucking love story ever dreamed up.

I thought of Jen, and I thought of Evan, and of the Queen and even Loretta, all like part of a

"Never. I'm not going back to the Harpies. I swear it."

He pulled back, but I held his arms. I could never let him go again. "I knew you wouldn't stay with them, deep down."

"How? I was so close. I suck at being a person."

A little laugh out of the corner of his mouth, and I had to touch his lips. "Charity, you may have become the Harpy, but it could never become you."

I fell against him, every muscle in my body loosening, and if he held me forever, it could never be long enough.

"Hungry?" he said, like we'd been hanging out on his couch all night or something.

"Um, yeah. I am fucking starving, actually."

"Come on." He took me by the hand to the bonfire that continued to glow and spit. The big blanket from his bed was spread on the sand, and the throw pillows from his couch. A six pack of Guinness cooled in an ice bucket next to a hibachi and a shopping bag.

"You did all this?"

"I thought we both deserved a date. A real date."

"Oh my God. This is perfect."

Robbie pulled out a package of hamburgers and some chicken legs from the plastic bag. It was so utterly normal, but there, with him, I'd touched magic.

"What are you thinking about?" he asked as he unwrapped the meat. I looked down, recalling pulling raw meat out of my fridge, shoveling it into my mouth, counting the seconds that I wasn't the Harpy, desperate for the taste of flesh. It consumed me as much as I consumed it.

"I eat meat kinda like a ravenous hyena. Being the Harpy makes me… *hungry.*"

He smiled knowingly. "I know about you and meat. I've seen you scarier than the Harpy when invited to a barbecue." He threw the burgers on the grill top. "You remember the first time we met?"

I bit my filthy nails, staring at the sizzling grilltop. "Oh yeah! I was working at that deli! I don't remember the name of it now, but I fucking hated it there. You ordered bologna!"

"You handed me the package, and instead of giving me the free slice of bologna the kids always get, you ate it." He laughed that amazing laugh that tickled me like a breeze through the trees. It made me want to sing. "You've always liked meat, woman. Doesn't mean you have a taste for blood."

"Maybe not anymore," I mumbled. But I was still me. I'd still be the same in so many ways. And fuck anyone who didn't like it.

My wings would never be white, Harpy or not.

He handed me a burger, but I was pulling the chicken out of the package.

"You want me to cook that?"

I batted my eyelashes at him. "No, baby. I'll just eat it raw."

EPILOGUE

*L*earning lessons and being destroyed by them are the same thing. My goal was just to survive my life lessons after turning in my Harpy wings. It was a new thing for me to have goals. Goals were for people who had something to lose, not for people who worked actively at running away.

I ran in a vicious circle so many times that my feet were coated in its gristly blood and tangled veins. But I was finished running from fresh starts and old fears.

Don't think Psychiatrist bought that I could have had my abuser sentenced to life in the Wood of Suicides and decided against it. He didn't buy any of the story, even after I heard Jen Matthews called in the waiting room and collapsed, sobbing when she didn't walk through the door. Psychiatrist came out of his office himself, took my arm and brought me right back in for an extended session.

"I told you Jen disappeared. If that's real, why won't you believe the Harpies are?" I asked him.

"Do you also believe your unicorns are real?" he asked back with a smirk.

"Funny," I said, smirking back. "But if I analyzed this the way I think your Psychiatrist Log would like me to, I'd say that I think the innocence of belief is real, and the perversion of that belief is also real, and that reality is something different to everyone, whether it take the form of a blood bruise Harpy or a pristinely angelic unicorn. And I would tell you that now I believe in both."

He let out a deep sigh, trying to hide his smile but it turned into a laugh. I laughed with him. Not the kind of laugh that said I could take him in a fight, just the regular kind where I was happy to laugh.

When we were quiet, he said, "You've lost two people that mattered to you in a place that you define as Hell. How are you going to recover from this? How would you like me to help you?"

I shimmied to pull my skirt down some, the corset riding up as I did. Psychiatrist pretended not to notice. "I didn't lose them, I flew away from them. Thing about wings is that they can carry you in a lot of different directions."

"Very insightful," he said.

"Yeah, well, I've had a lot to think over. A lot of self-reflection creates metaphors and bullshit talk, I guess. Anyway, I've made my mistakes and I've been a product of a lot of them but I never let them change me."

"However, you claim that your past turned you into a Harpy."

My eyes got as hot as my heart, the violence in my voice undisguised. "But. They never. Changed. *Me.*"

He cleared his throat. "Yes. I see what you mean. You are Charity Blake and nothing can take that away from you." I saw the bead of sweat on his forehead before he smiled and we said goodbye.

~

*K*eegan sang his loudest when he was inside his cage. I understood. Being in a cage wasn't the same as being pinned by the wings. It was an acceptable soul-crushing.

I hoped Jen could sing in the Wood of Suicides.

I'd moved into Robbie's apartment right after our beach date that had been rudely interrupted with a Harpy fight. My cage hadn't had bars, and I'd made it myself. Believing Robbie when he said that I was better than what I'd become had released me. The four new walls didn't hold me in, they freed me from myself.

It's not like I became some religious fanatic or some shit. Robbie told me that Jen and Evan had created their own circumstances, even if I'd been their gateway drug. He saw a dismal beauty in it, I think, that I could lead people so astray. The Queen had liked it, too. I couldn't survive living in the hearts of the monsters I'd run from, and I couldn't save the people I'd left behind —or underfoot.

Jen and Evan made their choices, but Painter's daughter, Maggie, hadn't. Harpy or not, I couldn't get her off my mind. I wanted to help her. I could figure out how.

All these thoughts and so many more clawed through my head over the scars of before, that first morning I woke up in my new home. Robbie was gone. Even the silence was bursting full of him.

I took Keegan out of his cage that morning, brought him with me to the coffee pot. I needed to hold him, to breathe in the possibility that I could wake up every day and be gentle.

My flying monkey coffee mug sat right next to the full pot. ("Flying monkeys are so ugly," I'd said when Robbie gave it to me. "Who says they're ugly?" he answered.) I smiled at the memory.

Then my eyes caught the note, honed in on it, and had to stop myself from squeezing Keegan to death.

It couldn't say anything awful, it couldn't say that he was gone, that he changed his crazy mind for ever wanting me to stay.

I set the little bird down on the counter, his nails scratching for something to hold on to. I only watched as I slid the note from under the mug. Robbie's chicken scratch that I'd see a hundred times, writing song lyrics, so many about me. Tears welled in my eyes but I focused and read, Keegan fluttering like my heart.

"The path to paradise begins in Hell. –Dante" Your *paradise starts with this cup of coffee. Love, Robbie*

I let out a sob, dropping the note and lifting the bird. I sunk to the floor and cried and laughed, and I sang, for just a while.

The coffee was burnt, just the way I liked it. But I no longer was.

ACKNOWLEDGMENTS

This book has waited a long time to see the world, and now it's a world of its own. I want to thank Summer Wier for championing it from the second she had it in her hands, as well as Nicole Tone, and Ashley Ruggerillo. Thank you, Jolene Haley, for never letting me down. My thanks to Joe Hart for being such a kickass friend and willing to field every question I threw at him, and not holding it against me when I never respond. Thanks forever to John F.D. Taff, Amy Lukavics, and Mark Matthews who make me believe in horror and myself. I want to thank my stepdad, Wayne Nelson, for constantly begging me to get the book out already. May Harpy wings fly you wherever you wish to go.

Never Miss A Release!

Thank you so much for reading **The Harpy**. I hope you enjoyed it!

I have so much more coming your way. Never miss a release by joining my free newsletter where I'll be sure to keep you updated on upcoming books!

To sign up, simply visit
https://juliehutchings.net/

Thank you for reading THE HARPY! If you enjoyed the book, I would greatly appreciate it if you could consider adding a review on your online bookstore of choice.

Reviews make a huge difference to the success or failure of a book, especially for newer writers like myself. The more reviews a book has, the more people are likely to take a shot on picking it up. The review need only be a line or two, and it really would make the world of difference for me if you could spare the three minutes it takes to leave one.

With all my thanks,

Julie Hutchings

RUNNING HOME
BOOK 1 IN THE VAMPIRES OF FATE SERIES
BY JULIE HUTCHINGS

Death seems to follow Ellie Morgan. Now someone's out for blood.

Tucked away in rural New Hampshire, awkward booklover Ellie lives a simple life, keeping herself detached from others. With just a single friend in a world that has taken her family from her, a part of Ellie longs for something more than nights on the couch and dull days working in a gift shop.

Enter Nicholas French.

Something about the new guy in town sparks a burning desire within Ellie, something more than his rugged good looks and piercing gaze that can see into her lonely soul. Fate has led him to Ellie's small town, and Nicholas' interest in her is more than undeniable attraction.

As Ellie learns more about Nicholas' dark yet noble nature, she discovers a part of herself she never knew existed, and why the threads of her destiny feel intertwined with his. But Ellie's chance at a new life comes at a cost, and in the end, fate may be the one to decide if she'll live or die.

RUNNING HOME is the first book in the dangerously passionate and deeply romantic Vampires of Fate series where not all monsters are evil, and love comes with a bite.

Get your copy of RUNNING HOME today and delve into the new and seductive paranormal romance series everyone is talking about.